Pl.___

"In his latest Penns River crime novel—*White Out*—a Black officer and a seemingly unarmed white supremacist sets off the proverbial spark that threatens to become an inferno. With protestors and counter-protestors arriving, along with the news media and agitators, the strained police department desperately works to keep the peace as an approaching snowstorm and a casino poker tournament complicates matters even further. A gritty crime novel that deserves wide attention."

—Brendan DuBois, award-winning
and *New York Times* bestselling author

"It's been a long time since I read a book that pulled me along as urgently as Dana King's latest Penns River novel *White Out*. King writes about his cops and their town with the kind of real affection that has you not just wanting, but needing, to know what happens to them next—and there's plenty happening in this fast moving, deftly written thriller. Highly recommended."

—J.D. Rhoades, bestselling author of the Jack Keller series
and the Cade and Clayborne historical thrillers

"We've all heard the stories of White cops shooting and killing unarmed Black men. But what happens when the scenario flips? In *White Out*, Dana King kills in this gripping behind-the-badge drama. One cop I know wonders how Dana is able to get it so right."

—John DeDakis, Novelist, Writing Coach, and
former Senior Copy Editor for
CNN's "The Situation Room with Wolf Blitzer"

# PRAISE FOR THE
# PENNS RIVER CRIME SERIES

"King has created vividly drawn characters, a plot the late Elmore Leonard would appreciate, and dialogue that hits all the right notes. Let's hope *Grind Joint* is the first in a new series chronicling life and crime in the Alleghenies."

—*Booklist*

"Dana King's *Resurrection Mall* is a patchwork of desperation from a depressed river town written with genuine style and grit."
—Reed Farrell Coleman, *New York Times* bestselling

"Dana King's *Ten-Seven* is a propulsive mystery thriller that showcases his ear for dialogue, penchant for wry humor, and mastery of the police procedural."
—Eryk Pruitt, Anthony Award-nominated author of *What We Reckon*

"An extraordinary voice. A mix of Pelecanos, Leonard and Wambaugh."
—Colin Campbell, author of the Jim Grant novels, for *Pushing Water*

"Dana King's *Leaving the Scene* is a slow burn that will leave you wanting more. A great read!"
—Bruce Robert Coffin, bestselling author of the Detective Byron mysteries

To Gary,
Nan @ the Vine
7/26/22

# WHITE OUT

Let's be careful out there

Dana King

# BOOKS BY DANA KING

The Penns River Novels
*Worst Enemies*
*Grind Joint*
*Resurrection Mall*
*Ten-Seven*
*Pushing Water*
*Leaving the Scene*
*White Out*

The Nick Forte Novels
*A Small Sacrifice*
*The Stuff That Dreams Are Made Of*
*The Man in the Window*
*A Dangerous Lesson*
*Bad Samaritan*

Standalone Novel
*Wild Bill*

# DANA KING

# WHITE OUT

A Penns River Crime Novel

Down & Out Books
3959 Van Dyke Road, Suite 265
Lutz, FL 33558
DownAndOutBooks.com

Cover design by Dana King

ISBN: 1-64396-269-8
ISBN-13: 978-1-64396-269-6

*To The Beloved Spouse.*
*Really, all these books are for you.*
*It's time I said so.*

# 1.

Stan "Stush" Napierkowski sipped the head from a frosted mug of beer. "That Beattie kid can wrestle, can't he? Makes me wonder what Dan Gable must've been like in high school."

Ben "Doc" Dougherty cradled his mug in his hands, feet on an ottoman. "He's the goods. I need a video of that reversal move he likes. Must've seen it thirty times and I still can't figure how he gets his hand around. Can do it either way, too. I gotta have slow motion."

"His uncle—you know Tom Yockey, don't you?—says Oklahoma State is after him hard."

"Don't even talk like that. I want him to go to Penn State. Be worth the trip to Happy Valley a couple times a year just to see him." Doc looked around Stush's basement as if searching for something. "Is it cold down here or is it just me?"

"I forgot to turn the space heater on before I left. Give it another few minutes."

"There's no heat down here?"

"Never has been. You must be getting old if you just now noticed it." Doc shot him a look. "This was unfinished when the furnace went in. I had no idea we'd have such luxury here someday."

Stush's idea of luxury was a recliner on either side of a seven-foot couch facing a fifty-inch television. Behind the seats a small dry bar and refrigerator with a beer tap built in. The space was

1

also the only way into Helen Napierkowski's laundry room, which diminished the ambiance on wash days. "We're getting a new furnace in the spring when prices go down. Gonna have them put a vent right there," he pointed, "so's Helen stays warm while she's folding laundry. Should heat this whole area."

"Honest to God? You lived here how long?"

Stush did math in his head. "Thirty-four years. No, thirty-five. We burned the mortgage around the time you made detective."

"And no heat in the cellar all that time."

"I'd of done it sooner if I knew how miserable you were every time you came over."

They sat in companionable silence. Penns River was still a township when Doc's father and Stush began their friendship. Doc passed up several lucrative opportunities so he could come home and work for his "Uncle Stush" when he was chief of police. Retired over six months, Stush was still getting the hang of it. "How are things at the house? That new kid, Boston. How's he settling in?"

"Trevor Boston's not close to being the new kid anymore. No offense, but I was shocked to see how many guys only hung around because of you. Retirement paperwork's piling up on Sullivan's desk like he's quality control at a paper factory. Four gone already and three more on the way that I know of. Long as I worked with these guys, I had no idea how long some of them had been around."

"I wouldn't think Sully'd be that hard to work for."

"He's not. It's the job. I guess a lot of people either didn't notice how it's changed, or were willing to overlook it so long as you were around. Add that to Sully's difference in command style and guys who had the time in are bailing."

Stush stared into his mug. "You sound like you're about half ready to bail."

"Not me. I'm management now. Remember?"

Stush pretended to laugh. "How're those sergeant stripes fitting you?"

"Kind of tight." A pause. "To be fair, I understand why Sully promoted me. And I guess I was the logical choice, considering the options. I still don't like it."

"It'll grow on you. Now what about Boston?"

"He's coming along. Mike Zywiciel does some mentoring. Sends him on calls with Sisler when he can."

"Sisler's about as excitable as a toad."

"That's the plan. Take some of the edges off."

"Is it working?"

Doc rolled his neck. "It's a work in progress, but yeah. Generally. Nancy Snyder told me he took a shit ton of abuse at a domestic a couple weeks ago and defused the situation without any help from her."

"What happened?"

"Some jagov husband kept Trevor standing on the porch freezing his balls off instead of letting him in to make sure everyone was all right. Time was Trevor would've knocked over the guy, the door, and probably some furniture gaining entry. Nancy told me he kept his cool when even she was losing patience. Said she was proud how hard he's working at it."

"How is Nancy, anyway?"

"Her face healed up nice. The little bump on her nose gives it character."

"What about the broad hit her with the…skillet, was it?"

"Cast iron." Stush winced. "Got a year's probation. Her and the old man both."

"That's all? For hitting a police officer in the face with a skillet?"

Doc made a *What are you gonna do?* gesture. "Judge Molchan said justice would best be served by giving them something to think about as they went through life or some bullshit like that. Set a condition that the next call we answer at that address, they both go in for the rest of the term, which sounds to me like the next complaint will be a homicide, but I'm not a trained legal professional, so what do I know?"

"What's Snyder think about that?"

"Whatever it is, she keeps it to herself. I know what I'd be thinking." Stush opened his hands. "I'd be thinking I'm the deputy chief and don't need to back up domestics in the middle of the goddamn afternoon anymore."

They watched the final minutes of a college basketball game that might have been exciting had either team been able to put the ball through the hoop if they were sitting on the backboard. The buzzer sounded and Stush asked if Doc wanted a fresh head on his beer. Doc took a swallow, checked the level, and passed. Stush topped off his own and took his seat. "Sully still bringing in people he worked with in Boston?"

Doc wiped foam from his lip. "Not all. Maureen Tilghman, she's the new detective, she worked with him there."

"How is she?"

"At least as good as I am."

"You mean before or after you made sergeant?"

Doc flipped him off. "She worked Homicide and Major Crimes in Boston. Knows her stuff."

"What's she doing here, then?"

"Retirement home."

"Like Willie Grabek."

"Oh, no. Willie took his retirement more seriously than the job. Mo Tilghman works."

"Anyone else slumming?"

"Be nice. I don't know Barney McGinniss well yet, but he seems okay. The other two newbies are straight out of academies. Holtzclaw's from Indiana and Obidowski's from Allegheny County. Or the other way around. They're so new I can't tell them apart yet."

"At least Obidowski's maintaining the Polack ratio. I was worried Sully'd turn it into a mick department."

"Depends on how many Boston retirees he can talk into moving here. I overheard the three of them talking about old times the other day. Sounded like they were calling roll for the

St. Patrick's Day parade."

"How's the new mix working out?"

"You know how it is. You got new guys trying to establish themselves and guys who've already paid their dues trying to adapt to a new situation. Gets interesting some days."

"Interesting is good."

"So long as things don't get fascinating." Doc snapped his fingers. "I almost forgot. Neuschwander's wife is pregnant."

"How many is that? Five?"

"Yep."

"I thought he had himself fixed."

"He did. Guess he was too much man for the procedure."

"How're they taking it?"

"About how you'd expect. Rick's lining up doctor's appointments and trying to decide if they should remodel or buy a bigger house. Hildy's looking for lawyers."

"Divorce?"

"Malpractice. She says she wanted a family, not a basketball team."

"I'll bet Ricky's in hog heaven."

Doc was about to answer when his phone sounded the *Official Business* ring tone. "Dougherty. Yeah, Chief...Where?...Is he okay?...I had a couple beers with Stush after wrestling but I'm fine. Where can I find you?...Understood. I just left. Ten, maybe twelve minutes."

Doc tapped the phone into his palm. "Trevor Boston just killed a guy behind Fat Jimmy's bar."

# 2.

Trevor Boston hit the ground running on his four-to-twelve shift. Almost T-boned by an SUV as he turned onto Leechburg Road from the parking lot. Pulled the guy over at the light for Chester Drive. Anthony Thomas, thirty-eight-year-old white male. No open warrants. A court date with Kathy Burrows in two weeks for a rolling stop. Thomas gave Boston attitude and drove away with citations for running the light, speeding, dangerous driving, and crossing over a double yellow line, which Boston threw in because the guy was an asshole. Made a note to talk to K-Bar about him before the court appearance.

Broke up a fistfight on Florida Drive over a fender bender. Fender scratcher was more like it. Each car's damage required no more than a good wash and a craft-sized bottle of touch-up paint, but the men lived across the street from each other and had only just learned the woman they were both putting it to over on Mintwood Drive was not exclusive property. The ill feeling that started when they both showed up at the same time last week carried over until today, when neither would let the other go first, leading to a collision that might have broken an egg, assuming it was already cracked. Hilarity ensued.

Boston planned to eat his meal at Round Back, wrestling Wednesdays not busy if you got there during the match. He was unaware of a catechism-related event at St. Margaret Mary's that ended half an hour before he took his break. Every ten-to-twelve-year-old Catholic kid in town beat him to the restaurant. With their parents. And grandparents. And stepparents, if available. The line to get in resembled a Depression-era soup kitchen by the time Boston rolled up at eight thirty. He ate at Subway, which was okay, but he'd had his mouth set for a Round Back giant fish sandwich.

Still settling himself in the car when a call came for a prowler on Oak Street. Went to the house, got the information, idled through the area shining the spotlight between houses until motion made him look twice. Got out to investigate and heard movement in the underbrush leading down Edgecliff Hill. Easing his way into the woods when the siren went off at the Number 3 firehouse and about shit when a good-sized buck came out of the thicket like a rabid grizzly was chasing him and knocked Boston on his ass.

The car seat didn't have time to warm his butt before the call came to go to Fat Jimmy's. Obidowski's sector that night, but he was handling the accident that prompted the alarm that almost got Boston gored by Bambi's father. Light snow falling, temperatures dropping, black ice a definite threat, Boston was half surprised he hadn't handled a weather-related accident yet. Rolled Code Two down the bypass, no siren or lights but not taking his time.

Fat Jimmy's didn't look any more depressing than usual. Block building, tiny windows too high to look through and too dirty to see through even if you could. Flat roof. Could pass for an adult bookstore if not for the neon beer signs in the windows. Boston parked near the front door, put on the lights on to indicate he was on official business.

Bigger crowd than he expected until he remembered the wrestling match would be over by now. Bar along the wall on the right, booths on the left. Tables scattered around the floor, with a couple tipped over. Two pool tables in the back left. The building smelled of stale beer, old cigarette smoke, and sweat.

Fat Jimmy himself sat on a stool behind the bar displaying

the lack of irony in his nickname. Dipped his chin an inch when he saw Boston and said, "Pool tables." Boston never stopped walking, Jimmy not much for small talk with cops except for his old schoolmate Ben Dougherty.

The corner behind the pool tables contained what appeared to be an unconscious man bleeding from the head. Another man pressed a folded bar towel to the wound. Two others engaged in animated conversation with a short, undernourished gent holding a broken cue stick.

Boston's approach stifled the conversation. He pointed to the man on the floor and asked the one with the towel, "He all right?"

"He might need stitches, but his breathing and pulse are stable." Boston's face showed the question. "I was a corpsman in the Army."

"He conscious?"

"Not really. Grumbles a little."

Boston keyed his shoulder microphone. "Base, this is PR-Eight. Request an ambulance at—" surprised he didn't recall the address, as many times as he'd been here. Realized he didn't need it. "Send it to Fat Jimmy's. Unconscious man in the back by the pool tables may need stitches. His vitals look good, though." Winked at the man with the towel, who smiled.

"Ten-Four, PR-Eight. They're on the way."

"PR-Eight, copy. Thanks." Boston asked the man with the towel to keep an eye on the victim and let him know if anything changed. Turned to the three men standing. "What happened here? And you." Pointed to Cue Stick. "Put that down." Tapped two fingers on the felt.

The man did and Boston rolled the broken cue out of reach. "Who wants to go first? Only what you saw and can swear to. Not what you heard or think."

The man who spoke wore a flannel shirt open over a Penn State tee, jeans, and Red Wing boots. "What I heard was hollering, so I come back to see what was going on."

Boston said, "You working security tonight?" Half smiled as he said it. Flannel Shirt and the man next to him snickered. "Security" at Fat Jimmy's was a souvenir baseball bat from Three Rivers Stadium Jimmy kept behind the bar.

Flannel Shirt had humor in his voice. "Ain't that your job, often as yinz is here?" Boston showed rueful acknowledgment. "Anyways, I heard hollering and a couple of 'cocksuckers' from back here and one of the voices sounded like Pete." Pointed to the bleeding man. "We go way back, so I come over to see did he need some help."

"Where were you sitting?"

Flannel Shirt pointed. "That knocked-over table there. The one on the left."

"You knock over the other one, too?"

"Yeah. I kinda got tangled up."

"Before we go on, what's your name, sir? I need it for the report."

"David Regner." Spelled the last name.

"Okay, Mr. Regner. What happened next?"

"I got back here quick as I could and saw this one," pointed to Cue Stick, "swing that pool cue and hit Pete up against his head."

Pool Cue said, "I was provoked."

Boston moved his head a quarter turn. "I'll get to you. What happened next, Mr. Regner?"

"I seen him look like he was gonna hit Pete again so I grabbed him before he could do real damage with the broken end."

"Was Pete down by this time?"

Regner nodded. "Bleeding pretty good, too."

Boston looked at the remains of the cue on the table. No other pieces in sight. "That the end he was holding?"

"Yeah."

"So he held the butt and hit Pete with the narrow end?"

"Gives you an idea of how hard he hit him, busting the stick and knocking Pete out like that."

"Then what?"

"I pushed this asshole up against the wall—"

Pool Cue took offense. "Who you calling an asshole, asshole?"

"You, for using the damn thing as a weapon."

"You one a them, too?"

"One of them what?"

Boston raised a hand. "Enough." Left time for suitable eye-fucking. "Then what?"

Regner said, "I was about to give him what for—"

"Try, maybe," Pool Cue said. Looked like he had more to say until Boston cut him in half with a glare.

Regner went on. "Like I was saying, I was about to kick his ass when this one," pointed to the man who had not yet spoken, "gets in between."

Boston asked the other man his name. "Mike Fantuzzo. I'm just a guy shooting pool. I couldn't believe they'd fight over something like that or I would've come over sooner."

"What were they fighting over?"

Fantuzzo looked at Cue Stick. Spoke as if he'd rather not. "This guy, I think his name's Richie…"

"That's good. Act like you don't know me."

"I never seen you in my life till an hour ago." Then to Boston: "He said something about, you know, a racial thing, and Pete there in the corner didn't like it."

Richie called bullshit. "You're just saying it was racial to get this colored cop on your side. There wasn't nothing racial about it."

Boston had had enough. "I'm not going to tell you again. You can either be patient and maybe we can sort this out here, or I can take you in to talk to a detective in the morning. All the same to me." Based on what he'd seen and heard so far, Boston didn't see any way Richie wouldn't spend the night as a ward of Neshannock County. Thought it better to keep that to himself for the time being.

Richie pulled back what would surely have been a clever rejoinder. Boston glared a few seconds before addressing Fantuzzo. "What did Richie say that irritated Pete?"

Fantuzzo looked more uncomfortable as he went. "The fourth guy was playing eight ball had to go. No one else was up for a game, so we started playing cutthroat. You know, where each guy gets five balls and you shoot everyone's except your own?" Boston knew how to play cutthroat. "I didn't have a shot, so I played safe and stuck the cue ball behind a couple a Richie's balls. Left him no shot at all." Paused. "He had something to say about it."

"What'd he say?"

Fantuzzo looked around. Richie glared. Regner shrugged. Fantuzzo didn't meet Boston's eyes. Opened his hands as if apologizing in advance. "He said that was nigger pool and that I should play like a white man."

That might have bothered Boston more had he been at the table and off duty. Now it was just a witness statement. His eyes flicked to Richie, then to Pete, who appeared to be coming around. "How does that end up with Pete on the floor?"

Regner spoke up. "Pete's sister is married to a Black dude. Nice guy. Everyone knows him, likes him. Thing is, Pete's sister— hell, the whole family—takes grief over it. Her husband being Black, I mean. Pete's a little touchy about it. He might've had something to say."

"Did he?" Boston asked Fantuzzo. "Have something to say?"

Fantuzzo looked like he wished it was him on the floor unconscious. "Yeah. It was, you know, nothing serious. It was like, he didn't appreciate that kind of language and Richie should cut it out."

"What did Richie do?"

"Hey!" Richie said. "I'm standing right here, asshole."

Boston wheeled on him. "Do you *want* me to hook you up? Interrupt one more time and you'll be cuffed and in the car while I sort this out. Do you understand?"

Richie said, "That'll be the day," then mumbled something Boston didn't catch. He would have let it pass but for seeing Regner and Fantuzzo flinch. "What was that last part?"

"Nothing."

Boston stepped into Richie's personal space. "You want to talk, here's your chance. Tell me what you said."

Richie straightened himself to his full five foot eight. "I said, 'That'll be the day.'"

"For what?"

"Huh?"

"That'll be the day for what?"

"I ain't saying shit now that these two got you prejudiced against me with that 'nigger pool' comment. Which ain't a racial thing at all the way they're playing it up, not in that, uh, whaddaya call it, context."

"You'll have all the time you need to tell your side. Let me finish here."

"It ain't right, you getting their stories first and making me defend myself when I ain't done nothing wrong. They only made a big deal out of that 'nigger pool' thing because they seen you was Black and wanted you on their side."

"Did you say it?"

"Say what?"

"Nigger pool."

"Well, yeah. But not insulting like they let on."

"Then how about you let me get from them how they took it, then you can explain how you meant it. Remember, though, what I really care about is who knocked who unconscious with a Cue Stick." Boston gave his attention back to Fantuzzo. "What happened after Pete said he didn't appreciate that kind of language?"

Fantuzzo might never shoot pool at Fat Jimmy's again. "Richie said, 'What kind of language you talking about?' and Pete said, 'That word,' and Richie come back with, 'What word?' like he didn't know and Pete said, 'The N-word,' and Richie said, 'You mean nigger?' and Pete said 'yeah.'" Fantuzzo ran out of gas.

"And?"

"And Richie asked why Pete was taking it so personal, it's not like he's one."

"That's what he said? Pete wasn't one? Not that Pete wasn't Black or was white?"

Fantuzzo looked to Regner for confirmation. Regner nodded. Fantuzzo said, "Those exact words: 'You aren't one.' So Pete says his sister is married to a Black guy and he's not going to put up with that kind of talk and Richie comes back with..." the sentence tapered off.

"Go ahead," Regner said. "Tell him."

"He told Pete not to be so sensitive about it, how it's not his fault his sister's a whore."

"I never said his sister was a whore."

"You're a lying sack of shit."

Richie stepped forward. Boston stopped him with the palm of one hand, "Open your mouth one more time before I tell you to and you're going in. Period." Richie gave a look that would melt steel, but backed off. Boston asked Fantuzzo, "What then?"

"Then's when it got loud and names started getting called and Pete got hit."

"Did Pete come at Richie? Threaten him in any way?"

"There was some yelling and pushing and shoving. Hard to say who did what first."

"That how it looked to you, Mr. Regner?"

"I couldn't say. Pete was already on the floor by the time I got back here."

Richie couldn't resist. "It was self-defense. It was the three of them against me and alls I had was the stick, so I used it."

Boston stuck a finger in Richie's face. "Goddamnit, I told you to shut your mouth until I said different."

Richie slapped Boston's hand away. "Who the fuck're you to tell me anything?"

Boston reached for his handcuffs. "That's it. You're going in. Turn around."

"Like hell. A real cop's going to have to take me in. Not some nigger with a badge."

Boston reached for a wrist to cuff. Richie slapped him open handed across the face and ran for the front of the building. Took Boston half a second to recover from the shock before he began pursuit. Almost collided with the ambulance crew on their way in. They'd been to Fat Jimmy's before and knew the drill. Stepped back to make room. One pointed to Boston's right. "He went that-a-way."

Footprints in the fresh snow led around the side of the building. Boston took his time, stayed away from the corner, flashlight in hand. Clear. Followed the tracks to where they went around back. Moved at an angle to give himself room in case Richie was hugging the wall. Saw a horror show of empty beer and whisky cases, pallets, and an overflowing dumpster that created an alley along the back side of the building. Stray bottles, broken glass, bottle caps, and pieces of paper and cardboard littered the path.

The cases and pallets stacked on either side would limit Boston's freedom of movement if he walked between the dumpster and building. Going around the outside limited his line of sight and could allow Richie to run back the way he came without being seen.

Boston paused to listen for movement. Nothing. Drew his weapon, finger outside the trigger guard. "Penns River police! Show yourself with your hands up."

Nothing.

Boston considered his options and moved into the path defined by the bar's detritus. Flashlight in his left hand, gun in his right. Small steps, head on a swivel. No ambient light. The snow, coming down harder, reflected the flashlight beam into his eyes. Paused after each step to allow space between crunches in the snow, alert for any sound.

There. To his left. Near the dumpster.

Quiet again. Cat, maybe. More likely a rat.

Or a man shuffling his feet.

Glass broke and Boston froze in place. Raised the gun. Eyes scanning between the rows of garbage, looking right when Richie came from behind the dumpster on the left. He turned. Would have said *Freeze* or *Stop* but Richie was too close. Boston fired. Richie appeared to slip, came up lunging. Boston fired twice more. Richie dropped to his knees with an expression equal parts rage, pain, and disbelief. Fell hard enough for Boston to hear his nose break as it bounced off the hardpack and gravel.

# 3.

Barney McGinniss stood smoking a cigarette on the public side of the crime scene tape when Doc arrived. "What do we have, Barney?"

"The nightly fight. Some guy got knocked out. Boston escalated the situation and this one's dead." Gestured over his shoulder toward the body, face up with snow starting to lay on the hair and clothing.

"That's all?"

"I been securing the crime scene."

Doc would have liked a more attentive attitude. "Anyone else here?"

McGinniss flicked the butt toward the parking lot. "Obidowski's inside taking statements."

"Anyone touch the body?"

"The EMTs had to turn him over. Apparently he was flat on his face when they got here."

"The victim have a weapon?"

"Not that I saw."

"Any chance someone walked off with one?"

McGinniss shook his head. "Boston says he was with the body until I got here."

Doc looked past McGinniss to the corpse. "You said the EMTs have been here already?" McGinniss nodded. "How'd they make it so fast?"

"I think they were already inside. You know, for the guy got hurt in the fight."

"Where's Boston?"

"In his shop by the front door. You probably walked right past him."

Police lights lit Fat Jimmy's parking lot like hell's Christmas by the time Doc returned to the front of the building. Nancy Snyder saw him first. "What's it like back there?"

"McGinniss has the scene secured and I guess Obidowski's taking statements."

"I sent Shimp and Tilghman in to help. The chief called in extra uniforms to handle any rubberneckers and keep the media back."

"Where's Sully?"

"He's coordinating from the house. I think he already has the state police on the phone. We're on hold to see if they're going to send someone tonight or tomorrow morning."

"Does he want me to wait until he hears back?"

Snyder shook her head. "It's your crime scene until further notice." A pause. "Do you want to talk to Trevor?"

"Is the union rep here?"

"No."

"Then no." Saw Snyder's expression. "Anything he tells me I have to report to the staties. I don't want him thinking he can confide in me because we've had beers together. How shook up is he?"

"Pretty bad. McGinniss found him on his hands and knees looking for the weapon he swears he saw. Barney had to lead him away."

"That's exactly why I don't want to talk to him. I understand why he did it, but he messed with the crime scene. We're going to have to note that and there's no way to make it look good. Neuschwander here yet?"

"He was getting his gear out of the van when I saw you."

"And it's still my crime scene, right? I can run it how I see fit until someone says different."

"I already told you that. Where are you going with this?"

Doc pointed skyward. "The snow's picking up and we have to assume the state investigators won't be here until morning at the earliest. I don't want to have to start from scratch with six inches of snow on the ground. We need to be able to reconstruct the entire scene indoors if we have to."

"You're not worried they'll think we doctored the evidence?"

"I'll burn that bridge when I get to it. Right now all I know to do is what I'd want done." Looked up into the snow. Shook his head in disgust. "I'd like to think I've established a reputation. A good rep's not worth anything unless you get to draw on the account once in a while." Saw Rick Neuschwander approach. "I gotta talk to Noosh before he goes back there. Anything else for me?"

"You know what to do. I'm going inside to help herd the cats. You're in charge out here."

"Let's touch base before either of us leaves, if not before." Snyder nodded and made for the door. Doc whistled through his teeth. Waved Neuschwander over.

To Doc, Rick Neuschwander was the most valuable cop in Penns River. The town had no budget for a crime scene unit. Whoever worked the case owned the responsibility for collecting and preparing evidence to send to either the state crime lab in Harrisburg or an independent testing center. Neuschwander wasn't great at interviews and his ability to build a case didn't kick any ass. No one cared. Gathering and packaging evidence was his superpower. The labs loved working with him because his samples were so well prepared. He was also immune from the standard cop disease of insisting his case was the most important thing in the world. The labs all knew that if Rick Neuschwander in Penns River said something was urgent, it was, and they'd do what they could for him.

He lugged his kit over to Doc. Pointed to where McGinniss put fire to another cigarette. "I heard Boston shot a guy." Doc nodded. "He have a weapon?" Doc shook his head. "Fuck."

"Don't take this the wrong way, because I know you only ever give your best work, but we need your best best work tonight. We'll have to hand everything over to the state police when they get here, and I don't want anyone to be able to even hint we mishandled anything."

Neuschwander nodded. "Medical Examiner here yet?"

"No, and I don't expect one anytime soon. I hear the snow came from the west and the roads are worse in Allegheny County."

Neuschwander took two steps. Stopped. "How's the light back there?"

"About what you'd expect from the ass end of Fat Jimmy's. Let me check a couple things and I'll come back and be your gaffer."

Neuschwander peered over his glasses. "Don't get above your raising. I'm the gaffer. You're the best boy." Winked and went on his way.

Doc was perusing the activity at the front of the building when an Allegheny County Medical Examiner's vehicle pulled in. Penns River was pretty much all there was to Neshannock County and with a crime scene team unaffordable, a medical examiner was out of the question. Allegheny County handled all unnatural deaths. For a fee.

Doc recognized the driver as she turned his way. Waved her over. Extended a hand. "Sorry to get you out on a night like this, Dr. House." Tried too late to pull it back. Michelle House despised anyone calling her "Dr. House" because of all the jokes that naturally flowed from the name. "Sorry," wasn't going to get him out of it.

"No need to apologize. *Benjamin.*"

Doc hung his head. Only blood relatives and Stan and Helen Napierkowski could get away with calling him any form of his given name. "My bad, Mike. I'm still sorry to get you out."

"What do we have?"

19

"Officer involved." Doc saw her cringe. "Cop's fine. Here's the thing: we're going to need your unique combination of speed and sensitivity on this one. The cop's Black and the victim's white. Oh, and we haven't found a weapon."

House squeezed her eyes shut. "Anyone I know?"

"Trevor Boston?" She shook her head. "Uniform. Been in the department maybe a year."

"How is he?"

"Haven't talked to him." Doc pointed around the side of the building. "Rick Neuschwander's back there with a uniform. I'll help him set up his lights in a bit so hang loose if it's too dark to do much." About to turn away when his Western Pennsylvania roots kicked in. "How're the roads?"

"Not too bad. I live on the Penn Hills side of Plum. Coxcomb Hill was a little slippy coming down."

"Won't be much fun going back up if this doesn't stop soon."

House pointed to the SUV. "Four-wheel drive. Together we will make Coxcomb Hill our bitch."

Doc couldn't help laughing. "Okay, Dr. Badass. I'll see you around back. Try not to injure anyone till I get there."

House left and Doc reached out to grab Mike Zywiciel by the arm. Patrol sergeant, Mike was so close to forty years on the job he could complete the retirement paperwork and be gone before the ink dried. No more pension bumps after forty and Mike—"Eye Chart" to his friends—had shown decreasing taste for what the job had become. He asked if Doc was finished with Boston.

"The union rep here?" Zywiciel shook his head. "Then I'm done with him. Right now I'm the investigating officer, not his softball buddy. Anything he says to me has to be on the record."

"You mind if I take him back to the house?"

Doc shook his head. "I know you know this, but conscience demands I say something about not letting him talk to anyone— *no* one—until he's lawyered up. You know how Trevor likes to unburden himself."

Zywiciel nodded. "State cops here yet?"

"Some time tomorrow is my guess. Depends on whether they send someone local or from Harrisburg. Interracial shooting like this, my guess would be Harrisburg. How's Trevor holding up?"

Zywiciel gave it thought. "About how you'd expect, I guess. He never shot anyone before. Sure as hell never killed anyone. I better get him out of here before the goddamn media shows up."

Doc was halfway along the side of the building when Nancy Snyder caught up to him. Pointed to a police car turning right onto Greensburg Road. "Is that Trevor?"

"Eye Chart's taking him to the house to wait for the union lawyer."

"Did Mike say how he's doing?"

"I asked. He said, 'About how you'd expect.' Whatever that means." Doc noticed how harsh that sounded. "I guess he's still processing. You ever shoot anyone?"

"Winged a guy once."

"How'd it make you feel?"

"It was a good shoot and he walked himself to the ambulance. I got over it."

Doc looked at her in the macabre light. Recognized what he saw. "Still think about it, don't you?"

"I think about the situation. How I might have handled it differently so I wouldn't have had to shoot him."

"Come up with anything?"

She shook her head. "He was an asshole. He's just lucky I'm not a better shot."

"I've seen you shoot. He was goddamn lucky. Can you excuse me? I need to help Neuschwander and the ME."

"Do you have a minute for Jimmy first? He asked for you."

Doc still looking toward where Neuschwander and House waited. "Sure. I guess so." A Kia that had seen better days pulled into the lot. A woman in her late twenties got out. Slipped a lanyard holding a laminated badge over her neck. Doc pointed Snyder that direction. "Now you get to earn that exorbitant deputy's salary."

"Who's that?"

"Press. Part-timer for the *Tribune-Gazette*. She's okay but I need you to keep her away from me for the time being." Snyder went off to intercept.

Doc found Fat Jimmy at his usual perch behind the bar. "What's up, Big Man?"

Jimmy looked unwell. "What's it been? Six months since Patty Polcyn was killed, here the last place anyone saw her alive?"

"About that."

"And now this. I mean, I saw it start. I didn't figure Richie to use a cue on that guy, but I knew a fight was coming. Seen enough of them in here."

"Relax, Jimmy. None of this is on you."

"I should've warned that cop."

"About what? He's answered calls here before."

"Richie has some serious racial issues. I should've figured he wouldn't let a Black cop take him in without a fight."

"It's part of the job. Just because it doesn't often happen doesn't mean we're not prepared for the worst. Trevor Boston knows that."

Jimmy stayed quiet long enough for Doc to consider going back to work. About to speak when Jimmy beat him to the punch. "I have no delusions about this place. It's a shithole and decent people wouldn't be caught dead here." Grimaced at the inadvertent pun. "It's *my* shithole, though. Whatever happens here, there's a standard."

"I know, Jimmy. We all do."

"Don't just say it. It's important to me that you of all people understand."

Doc waited for eye contact. "Every cop in town knows you let things go on in here as part of the cost of doing business. We also know you're not a skel and we'll hear about it if certain lines get crossed. You went out of your way to help us with Patty Polcyn. What went on here tonight falls under the category of 'shit happens.' Could just as easily been the Inn or the Edgecliff."

"But it wasn't."

"Tonight your number came up. Now it's over. We'll have to poke around for a few days, but in a week this will be a conversation piece. It's not like you're caught in the middle of a gang situation." Doc placed a hand on top of one of Jimmy's resting on the bar. "It's a hell of a thing. I know. You give your statement yet?" Jimmy nodded. "They tell you to stick around?" Jimmy shook his head. "Go home. Drink a little of that apple pie shine you like so much and get some sleep."

"I have to lock up."

"Give me the keys. I'll be here till damn near daylight, anyway. You'll be closed as a crime scene for a couple-three days. I'll drop them off when we're done."

"You sure?" Doc nodded. Jimmy took a ring of keys from his pocket. Started to remove some. Stopped and took what appeared to be his truck and house keys. Gave Doc the rest.

Doc nodded thanks. "I'll bring them to the house first chance I get. Can I ask a favor before you go?"

"Whatever you need."

"You mind if we come inside from time to time to warm up? Colder than a penguin's balls out there."

Jimmy pointed to the coffee pot. "Beans and filters are in the cabinet under if you want them." Lowered his voice. "You want to liven it up with a shot or two, the place is yours." Hefted himself off the stool. Extended a hand.

Doc accepted the offer. "Wouldn't surprise me if you were open as soon as Saturday. Be like it never happened."

"I hope so. Richie had friends I'd rather not have to mess with. I hope they don't decide to stop by and check out what I might've done different."

# 4.

The state police investigators from Harrisburg walked into Sullivan's office at 10:08 the next morning. Six people crammed into the small room by 10:15: Sullivan, the chief; Nancy Snyder, his deputy; Mike Zywiciel, patrol sergeant; Doc, detective sergeant and lead investigator until now; and the two staties, Thornton and Rothermel. Running on two hours' sleep, Doc forgot which was which before he'd finished shaking hands. Everyone had coffee. Everyone had a donut. Sullivan changed a lot of Stush Napierkowski's policies, but the daily donut run remained inviolable. Went out himself this morning after sleeping on the couch in his office.

Introductions out of the way, the locals deferred to the state troopers. Thornton took charge. "First off, Trooper Rothermel and I want to thank you on behalf of the Pennsylvania State Police for the cooperation you've already extended. We know you'll continue to do so. Thank you, Detective Dougherty, for emailing the reports to us overnight. We read them to each other driving in on the Turnpike this morning, so we're pretty well up to speed. Please thank Detective Neuschwander for his assistance. An investigation like this is hard on everyone, so we'll try to stay out of your way as much as possible. Along those lines, Chief Sullivan, is there someplace we can work that's away from the flow of traffic?"

*Where none of the locals can look over your shoulder,* Doc

24

thought. Sullivan said, "The district attorney volunteered space on the county side of the complex. That will be more comfortable than what we have here, but not as convenient to anything we have you might need."

"The DA's space is fine. No offense, but if we need anything from your department, we'll let you know."

"None taken. What else can we help with? Phones? Computers?"

"Phones and computers we got. Everything else we'll arrange with the DA. All we need from you is a detective to serve as liaison. We won't need him full-time, but he needs to be available whenever we ask for him, which might make it hard to keep him in whatever rotation you have for catching calls."

"I'm detailing Detective Shimp. She's worked homicides before and knows the drill." Thornton might have sighed on *she*. "Anything else?"

"We'd like to see the crime scene and whoever worked it last night."

Sullivan thought over the department's current disposition. "Detective Dougherty took the lead until you got here. The other detectives have the morning off, though Shimp is on her way in. The uniforms pretty much worked double shifts or more. I sent them home. They'll start coming in at noon."

"Any of them do more than preserve the scene?"

Sullivan deferred to Doc. "A couple took statements, but they all got there after it happened."

Thornton looked to Rothermel, who shrugged. "Let them sleep. We'll catch up through the day if we have questions. Where's Officer Boston?"

Sullivan said, "Home on administrative leave. He lives not a mile from here so we can get him whenever you want. The union lawyer's in Pittsburgh and asked for at least ninety minutes' notice."

Neither trooper had a problem with that. Thornton said, "We'll see him this afternoon around one or one thirty. We can push it back to as late as three if that's too tight for the lawyer, though I don't want to go any later than that."

Teresa Shimp caught up with Doc as everyone was preparing to drive to Fat Jimmy's. "What does a liaison do in a situation like this?"

"I could pretty it up for you, but since we're friends, I'm going to give it to you straight: it's a glorified gofer job, more gofer than glory. You work with the troopers—who don't strike me as having sticks too far up their asses—to tell them where things are, who's who, and communicate between them and Sully. Maybe some of our procedures they're not aware of. What you are not is an investigator. That's their job. It's officially a part-time detail, but they're going to want you around pretty much full-time for at least a few days. We'll cover you back here."

He saw the question on her face. "I'd do it if I weren't sergeant. We need Neuschwander for crime scenes and Tilghman hasn't been here long enough to know some of what they're likely to ask. That leaves the short straw for you." He shrugged in apology. "Look on the bright side: it's like winning an all-you-can-eat at the Overtime Buffet. OT is pre-approved because the state picks up the tab. You don't even have to request it. Just don't be in a hurry to collect." Made a mental note to find a way to make it up to her after this shit detail ended.

Shimp stopped short of Sullivan's doorway. Put a hand on Doc's arm. "How much of a two-way street is this liaison job?"

"Officially, not at all. While you're with them, you are a deputy state trooper, though they won't swear you in. You're not to share anything with us you wouldn't share with a civilian." Paused for effect. "That said, if something troubles you and your conscience demands it, feel free to avail yourself of Father Dougherty's confessional service. Off the record, of course, and preferably hypothetically."

Shimp resumed walking. Doc blocked her way. "So we're clear, I do not expect, and do not want, progress reports. Nothing can taint this investigation. I want to see Trevor cleared because it was a good shoot, not because he's one of us."

"You worked the scene. Do you think it's a good shoot?"

A question Doc had avoided asking himself. "I want it to be. I know Trevor and I can't believe he'd go back there to ace an unarmed man, no matter the provocation. That's why we don't investigate our own shootings."

"I know you too well to think you'd tank an investigation."

"I wouldn't. But what might I miss, or dismiss, because I know Trevor and it doesn't match my impression of him? No one knows anyone that well. Not even ourselves." Thought of his cousin the private investigator in Chicago. Nick had killed half a dozen people Doc knew of. All "good" shootings. But Doc had seen things when his cousin was in town a few years ago he would never have suspected, and they grew up together, close as brothers. "Let's go. We don't want to keep them waiting."

The little convoy drove to Fat Jimmy's on roads already cleared from five inches of overnight snow. Penns River won an award a couple of years ago for having the best snow removal of any Class Three city in Pennsylvania. As a Penns River boy born and bred, Doc was proud of that. The head of Public Works was a good friend. Still, he felt for the poor SOB who had to compile the statistics.

Fat Jimmy's parking lot was empty except for Lester Goodfoot leaning against his patrol car drinking coffee from a Tervis. The lone Native American in the department, Lester and his wife were the only two in Penns River. He worked graveyard by request in an attempt to make a virtue of his insomnia, though if asked he would say he did it because he saw better at night than the white-eyed devils. He'd also requested a special out-of-grade raise for juicing the department's indigenous demographic to 2.5% in a town where Native Americans made up only 0.007% of the population. City council had yet to succumb to his logic. The other patrol officers bought Lester a case of beer and a fifth of Jim Beam each year at Christmas to thank him for eating the shit shift.

Doc made sure he got to Lester first without appearing to hurry. "How's it look, Lester?"

"Same as you left it. Cold as my mother-in-law's heart out here, though."

"Thanks. Go home and get some sleep. We'll be here a while."

Snow crunched under Lester's tires as he drove away. Doc lifted the crime scene tape to pass through. Everyone else stayed on the other side.

Thornton said, "Lay it out. We read the reports, but tell us what a night's reflection showed you."

Doc wasn't sure how to take the "reflection" comment. "Understanding I have no statement from Boston—"

"Understood."

"He answered a call for a fight inside. Man knocked cold with a pool cue." Thornton and Rothermel said they "read" the reports on the Turnpike, which Doc knew meant one scanned them while the other drove. "All the background we have on Richard Johnson so far is that he was thirty-eight years old. Divorced with no kids. He worked as a driver for a uniform company. You know, picking up dirty and dropping off clean."

Rothermel asked what started the original fight. "Johnson used a racial slur and one of the guys he was shooting pool with took offense. Things escalated from there. The guy who got hit, Pete Less—"

Thornton interrupted. "I wanted to ask about that. You're telling me Dick Johnson knocked out Peter Less? Who's in charge of naming kids in this town?"

This was the kind of opening Doc usually lived for, an opportunity to lighten the mood for a couple of minutes. In bed at six and up at eight, his sense of humor was even more sleep deprived than the rest of him. "I just report them. I don't make them up. Besides, Johnson preferred 'Richie.' You mind if I go on?"

Thornton did not, though his expression suggested he thought Doc was a humorless prig.

"Boston was getting stories from the other two guys involved in the fight—neither of whom had entertaining names, so I'll leave them out for now—and Johnson's pissing and moaning all the while about how they're slanting the story to make it more of a racial thing than it ought to be, like they're playing up to Boston. Finally Johnson runs his mouth one time too many and Boston puts a finger in his face to show he's had enough." Doc demonstrated, index finger extended, thumb touching the middle finger. "It's one of his moves. Usually pretty effective."

Thornton said, "Not this time, though."

"Not this time. Johnson slaps the hand away and Boston runs out of patience and starts to hook him up. Johnson said," Doc checked his notes, "'Only a real cop can take me in, not some nigger with a badge.'"

Rothermel was impressed. "Honest to God? He said that to a cop? How drunk was this guy?"

"Lab results aren't back yet. Oiled up pretty good from what I heard."

"And Boston didn't kick his ass right there?"

"I know it would've crossed my mind." Doc dismissed an idea to mention how well Boston had done with his temper of late. "Turned out he never got a chance. Johnson slapped him across the face and split."

That impressed both troopers, neither of whom appeared eager to contradict Doc's low idea of how much of the reports they'd read. Doc continued: "The EMTs who came for the injured guy," Doc saw no need to mention Peter Less's name again, "almost got run over by Johnson on his way out. They directed Boston around this side of the building. Theirs are the last witness statements we have. Everything else has to come from the scene."

Thornton said, "Understood. Go on with what happened out back."

"It's not a good crime scene. The EMTs estimate there was an inch or an inch and a half of snow when all this happened. There's at least three times that much now. We got what we could but didn't want to brush much away for fear we'd disturb something."

"You cover it? A tarp or a tent? Anything?"

Doc shook his head. "We thought about it. Laying something directly on the ground might disturb trace evidence when we lifted it; melting snow will leave it behind. We thought of constructing a canopy, but we didn't have everything we needed, and there's not much room to work. We'd of stepped all over the scene getting it up. What we can do is get a guy out here from Public Works with one of those jet engine-looking heaters to melt the snow in place."

"We'll see. You find a weapon?"

"No. Boston told the first officer on the scene—McGinniss—he saw one, but nothing has turned up. McGinniss found Boston on his hands and knees looking when he got here."

"Convenient way to fuck with the crime scene."

"You're right. Messing with the scene makes him look bad. On the other hand, he had plenty of opportunity to plant a weapon, in which case he sure as hell would've left everything else exactly as he found it."

"Assuming he had a throw-down piece."

"Assuming he had one."

Neuschwander had staked out inner and outer crime scenes. The tighter line described the areas where the body had fallen, where Boston was when he fired, and the route Johnson took in his approach. The troopers stepped under the tape that closed off the entire back side of the building for a better look.

Rothermel said, "What will we see if you melt the snow?"

"About what you'd expect from what you see now. Trash, broken glass, paper, rat shit."

Hard to say which trooper looked more disgusted. Thornton said, "You said you can get this melted. How long will it take?"

"An hour or so once he gets set up. I'll send Neuschwander out with him to make sure nothing is disturbed. Joe's done this before. He knows the drill."

The troopers conferred. Thornton said, "See if you can get it done by midafternoon. For now we'll go back to your station and get set up. Bring Boston in by one, one thirty at the latest. We'll see what happens from there. Detective Shimp, you're with us." Turned and walked to his car, Rothermel and Shimp trailing in his wake like baby ducks.

# 5.

"Have we done everything to make this handoff as efficient and professional as possible?" Brendan Sullivan leaned his elbows on the desktop in his *Let's get down to business* pose.

Doc stifled a yawn. "As much as we can. It was a tough crime scene. Middle of the night, freezing cold, snowing like a bastard. As much trash outside the dumpster as in it. I've never seen Rick Neuschwander work harder or better. We'll go out with the troopers later to see what shows up after the snow's been melted. It's their investigation, but it's our crime scene."

"Shimp's with them now?"

Doc nodded. "They went straight over to the county side after visiting the scene. I think the DA set them up in his conference room."

"Who's he sucking up to?" The Neshannock County DA was well-known not to want law enforcement cluttering his office space.

"Rumor has it he's thinking of running for Congress when Schmidt retires. The money man he wants to impress is a state police jock sniffer, and the party chair in Harrisburg is the brother-in-law of the deputy commissioner."

"I never thought of Hagedorn having much political potential."

Doc said, "He'll find that's a common assessment once he starts poking around. Neshannock County has no juice in Harrisburg. What little there was negated by the loathing everyone has for Dan Hecker."

"I noticed that. Why does everyone in Harrisburg seem to have a hard-on for Hecker? I know why we do, but that's a couple of hundred miles away."

"Hecker gamed the system to get the casino. A lot of people looked bad when the word leaked out. Which they had to know it would, so there's no sympathy for them. Most of the DA's campaign support comes from Hecker. Harrisburg knows that. Mike Hagedorn's not going anywhere."

Sullivan rubbed his forehead. He couldn't have had much more sleep than Doc, and that on his office couch, where Doc found him after returning from the crime scene to start typing. Sullivan said, "What's on the agenda for the rest of the day?"

"The staties are coming this way around one or one thirty to talk to Boston. After that we're all going back to the crime scene."

"I thought they had that beautiful conference room set aside for them."

"They want to use our recording equipment and it's wired into the observation room."

"I must be tireder than I thought. When did Thornton ask me for that?"

"He didn't. He told Neuschwander on the way back this morning."

"Ah. Does this mean Neuschwander can get us a copy of the statement?"

Doc shook his head. "He's been told to set everything on autopilot and leave the room until summoned to turn it off." Sullivan showed disappointment. "They didn't expressly forbid him hooking us up with a direct feed we can watch from your office. He didn't mention he could do that, but he said they had a lot on their minds and he didn't want to burden them."

"Neuschwander's a good man. Fertile, too, from what I hear."

"You have no idea."

Sullivan rubbed his eyes with the heels of his hands. What he said was not a question. "No weapon."

"And no one disappeared one, either. Boston was still on hands and knees looking when Barney McGinniss rolled up. Barney had control of the scene until the rest of us got there, and we handed it off to Lester Goodfoot."

"Barney's a good man. I know he comes across as a burnout sometimes, but I guarantee he didn't let anyone who didn't have a badge get within fifty feet of that scene."

Doc was still unconvinced about McGinniss's virtues as a cop. Barney worked with Sullivan in Boston, one of what the holdover locals referred to as "The Winter Hill Mob" behind their backs. Doc worried how an East Coast big city mentality would wear on a borderline Rust Belt borderline Appalachian town like Penns River. "Anything else?"

"Now might be the time to get something to eat if you're interested. Bring me back a sandwich while you're at it. We can eat in here while we watch."

# 6.

Thornton asked if the recording equipment was working. Neuschwander rapped twice on the one-way glass. Thornton pointed to the glass, then swept his finger toward the door. "We'll call you when we're done. Lock up on your way out."

Doc and Sullivan settled in, lunches eaten, sipping the dregs of their pop through the ice in their cups. The "Conference in session" sign hung from a hook on Sullivan's closed door. His computer screen, turned so only he and Doc could see if someone were to barge in, showed the interview room, both troopers facing the door. They nodded after a few seconds, probably at some acknowledgment from Neuschwander that he'd left the observation area.

Thornton looked over his shoulder at the one-way glass as if checking to see if anyone had stowed away, not that he'd see even if they did. A man Doc knew as the union lawyer sat facing the camera to its right. Trevor Boston sat dead center. Dressed in an open-collared shirt, Boston looked as if he hadn't slept any more than Doc.

Thornton turned to face Boston and the lawyer. Cleared his throat. Checked his watch. "The time is one fifty-two p.m. on seventeen February. I am Trooper Evan Thornton. Also in the room are Trooper Douglas Rothermel, Penns River Police Officer Trevor Boston, and Joseph Migliorini, serving as Officer Boston's counsel. Does anyone have any questions before we begin?" No one did. "Outstanding. Officer Boston, please describe everything that happened from the moment you stepped out of your patrol unit at Fat Jimmy's Bar last night."

Boston's recitation had no surprises for Doc, who nodded from time to time when Sullivan looked at him for reassurance. Regner and Fantuzzo had been such good witnesses Doc fantasized about hiring them to travel around town to watch crimes.

There was nothing in the telling Doc didn't already know, though the story was more compelling in Trevor's words and voice. He showed nerves at first, no surprise. Desirable, even. Last thing he needed was for anyone to interpret detachment as a sign of sociopathic tendencies. He grew more comfortable as things went on and the troopers didn't badger him about details. That would come later.

Thornton and Rothermel knew their stuff. They allowed Boston to tell the story his way. Asked for the occasional "clarification," or for him to fill in a perceived gap. Doc had done this more times than he could remember. Let the suspect tell whatever story he wanted, lock him in, then come back later if anything didn't match the evidence or what they learned from other sources.

Boston's description of the events inside the bar complete, he paused for a drink of water. Didn't resume as quick as Thornton wanted. "What happened when you got outside?"

"The EMTs showed me the direction he went. I stopped at the first corner to ensure he wasn't waiting in ambush, then proceeded toward the back of the building."

"Was your weapon drawn?"

"Not at that time. I had room to move and time to respond if he was waiting for me."

Boston delayed, as if expecting another question. Went on when none were forthcoming. "I walked along the wall looking for fresh tracks, but the snow was coming from the other side and there wasn't much that close to the building. When I got to the end I stepped back and looked around the corner to see how things laid out. It's kind of—you've been there by now, haven't you?"

Rothermel said, "In daylight, with friends. What did you see?"

"Along the back wall are liquor and beer cases—cardboard boxes—lined up in piles of at least six feet high. Parallel about six or eight feet away is another row of empty boxes, not quite as high, with a couple of stacks of wooden pallets. A dumpster sits about halfway along this side. The path between is littered with broken glass, pieces of wood, paper, cardboard, all kinds of shit."

Thornton asked if there was a door along the back wall.

"I couldn't see one, but I knew there had to be. Emergency exit, if nothing else, but I also figured they'd want the dumpster convenient to a way out."

"Had you ever been there before?"

"To Fat Jimmy's?" Boston snorted. "It's a regular stop, especially on weekends."

"Ever been around back?"

Boston shook his head. "Never had reason to. The action's always inside."

The troopers accepted that. Boston went on. "I didn't see or hear anything, but I also couldn't see behind the dumpster and didn't know if there were gaps between the boxes where someone could stand." He paused.

Rothermel said, "Is that when you pulled your weapon?"

"About then. I was preparing to go back there when I heard a sound."

"What did you hear?"

"It's hard to say with the way the snow muffled everything. Could've been breaking glass. I also heard what might have been someone shuffling their feet, so I thought maybe he stepped on a bottle or something."

Thornton: "When did you announce yourself?"

Boston thought. "Either right before or right after I drew my weapon. A second or two either way."

"Did you have your flashlight on?"

Boston nodded. "Not that it did me much good. It was blowing harder around back so all I really saw were snow-flakes reflecting the light into my face." No objections. "I was about to move forward when I saw the suspect—"

"Victim."

Migliorini spoke for the first time. "Not yet he isn't. In the timeline of this narrative, he's still a suspect."

Thornton sat back, disgusted. "Let's not quibble, Counselor."

"Let's not editorialize."

Thornton breathed to speak. Rothermel got in first. "No one wants to waste time here. We still need to get to the crime scene while there's daylight." Neither combatant argued with the logic, though both appeared willing to continue their discussion, outside if necessary. "Officer Boston?"

"He came from the far side of the dumpster, moving pretty fast. I turned that direction and raised my weapon and he...he slipped, or something. Like a stumble, but he kept coming. I ordered him to stop. When he didn't, I shot him."

"How many times?"

"Three. I think." A pause. "Yeah. Three. I'm sure."

"Did he go down right away?"

"Maybe a couple steps, but he already had momentum moving my direction."

Thornton: "How long before you shot him did you order him to stop?"

"It was so quick. I know I started to tell him, but I don't know if I got everything out before I fired."

"So he never had a chance to comply?"

"He was on me. There wasn't time."

No one spoke for a minute. Thornton said, "Did you identify yourself as a police officer?"

"Like I said, right around the time I drew my weapon. Before I stepped off to go behind the building."

"Did he hear you?"

Sullivan said, "Jesus Christ," under his breath.

Boston looked toward Migliorini. *Seriously?* "I said it loud enough and he knew I was coming after him, so I assume so. Am I one hundred percent sure? How could I be?"

"How would he know you were coming after him?"

Sullivan said, "Fuck you."

Boston's confusion showed. "He assaulted a police officer and ran. He had to know I was coming for him."

"Called you a name, too. Didn't he?"

"I've been called worse. It's part of the job."

Rothermel opened his mouth to speak. Thornton cut him off. "You said he had to know you were coming for him. What did you mean by that?"

Boston and Migliorini exchanged looks. The lawyer shrugged. Boston said, "I guess I meant common sense says if you slap a cop and run, he'll pursue."

Sullivan said, "And bring an ass-kicking with him." Doc sensed the chief's Irish coming up, which would not be good for anyone.

Thornton: "This time you said, 'pursue.'" Left it for Boston to pick up.

"Pursue, come after. Same thing."

"You didn't say 'come after' the first time, either. You said, 'come for.' That's a whole different connotation."

Migliorini said, "As we lawyers like to say, that's a distinction without a difference."

"Is it?" Thornton left time for disagreement. Doc knew Sullivan would have obliged had he been in the room. "Someone says they're coming after you, they mean to catch you. Someone says they're coming *for* you..."

Boston rolled his eyes. "Okay. Bad word choice. Let's say he had to know I was in pursuit. You happy now?" Boston's expression implied Thornton was not.

Rothermel's turn. "Did it occur to you there might be someone else back there?"

It had not, based on Boston's reaction. "I had no reason to believe anyone else might be in the area."

"You said you figured there had to be a door. It never occurred to you an employee might come out the back to drop off some trash? We've seen the bar. Kind of place, the line for the men's room got too long, it wouldn't surprise me if that area served as the emergency urinal."

"It never occurred to me. I was focused on the subject."

Thornton: "What about the background?"

"The background?"

"People walking behind the target. Houses downrange. Anything and anyone within twenty-four hundred yards is potentially in danger."

Sullivan stared at Doc, dumbstruck. Doc said, "Let's see how Boston handles it."

A brief attorney-client conference. Boston sat back and cast a questioning look. Migliorini thought, then shrugged. Boston said, "It'll only go that far if you put some trajectory to it. I was firing more or less parallel to the ground at a target less than twenty feet away. Slightly downhill, even."

"The round would still travel several hundred yards."

"More like two hundred. Maybe three. Either way, I didn't have time to make the calculation. Like I said, he was on me. It was him or me."

The troopers let it lie on the table a few seconds before Thornton said, "What was it that made him such a mortal threat? I mean, you skipped over the use of force continuum and went straight to lethal."

"That's not true. I tried verbalization and empty-handed control in the bar. He resisted."

"There were less-than-lethal options."

"I didn't have time."

"Which brings us back to my original question: what made him such an immediate and urgent threat? Did he have a weapon?"

Boston swallowed hard. Migliorini leaned in, shielded his mouth from the detectives and the microphone. Sat back. Boston said, "I thought he had a knife."

"Was a knife found at the scene?"

"Not to my knowledge."

"Was any kind of weapon found?"

"Not to my knowledge."

"So he wasn't armed."

"I had reason to believe he was." Thornton arched an eyebrow. "I saw something in his hand."

Another pause, longer than the others. "You shot him. He's down. What did you do?"

"I maintained a sight picture until I was sure he wasn't moving. I then checked for a pulse and didn't find one, so I got on the radio and called for an ambulance."

"Which you knew was already there. You said it was the EMTs who pointed out which way Johnson went."

"I didn't want to leave the scene unsecure."

Sullivan grunted. "As he was trained."

Thornton: "How long did it take for the EMTs to get to you?"

"Less than a minute. They came out the back door. We weren't fifteen feet from it."

"Why didn't you go to the back door and call for help?"

"I didn't...I thought...I guess I figured a place like Fat Jimmy's, the door would be locked from the inside."

"Did you check? Before you used your radio to call for the ambulance?"

"I didn't know exactly where the door was until the EMTs came out. I hadn't gone that far along the back."

"It still would've been quicker to get them yourself, even if you had to go around front to do it. Wouldn't it?"

"I didn't want to leave the body unattended."

"It wasn't a body yet. Far as you knew it was just a GSW."

"I checked his pulse! He was dead!" Migliorini laid a hand

on Boston's arm.

"What you mean is that he had no pulse you could detect."

"There wasn't anything I could do for him."

"Did you attempt CPR?"

"He was on his face."

"Did you turn him over?"

Boston clenched his fists on the table. "He was dead!"

"Did you turn him over?"

"There was no point!"

"Counselor, direct your client to answer the question."

"Can we have a minute?" Thornton assented with a disgusted hand gesture.

Boston and Migliorini turned to face each other. Boston rested his elbows on his thighs. Hung his head. Migliorini spoke with some urgency into Boston's ear, keeping his head between the attorney and the detectives.

Everyone in position again two minutes later. Thornton said, "You ready?" Boston nodded. "Did you turn him over?"

"No." So soft Doc wasn't sure he hadn't read Boston's lips.

"Speak up for the recording."

Boston spoke louder. "No." Realized how that sounded. "I didn't turn him over."

"Why not?"

Migliorini said, "Asked and answered."

"We're not in court, Counselor. You're here to protect your client's rights, not steer the questioning."

Doc recognized the lawyer's expression. Were Boston a civilian, this is where Migliorini would make a dramatic gesture of putting any papers into his briefcase, then snapping it shut with authority as he said, "We're out of here." Thrown his two-thousand-dollar Burberry coat over his arm and left, tossing, "Charge him or release him" over a shoulder on the way out. Boston waived certain rights when he took the police oath. He could lawyer up, but he didn't have the same right to stop talking as the average knucklehead.

The sides exchanged hard looks. Thornton spoke after allowing time for the intensity to drop. "Did you turn him over?"

Boston sounded deflated. "No. I told you that already. No."

"Why not?"

"He was d—I thought he was dead. I wanted to protect the scene."

"Knowing the first thing the EMTs would do would be to turn him over."

"I guess I wasn't thinking that far ahead."

Thornton appeared to have made his point. "Let's go back inside the bar. Johnson called you a nigger to your face."

"No, he didn't."

Both troopers raised eyebrows. Thornton said, "You told us he said only a real cop could take him in, not some nigger with a badge."

"You said he called me a nigger to my face."

"Explain."

"I didn't take what he said—about who could take him in—I didn't take that personally. Not like he called me that."

Rothermel nodded. "This sounds like another distinction without a difference, but all right. You're saying you took no personal affront from the language he used."

"That's right."

"What *did* you do? I mean immediately after he said that."

"I attempted to place him in handcuffs."

"Yet you didn't take the comment personally."

"He continued to interfere with my investigation after multiple warnings to stop. He disobeyed several lawful requests. It was time."

Thornton, with a sneer: "You're telling us you were upholding the honor of the uniform."

"I was doing my job as a sworn officer. He would've said something like that to me off duty—I'm saying to me personally, not knowing I'm a cop—I'd have knocked him on his ass."

Doc and Sullivan recoiled. Both understood what he meant.

Both agreed with it. Having to put up with things while wearing the bag that the average guy would never tolerate was a common topic of conversation among cops. Not in front of two investigators tasked with determining if your temper led you to kill a man.

Boston's comment hung in the air like a stale fart. Not offensive enough to comment on, memorable enough to resurface later if a point needed to be made.

They took him through it again. Nothing changed worth mentioning. Everyone did their jobs. The troopers locked Boston into a story. He told it with the right mix of precision. Not so much it sounded rehearsed, not so little it wouldn't hold water. It didn't matter much. Few facts were in dispute; none would be after the crime scene report and lab results were in. Only two things mattered:

1. Did Boston see something he could reasonably consider to be a weapon?
2. What was in his heart when he went back there?

Doc felt bad for the young officer. This took a lot out of him, no matter how well he thought he did or didn't do. The next interview—the one after the troopers had digested the reports and viewed the crime scene without five inches of snow—that chat would make what happened today seem like a first date.

# 7.

Warmer at the crime scene than it had been that morning. Balmy compared to last night. "Cold and a half" on what Doc thought of as the Bill Ray Coldness Index, devised by an Army buddy:

Cold
Goddamn cold
Goddamn fucking cold
Jesus Christ is it goddamn fucking cold
Go to hell

Doc had just about made up his mind to go inside and pee when his cell went off. Brendan Sullivan. "Get back here right now."

"I don't think they're finished with me yet."

"Shimp's the liaison. Get your ass back to the house forthwith."

The troopers threw him looks that would have dropped a lesser man, fazed Doc not at all. Walked into Sullivan's office eleven minutes later, the station even more subdued than when he'd left.

Sullivan spoke before Doc could knock. "You hear the news?"

"I been kind of busy, what with Boston shooting that guy last night and the state police up our asses all day," Doc said in his *I've had two hours' sleep and can live without the* Guess what? *bullshit.*

"Car radio?"

"Over-the-air radio is a mix of shitty music and fascist abuse of the First Amendment." Doc trying to show proper respect to the chief while teetering on the brink of a hearty, *Cut to the fucking chase already.*

"I saved it for you."

Sullivan pointed a remote control at the television in the corner of his office. Some CNN midday show with the standard cable news-attractive female host. "Breaking news: This video was posted half an hour ago on social media by an organization calling itself 'Potentia Albus.' The white nationalist group is led by Spencer Richards, who is speaking in the video, which was posted in response to the shooting of a white man by an African American police officer in Penns River, Pennsylvania last night."

Doc said, "Richie Johnson was a Nazi?" Sullivan pointed to the television. "With a name like Richie?" Sullivan jabbed a finger at the screen and Doc decided he'd been clever enough for the time being.

The man on the screen appeared to be about Doc's age, early forties. Square head framed by dark hair cut short on the sides. He spoke with a slight lisp in a semi-honky voice that dripped with condescension. Wore the aura of a man who knew his shit not only didn't stink, it tasted like Dove Bars. Not that he'd give you any.

"Last night in Penns River, Pennsylvania, one of our brothers, Richard William Johnson, was murdered in an incident that cannot be explained in any way other than as a government-sanctioned assassination of a white man by a Black. The Democrat governor has already dispatched members of Pennsylvania's deep state to blackwash the entire incident, which will be deemed a legitimate use of police force regardless of the surrounding facts.

"We cannot allow this to pass, as we have so often in the past.

Too long have we stood by while our birthrights were eroded. We draw the line at open warfare. I call on all like-minded— better, all *right*-minded—people to demonstrate their outrage by coming to Penns River this weekend. The funeral arrangements are still pending because the coroner—a Jew from the neighboring county—has yet to finish desecrating Richard's remains. In the interim, the sham 'investigation' continues." Richards made air quotes as he said, "investigation."

Doc taken aback to learn Allegheny County Coroner Andy Wang was Jewish. Richards droned on. "We must draw a line to let racist authorities know we stand at a precipice. Our only choices are to step into the abyss like lemmings or to pick up the gauntlet and fight. Push back from the brink to reclaim what is ours. Let Penns River be this generation's Pearl Harbor, the event after which we can no longer naively assume good will from those who oppose and oppress us.

"We must rise up to accept our God-given responsibility, our mandate, to return America to its leading position in the world. It is neither accident nor coincidence that the rise of the Black and the brown coincides with the eclipse of American authority and respect in the world. This weekend will be the first step along the path toward reclaiming our mantle. I look forward to seeing all of you in Penns River."

Sullivan thumbed the remote. Doc continued to look at the blank screen. "Who the fuck is Spencer Richards? And what the fuck is a potential albumin or whatever?"

"Potentia Albus means 'white power' in Latin." Doc was impressed. Sullivan said, "I looked it up while you were driving in."

"What about the guy? Spencer Richards? What does he mean?"

"Apparently he's an up and comer in the alt-right. Has disturbing ideas on all the usual stuff. Holocaust denier, racial purity, God put white people on earth to rule. The usual and then some. Started off billing himself as the twenty-first century

George Lincoln Rockwell. Now he says Rockwell was a pussy."

"And this guy was? Rockwell, I mean. Sam's the actor. Right?"

"George Lincoln Rockwell was the head of the American Nazi Party for years. Founded it, for all I know. He might also have been the first to use the phrase, 'white power.'"

"A role model, then."

"Exactly."

Doc played with a shoelace that had begun to split. "What's the plan?"

"No vacations until further notice. No approval for requests for time off. Scheduled days off are okay, subject to one-hour recall. No cashing in lost time. I'm also going to ask the mayor to see if the state police will provide support, or at least have people on standby till we see how bad things get. Tell the detectives to have their bags ready to wear in case I call them out. Mike Zywiciel is checking the riot gear now."

"We don't have near enough for everyone."

"I know. He's looking to see what we do have so we can come up with a plan of who gets what and who goes where."

"What about Shimp?"

"What about her?"

"She's the liaison with the state investigators."

"Right." Sullivan leaned his elbows on the desk. "She works intake as much as they'll let her. Let's hope they're sensitive to our situation."

The phone interrupted. Sullivan answered on the first ring. "Yeah, Val. I was just about to call him. Put him through." Mouthed to Doc: "The mayor." Said into the phone, "Hello Mr. Mayor—right. Chet. I was just about to call you...yes, I saw it on television." Sullivan's face clouded and Doc didn't need to hear Chet's side of the conversation to know what came next. "Are you sure that's how you want to do it? I mean, we have no idea how many are coming or how aggressive they'll be...I suppose it does depend on the weather somewhat...uh-huh...uh-huh...you're the boss…that's right…yes, I understand. No calls to any barracks or to Harrisburg…Yes, sir. Mr. M—Chet, I have Ben Dougherty with me now and Mike Zywiciel will be here any minute so we can start getting ready…I'll call you if anything new comes up…understood. Thanks for the call."

Sullivan didn't hang up. Stared at the handset. Doc said, "Let me guess. You're under no circumstances to call for any state police assistance."

"How did you know?"

"This isn't the first time whoever sat where you are now got a call like that. I knew what he wanted as soon as you told me who it was."

Sullivan looked at the handset as if he didn't remember picking it up. Slipped it into its cradle. Blew air from his cheeks. "What's going on here?"

"We talked about the DA's political future this morning." Sullivan nodded. "How strings got pulled for Dan Hecker to put his shitty little casino here." Another nod. "That animosity runs both ways. Hecker never forgave Harrisburg for making him open here instead of someplace more glamorous, like Erie. This is his way of showing the Commonwealth we don't need them. Been that way since Hecker bought Chet the mayor's job."

"You called a traffic examiner in for the hit-and-run last summer."

"We can get away with one-offs like that so long as we keep them under the radar. Stush had personal relationships with a lot of staties. So does Mike. I have a few. We go direct and by the time it floats up to Chet—if it does—the job is done. We may have to eat a dessert-sized bowl of shit over it, but nothing too onerous."

"We're on our own, then."

"Unless the governor takes it upon himself to send in troopers. Or calls out the National Guard if things go to hell altogether. What breaks Hecker's balls is that we're still subservient to Harrisburg. Like with this Boston situation. The state police handle all police shooting investigation for cities under a certain size, which means pretty much everyplace except Philadelphia and Pittsburgh. Scranton, maybe. Wilkes-Barre. Allentown, I suppose."

Sullivan rocked back in his chair. Rested a heel on the corner of the desk. "Stan Napierkowski told me this would be a nice place to retire."

"He wasn't lying." Sullivan shot Doc a look. "He's retired here. He loves it. That's how you got the job."

# 8.

The phone was already ringing when Doc got back to his office.
"Dougherty."

"Hi, Sergeant. It's Katy Jackson from the *Tribune-Gazette*. Have you heard the remarks by Spencer—"

"No comment."

"You can't even tell me if you heard them?"

"Sure I can."

"Okay. Have you heard what Spencer Richards said about last night's shooting?"

"No comment."

"You just said you could comment on that."

"It's not that I can't. I'm not going to." Katy Jackson worked her way up from stringer to part-time to full-time as the Neshannock County reporter for the Pittsburgh *Tribune-Gazette*. She was smart, eager, conscientious, and ambitious. She and Doc had crossed paths before and knew each other well enough he could mess with her and she wouldn't worry about getting scooped.

"Is there anything you can comment on?"

"The weather's shitty."

"I was thinking more along the lines of the current situation. You know, Black cop shoots unarmed white—sorry, allegedly unarmed white supremacist? Neo-Nazis converging on the town? That sort of thing."

"All official comments come from Chief Sullivan's office."

"I called there already. Whoever answered the phone said a statement would be forthcoming."

"So you called me, hoping I'd put my head in a noose and talk out of school to further your career and ruin mine."

"That's not how I would've phrased it, but yeah. Pretty much."

"Then you're out of luck. I will not comment. Nor will I be a highly placed police source who requested anonymity."

"You're not that highly placed."

"I am management, though."

"You are."

"Here's the thing: I can't be any kind of police source. I can't be a source at all. What I'm about to tell you is not only not for attribution, it's not for publication. What I think you ink-stained wretches call deep background. You may only use it to inform your reporting and it can never appear in print without my say-so. Do we agree on that?"

"Yes." They'd played this game before. She knew if she went along he'd give her stuff no one else had when the time came. It was working with Doc as much as anything that got her the full-time job. She told him as much one day when he refused to let her take him to dinner as a thank you.

"I never heard of Spencer Richards before Sullivan showed me the video. Sully admitted he had to look the guy up."

"He's supposed to be a big deal in the alt-right."

"That's what the CNN chick said. He strikes me as the kind of guy social media allows to have a disproportionate effect on public opinion. I just hope he doesn't have a disproportionate effect on events."

They danced a while longer and ended where they always did: Katy promised not to bother Doc (too much) and Doc promised to give her advance notice before something went public. Both understood they'd get together when the snow settled and she'd get pretty much whatever she wanted to know in a combination of on the record, off the record, not for attribution, and background statements. Sullivan knew of their arrangement and did not disapprove. Once Sully even fed Doc information to give to Katy as coming from a "well-placed police source." Sullivan didn't rise to the rank of captain in Boston without learning how to play the media better than anyone Doc had ever worked with.

Time check: three thirty. Half an hour from end of watch, running on fumes, Doc thought about signing himself out. Almost did, until he remembered all the paperwork lounging on his desk while he'd been chasing his tail. Another half hour wouldn't kill him. Gave it up when he'd read the same paragraph four times and it still didn't register.

# 9.

Teresa Shimp declined the troopers' invitation to dinner. She hadn't had much more sleep than Dougherty, so she showed them the back way in and out of the city-county complex and asked to be dropped off out of sight of the media. Then she went home, ate a frozen dinner, and took a coma for an hour and a half. By seven thirty she'd showered, changed, and stopped by the detectives' office to check messages and get a fresh notebook.

Nearing the tunnel that connected the two sides of the building she encountered a man she didn't recognize who looked lost. It wasn't unusual to see civilians in this part of the building during the workday, but not with all the offices closed for going on three hours. He didn't wear anything that identified him as any kind of civilian employee and Teresa knew all the local law enforcement personnel. He was a mystery, and she was a detective. Show time.

"Can I help you?" Her voice resonated along the almost empty hallway.

He seemed as much disgusted as anything else. "Where are all the cops?"

Teresa gestured back over her shoulder. "You walked right past them. Back there."

"I saw those cops. I'm looking for the state troopers investigating that thing in the Flats last night. Woman sent me this way."

"They're in the district attorney's office. Come with me."

He gave her a long, appraising look. "Who are you?"

Teresa badged him. "Detective Shimp, Penns River police. What's your business with the troopers?"

"They're interested in what happened at Fat Jimmy's last night, right?" He fell into step with Teresa. "Not just out back where Richie got shot."

"You knew Mr. Johnson?"

"Not like friends. I'd seen him around."

Teresa didn't recognize the man from last night. She also hadn't taken every statement. "What's your name, sir?"

"Mark Bordonaro. I work over the beer distributor across the river."

Thornton and Rothermel were already in the conference room. Teresa made introductions, told them Mr. Bordonaro had some information, and stepped aside to do whatever it was liaisons did in these circumstances, which didn't appear to be much.

Rothermel indicated a vacant chair. "What do you have for us?"

"About last night. You looking into what went on before they took it outside? While everything was still in the bar?"

"Anything that might be relevant."

"What kind of thing would be relevant?"

Thornton was in *cut to the chase* mode. "Asking questions is our job. Stop beating around the bush, tell us what you know, and we'll decide if it's relevant."

Bordonaro looked from cop to cop for the friendliest face. Settled on Teresa's. A lot of people made that mistake. "How about this? As the cop's chasing the guy out the door, I heard him say he hoped no one was out there so he could shoot that motherfucker. Pulled his gun as he said it."

Teresa's bullshit detector shot up to eleven. She and Mo Tilghman took at least twenty statements at Fat Jimmy's. None indicated Boston pulled his weapon before going outside.

Thornton said, "Those exact words? You'll swear to it in court?"

"I don't know about swearing to the exact words. The gist of it."

"You heard him say that? 'I hope there's no one outside so I can shoot this motherfucker'?"

"Like I said, something close to that."

Rothermel said, "Where were you when he said this?"

"Where do you think I was? Fat Jimmy's."

"*Where* in Fat Jimmy's?"

"By the door. Cop passed within a few feet of me."

"Who were you there with?"

"Couple guys."

"Who?"

"I don't know their names." All three cops sent glares his way. "I went by myself. I got involved in a conversation with these other two guys."

Thornton: "How long did you talk to them?"

"I don't know. Ten minutes. Fifteen. Maybe less."

"And you didn't get even their first names?"

"You know what it's like in a bar. You talk to this guy; you talk to that guy. It's just bullshitting."

Thornton spoke to Shimp. "Anyone get his statement?"

She held up her phone. "Nothing from anyone named Bordonaro."

Thornton focused his full attention back to their witness. "Explain that."

"I was gone by the time the cops got there to start asking questions."

"Why did you leave?"

"It was getting late. I was already headed for the door to go home when it happened."

"All that excitement and you went home."

"I had work this morning. I would've come in sooner except I just got off and had to eat supper."

Thornton said, "Look at me." Took a picture with his phone when Bordonaro did.

"What was that for?"

"If we show this picture to the people who were at Fat Jimmy's last night, how many of them are going to recognize you?"

"I don't know. It's dark in there. People are drinking. Fat Jimmy's is the kind of place you don't look at people like you want to memorize them."

The room had the aura of a kitchen where the cook opened the package of porterhouse to find maggots on the underside. Rothermel said, "Would you sign a statement describing what you just told us?"

"You mean like swear to it? I told you I didn't remember word for word."

"Doesn't have to be exact, so long as you say that in the statement."

"I guess I could do that." Thornton slid a notepad across the table. Flipped a pen after it. Bordonaro looked at the pen like a snake might crawl out the tip. "I wasn't figuring on being here that long. Can't you just put what I said in your notes and we'll call it done?"

Rothermel said, "We don't need your life story. A few paragraphs will do. When you got there, who you were with, what you saw, what you heard, when you left."

"I told you I don't know them guys I was talking to."

"Then say that. Maybe describe them a little."

Thornton couldn't hold back any longer. "Listen, pal. I been up since four thirty this morning. Write or don't. Whatever you do, do it now or tell your story walking."

Bordonaro considered the pen again. Started to write. Slow at first, faster as he went on.

Thornton turned to Teresa. "I shouldn't break his balls like that. It amazes me people give statements at all. I should be grateful."

Teresa recognized the cue. She and Dougherty had done similar things often enough. "You should be. Most people have no idea the kind of trouble they can get into for making a false statement, even if they mean well."

"Exactly. Good Samaritan comes in, nothing to gain, says the wrong thing? Boom! They're in a jackpot."

Rothermel said, "Knock it off, you two. You'll scare him. Intent matters."

Thornton: "How do you mean?"

"Just because a statement is inaccurate doesn't make it a lie. Honest mistakes happen."

"Well, yeah. No two statements are exactly the same. People see and hear different things. Depends on where they were, how much they were paying attention. I worry more when statements agree too much."

Teresa sensed an opening. "What about a statement that comes in out of left field? Not like it's missing stuff others had, but has stuff no one else did?"

Rothermel waved an approving finger her direction. "Good point. We'd have to check that pretty close. Last thing we want to do is put someone away over a simple misunderstanding."

Bordonaro put down the pen. Pushed away the pad. Thornton picked it up. "You forgot to sign."

Bordonaro looked as if he'd poured sour milk on the last bit of cereal in the house. "I don't know if this is such a good idea."

Rothermel showed confusion. Thornton gave Bordonaro a five-hundred-watt cop stare. "You couldn't wait to tell us when you came in here."

"Yeah, I know. It's just—this Black cop. He could go to prison for this."

"It's possible."

"Or he might not."

"Also possible."

"I'm a little concerned what might happen if I give this statement. Am I gonna have to testify?"

Rothermel said, "I don't see any way you don't get called as a witness if this goes to trial. Based on the statements we have, you're the only person who can testify to Boston's state of mind when he went back there. Case like this, a jury will want to know if he had intent. Detective Shimp. You work with the local DA a lot. That sound about right?"

"Absolutely. I've seen Sally Gwynn plead out enough cases to know this never sees a courtroom without evidence of intent, and there's no way she can afford to plead out something this high profile."

Thornton, to Bordonaro: "There you go."

Bordonaro was sweating like a junkie two dollars shy of a fix. "I testify and he don't go to jail, I'm gonna have to spend the rest of my life looking over my shoulder for this cop."

Rothermel said, "There are a lot of cops in this town."

Bordonaro was close to panic now. Teresa raised an eyebrow toward the troopers. They nodded. She took the seat next to Bordonaro. Leaned in to create a sense of intimacy. She'd done this before and knew she did it well.

"Mr. Bordonaro, I've worked here for a few years and I know everyone in the department. We don't want a bad cop here any more than you do. If Officer Boston went back there with malicious intent, we want to know about it. We also know juries are unreliable. Guilty people get acquitted all the time. Tell the truth and you have nothing to worry about from the Penns River police, no matter how the trial comes out."

"I am telling the truth here."

"I'm sure you are."

"What I'm worried about is, like, what if someone decides I ain't, even if I am?"

"Cops are evidence-based people, Mr. Bordonaro. No one is going to decide one way or the other without investigating your statement first." Paused for effect. "We will look into it, you know. Any uncorroborated statement requires investigation."

"Maybe the rest of you are okay, but I still got to consider what could happen if I testify and this Black cop goes free."

Rothermel said, "Why do you keep bringing up that he's Black?"

"It doesn't matter if he's Black or white. Mexican, even. I had a few drinks. It was noisy. You know what Jimmy's is like after a ball game or a wrestling match."

Thornton's voice had the warmth of a meat locker. "Tell us."

"You've been there, right?" No acknowledgment. Bordonaro looked around the room. "None of you?" Teresa kept her experiences to herself. "It's—it's—it's noisy, is all. There's a lot going on. The light's not too good, either."

Thornton, with no hint of a question in his voice: "You're saying you don't want to sign the statement."

"Yeah, I want to sign. It's just...looking at it, writing it down like that, I'm not a hundred percent sure about what he said. The Black cop, I mean." Cringed a little after mentioning Boston's race.

Thornton opened the door. "Get lost."

"Hey! There's no need for that. I was trying to be a good citizen. I'm just being careful."

Rothermel came around, sat one cheek on the table next to Bordonaro. "Mr. Bordonaro, we appreciate people who step up to be witnesses, especially when they do so at some personal risk. We also take a dim view of those who show up out of nowhere to tell us uncorroborated stories they're not willing to stand by.

"You came in here claiming to have skipped out on the initial canvass. You have no names of anyone who might have seen you or talked to you. If we show your picture around and no one can vouch for you...we might have to check around. Find out where you *were* drinking last night."

Bordonaro stared at a spot halfway between his feet and Rothermel's. Thornton said, "You didn't waste too much of our time tonight, so I'm not taking it personal. We see you again and you're peddling a different story? I'll have something to say about that. Are we on the same page?"

Bordonaro nodded. Mumbled something.

"Good night, then."

No one spoke until the footfalls disappeared. Thornton broke the silence. "I hope that Hitler Youth asshole on the television today isn't going to cause us any more problems like this."

# 10.

Sean Sisler rolled down Oak Street with his headlights off. Answering a call from the same address where Boston encountered a deer the night before. Requests two nights in a row from the same house at the same time meant either

> 1. There was an innocent explanation (loose gutter, tree limb brushing window, raccoon loose in trash);
> 2. Someone in the house had a hyperactive imagination;
> 3. Someone was fucking with either the police or the resident;
> 4. The prowler had come back for seconds, which was cause for concern.

Sisler operated on Option Four, as none of the others carried legitimate risk of injury unless the coon was rabid, or turned out to be a bear. It was a lot easier to scale down the vigilance than to ramp it up. Assuming you got a chance to ramp it up.

Everything looked quiet from the front, which told Sisler little. Prowlers don't often try to break in the fronts of houses where the world can see them. Sisler turned off the dome light and got out of the car. Walked around the side of the house, flashlight in one hand, retracted baton held along his leg.

Well-groomed flower beds waiting for spring at the front of the house led to shrubs in winter mode around the side. Sisler walked heel-to-toe and kept as much weight as possible on the outsides of his feet to minimize the sound of his tactical boots crunching the frozen snow. Eased his head around the corner to look at the back. Nothing there except for the chimney jutting out halfway along.

He moved at an angle calculated to keep anything he encountered between him and the house. A flash of light in the woods caught his attention. Turned off his flashlight and waited. Saw it again. Binoculars, maybe. Altered his approach even more to come around whoever he was tracking. Hoped the houses and trees broke up the streetlight enough to prevent his uniform being too obvious against the pristine snow of the yard. His stealth well short of stalking, knowing the subject's only flight was into the woods that ran down Edgecliff Hill. Tonight's were not the conditions for such a dash unless you had a crush on an ER nurse.

Ten feet away, Sisler turned on the flash and said, "Freeze. Penns River police."

Of course, the guy ran.

Made it twenty feet before slipping and planting his face flush into—what else?—an oak tree. Dropped onto his back like a bale of flour.

Sisler took his time to approach, watching the man's hands all the time. "Stay right where you are." Saw as he got closer this was more like a kid. Sixteen years old, maybe. "What's your name?"

"Dennis."

"Dennis what?"

"Dennis Mitchell."

"How old are you?"

"Seventeen."

"What are you doing back here?"

"Nothing."

Sisler took a deep breath. Exhaled through his nose to give

Dennis the idea patience was in short supply. "Dennis, we can settle this right here, or we can go to the station and get people and paperwork involved. A lot of that depends on what happens in the next minute or so. Now, what are you doing back here?"

"Nothing. I'm just back here, you know?"

"Where do you live?" Dennis mumbled something. "It's not like I won't find out. Where do you live?"

"Royal Oak Drive." Around the corner.

"Pick up your binoculars and let's go."

Dennis mumbled something. Might have been *fuck*. Said for attribution, "I must've dropped them when you scared the shit out of me."

Sisler still had the eyesight—what Dougherty called "Ted Williams vision"—that served him well in Afghanistan. Found and retrieved the glasses. Scanned the back of the house for the hell of it more than anything. Dennis sagged against the tree.

The curtains were open in the right upstairs window; the shade was up. A young woman—a girl by Sisler's standards—stood near a lamp positioned so she could be seen from the outside. Sisler supposed she was attractive, not that he cared, being over thirty and gay. Well-developed for her age, no mistake about it dressed as she was, which was not at all. She slid a finger into her mouth, caressed a nipple with it. Her other hand was between her legs.

Sisler turned to Dennis. "Friend of yours?" Dennis mumbled something. Articulation not his strong suit. "Level with me. You were about a minute from whacking it. Be honest." No answer.

Sisler considered options while watching the steam of his breath dissipate. Wondered if how long it took depended more on the temperature or the humidity. "How long as this been going on?"

"Couple nights."

"Literally? Just last night and tonight?"

"Yeah."

More consideration. "Do they have a dog?"

"Little yappy thing."

"She have brothers?"

"He's away at college."

"Her old man have a gun?"

"I don't know. Maybe. He wouldn't shoot nobody."

"He's not the only one you'd have to worry about." Dennis looked confused. "I have a gun."

"You're a cop."

"Cops shoot people. Don't you watch the news?"

"They don't—cops don't, I mean, in a town like this, a cop's not gonna shoot, you know? That happens in cities and ghettoes. Not out like where we are."

"You mean cops shoot Black people?"

"Well, yeah. Mostly. Right?"

The job got harder every day. Broke Sisler's balls, people just assuming cops only shot Blacks. Not that he could blame them all that much, what you saw on the news. "You hear about the white guy got shot by a cop down the Flats last night?"

"I heard something. Didn't pay much attention. It was down the Flats, you know?"

Fucking kid. If it didn't happen to him or someone of personal acquaintance, it didn't really happen. "Here's something you don't know, Einstein. The cop that shot that guy last night? Guess where he was right before he went to the Flats." Left it there.

"How would I know?"

"You might've seen him. He was right here. Looking for you."

"That's bullshit."

"I'll show you the logs when I take you into the station." If the staties hadn't already vouchered them as evidence. Dennis didn't need to know that.

That got the kid's attention. "You're still taking me in?"

"I haven't ruled it out. I have to account for myself every time I'm dispatched. I'm going inside to talk to the father or mother or whoever made the call. Can I assume you don't want to get your girlfriend in trouble?"

"She's not my girlfriend."

"Kid, in some countries you'd have to marry her, what you two've been doing. You want me to keep her out of it? Maybe cut you a break at the same time?" This, Dennis was all in on. "You wait right here until I come back. Let me see how things go in there and maybe—maybe—I can cut you a pass this one time. But your ass had better be right here when I come back. It's not like I can't find you if I want to."

"Thanks. I really appreciate it, but can you hurry? I gotta piss something awful."

"You kept everything zipped this long. Another few minutes won't kill you." Considering where they were, nothing prevented Dennis from relieving himself where he stood. He could figure that out for himself.

The man of the house answered the door. Pushing fifty, in pretty good shape, losing the combover battle. Sisler identified himself. "I couldn't find anything, sir. Best I can figure is some deer are walking through there. The officer that responded last night about got run over by one."

"There were no tracks this morning."

"It was back in the woods a little."

"I could've sworn I heard something closer."

"You very well might have. It could be just about anything. Stray branch, hanging wire, loose gutter. All I can tell you is I gave it a good look and didn't see anything to worry about."

The homeowner didn't sound too sure. "I'll take a look tomorrow if I get a chance. Over the weekend, for sure."

"That's not a bad idea. So we're clear, I'm not saying not to call. You hear anything that worries you, tell the nine-one-one operator we spoke tonight, and that Officer Sisler said that whoever comes should bring backup and do a proper search. I'll enter it in my logbook, as well. I want you to know that me not finding anything tonight doesn't mean I'm not taking it seriously."

Mom spoke over her husband's shoulder. "That'd be great. Thank you."

Sisler waited to see if they had anything else to say. Filled the space himself when they didn't. "I wonder if I could speak to your daughter for a minute before I go."

Neither parent expected that. "Diane? What for?" came in unison.

Sisler lowered his voice. "It's not a big deal. She's not in trouble and I don't want to get her in Dutch here. It's just that, while I was looking around outside, I noticed she's not as careful as she might be with her window shades while she's getting ready for bed. I'm not suggesting it's my place to talk to her about it, but I know sometimes kids roll their eyes when their parents give advice or warnings. Even take it as a challenge. A kindly word from Officer Friendly might make the message take better, but only if you think so."

Mom was confused. "I don't understand why you're concerned about this."

"Ma'am, there are all kinds of people out there. The odds are against it—a thousand to one, maybe—but if someone happened by and saw too much of your daughter, they might get the wrong idea about her." Dad's expression implied maybe it wouldn't be the wrong idea. Sisler soldiered on. "This person finds out who she is, makes sure he runs into her somewhere? He might have certain expectations. If they aren't met...it's a shame girls have to be so much more careful than boys, but that's life. Even in a town like Penns River."

Dad said, "We've had a few talks, not about that exactly. Maybe you can impress the importance on her better."

Diane met Sisler in the living room dressed as if he'd disturbed her sleep in a convent. Flannel pajamas, terrycloth robe, bunny slippers. Sisler threw a quick look toward the kitchen to verify the parents' location. They nodded. He spoke to Diane so only she would hear. "Hi, Diane. I'm Officer Sisler, Penns River police. I'm sorry to bother you so late."

Diane sounded somewhere between unsure and scared. "What's all this about?"

"Do you know a boy named Dennis Mitchell?"

That snapped her head back. "From school. We're not close or anything."

"Diane, I have Dennis outside. In handcuffs," he added for effect. She had no concept of a poker face. "I don't want to get either of you in trouble, but the shows you're putting on have to stop. I catch him out there again, he's going to jail and it's going to come out why."

"I don't know what you mean."

"Yeah, you do. I saw. You understand? I saw you." Diane blushed so hard her robe glowed. "I'm not judging either of you. This may be your idea of safe sex. That's none of my business. An officer was almost injured here last night when he startled a deer." Paused for a second to wonder how different things might be today had the deer torn Boston up a little and kept him from going to Fat Jimmy's. "We get another call, we'll have to do something."

Back in the woods, Sisler found Dennis next to a puddle of steaming urine the boy had tried to kick snow over. Sisler waved for him to come along. "I spoke to Diane's parents. They don't know about what's been going on here. They won't, so long as it never happens again. I also talked with Diane to make sure she understood the potential consequences."

"Is she in trouble?"

"No. I put it to them that she's a little too casual about her privacy and I stumbled onto it while I was looking around. A tip for you: her father has suspicions about certain aspects of her conduct."

They stopped next to Sisler's patrol unit. Dennis asked what happens next. "I'll give you a ride home. Remember one thing: I ever get another call like this, I'm bringing at least one more cop and an ass-kicking before we take you to jail. Do you understand?"

Sisler made Dennis ride in back as a preview of potential coming attractions. Agreed when the kid asked to get out a couple of houses from his own. Watched him walk along Royal Oak Drive, thinking there had been advantages to growing up gay.

# 11.

Doc had phone in hand to call Fox's for a pizza when the doorbell sounded. The man on the front stoop held up credentials for easy reading. He was in his late thirties and about Doc's height and build, maybe a little more solid. A conservative suit, short hair, and the unmistakable aura of *fed* cemented the image in Doc's mind, so he was not surprised when the stranger said, "Detective Sergeant Benjamin Dougherty? I'm Deputy United States Marshal James Hensley. Can I have a little of your time?"

"Only if you agree to call me either 'Doc' or 'Detective.' I can live without 'Sergeant' or 'Benjamin' or 'Ben' altogether."

"Deal."

Doc offered a Coke. Hensley accepted. Doc retrieved two glass bottles from Mexico made with real sugar. Had to go all the way to Costco to get them. Filled two glasses with cracked ice and poured. Came back to the living room to find Hensley flipping through a book. "This any good?" Held up *One or the Other*.

"I like it. It's about a Montreal cop in the seventies. A friend noticed the similarity in names—Dougherty with an O is kind of uncommon—and bought me the first book in the series. This is the third and I'm enjoying it just as much. I'm a little disappointed the author doesn't seem to have written anything lately."

"The cop have any resemblance to you?"

"He's Canadian, so he's politer. Younger, too. I'm pretty sure I'm better looking." Doc sipped his Coke. "What can I do for you, Marshal?"

Hensley took a photograph from a pocket. "Does the name Karl Tucker mean anything to you? Sometimes goes by 'Bull.'"

Doc looked at the photo. Shook his head. "Should it?"

"Tucker did a nickel in Quentin for armed robbery. Hooked up with the Aryan Brotherhood and came out a true believer. Even changed the spelling of his name from 'Carl' with a C to 'Karl' with a K. That guy who wants to hold a Nazi convention here this weekend? Spencer Richards? He's the face of that Potentia Albus operation but Tucker's the driving force. Recruits, pushes buttons, raises the dark money."

"Why isn't he the front man?"

"Partly because his opinions on race make Richards look like Martin Luther King. Mostly it's because his name's on a fugitive warrant for possessing eleven thousand four hundred sixty-eight pounds of ammonium nitrate. ATF picked him up, but some old AB buddies shot up the convoy taking him to court and got him out. Killed a couple of marshals."

"I remember reading about that."

"It made all the papers once the media figured out he was carrying almost three times the nitrate used to blow up the Murrah Building."

"That had to be three years ago. He's still out?"

Hensley's voice showed what he thought of the chance to apprehend Tucker. His face showed the emotion of an accountant triple-checking a statement. "Number Two on the Most Wanted list. Dropped out of sight completely. Has a survivalist background, so for all we know he's living in a fucking cave somewhere. He's the American bin Laden."

"And you think he might show up here for Richards's big event?"

"It's more than think. We have reason to believe. Homeland Security passed us a tip. Might even have a man inside Potentia Albus, not that they're telling us."

"Of course not."

"If Tucker does come, it won't be to carry a tiki torch and sing the Horst Wessel Song. Something will break bad. It's what he does."

*At least it's not Super Bowl weekend.* "Thanks for the heads up. I'll pass the word."

"Do me a favor and pass it on the down low. No offense, but there seems to be a sympathetic cop or two in every jurisdiction. We're tired of Tucker knowing what we're going to do before we get a chance to do it. That's why I didn't make a formal appearance at the station."

"But you trust me."

"Remember an FBI special agent named Ray Keaton?"

"Well. We got along pretty good when he was working organized crime in Pittsburgh. I heard he was counterterrorism now."

"Still is, but on the domestic side. Works on a task force that tracks these guys. Called me when we got the heads up about this weekend and vouched for you."

"Not the chief?"

"He doesn't know the new chief."

"You want me to...what? Tell him? Not tell him?"

Hensley hesitated. "You worked counterinsurgency intel in Iraq. Use your judgment on how much to tell him and how to put it. We don't want anyone here to be caught unaware, but we also don't want Tucker to get wind we might be half a step ahead of him for a change. The best course might be to come up with some pretense to want to talk to a guy that matches Tucker's description. If you come across him, all I need is for you to hold him until I can get there."

"How long are we talking about? It could get busy here this weekend."

"I'll be in town looking myself, so it shouldn't be more than ten or fifteen minutes. After that I'll need an enclosed facility where I can watch him until reinforcements come from Pittsburgh. That'll be an hour or two, but he'll be my problem then."

"I think we can handle that."

Hensley set down his glass. Leaned forward. "No offense, but I want you to understand this is not without risk. We have people ready to scramble on a moment's notice, but you have to assume his friends will come for him and they'll be armed and extremely dangerous."

"Kind of puts my people at risk, all the more information you're willing to let out."

"It's a balancing act. Something simple like a traffic stop, they see a guy looks like him, call me and put a tail on him. Make sure your people know that if they become concerned for their safety, let him go. I'll get marshals here quick as I can once I know it's worth the trip."

Hensley seemed like a good guy and Doc wanted to help if he could, but Penns River looked to have a full plate this weekend without playing grab-ass with Public Enemy Number Two. "I'll do what I can. You understand we're up against it ourselves right now."

Hensley was nodding before Doc finished. "Don't make too much of this. Tucker's not one of those 'you'll never take me alive' assholes. He's tight with the AB and is proud of how well he can jail. That said, he enjoys violence. If he thinks hurting someone will get him what he wants, he'll hurt them."

"Bad as he needs to?"

"Bad as he wants to." Hensley saw Doc's concern. "Tucker's my fugitive. It just so happens that this weekend he may be both our problems. If all I get out of this is word that he was here, I'll take it. We're not going to have any more dead cops."

"We?"

"The Marshals Service. And you."

Doc and Hensley paused on the stoop to shake hands. Hensley took a key fob from his pocket. A Suburban a few spaces from Doc's car chirped and flashed its lights.

Doc said, "I thought marshals all drove black Town Cars."

"Only on *Justified*. Even then, only Raylan."

"Well, hell. You're not nearly as cool as I thought. I may have to reconsider my offer of unconditional assistance."

"Would it make a difference if I told you I have on my desk an autographed picture of me shaking hands with Raylan Givens? In the flesh?"

"Is he wearing the hat?"

Hensley nodded. "Taken on the range at Glynco."

"Damn, Deputy. If I'd known that I'd of let you sleep with my sister. If I had one."

# 12.

Trevor Boston opened the door wearing jeans and a loose-fitting pullover sweater. Doc displayed the pizza box. "Jeet?"

"Not hungry."

"It's Fox's." Opened the box to let the scent out.

Boston averted his eyes. "What's on it?"

"Pepperoni and sausage."

"No mushrooms?"

"I'd have to eat it myself if you weren't home, or threw me out. I hate mushrooms."

Boston looked into the box. "That would be a lot of pizza to eat by yourself."

"And I'll bet you haven't eaten all day. Must be starving."

"I don't have any beer." Doc held up a six-pack of Yuengling. The left corner of Boston's mouth turned up. "That's cheating. I won't be allowed to go back to Philly if I refuse."

"I'll tell, too."

Doc wasn't sure how many rules or protocols he was breaking by bringing a pizza and beer to Trevor Boston. Doc was a sergeant now, and a detective; Boston was a patrol officer. Not only outside the chain of command but, given the situation, Doc shouldn't talk to Boston at all. The kind of situation Doc complained about when Sully promoted him, the unofficial roles that would go unfilled.

Still, Trevor Boston was a cop who was hurting. Doc hadn't

been able to shake the look on Boston's face, sitting alone in his shop outside Fat Jimmy's. Never besties, they'd always got along. Boston had come for advice a couple of times before Doc got his stripes; Doc was always happy to oblige. Steered the single post-promotion request to Mike Zywiciel with considerable tact.

Doc put the pizza on plates while Boston poured the beer. "These are still cold."

"I bought them right out of the cooler at Mroczka's on my way to pick up the pizza."

Boston solved a robbery at Jake Mroczka's beer distributorship over the summer. "He's a piece of work. How's he doing?"

"He's good. Asked about you, as a matter of fact." Boston showed disbelief. "No, really. Asked me how that colored cop was doing, the one that caught those two assholes robbed him last summer."

"Colored?"

"It's a process. Eat."

They each ate a slice and drank a beer. Boston said, "You buying trouble coming over here?"

"Not if you don't tell anyone." Doc let the import of his comment settle. "I left my stripes in the car. My conscience is clear so long as we don't talk about anything that happened last night."

More eating. An occasional drink. The silence was as comfortable as could be expected with an elephant that size in such a small kitchen.

Boston said, "This is good pizza."

Doc flipped a strand of cheese over his lip into his mouth. "The Inn gives it a run for its money, but yeah. Fox's rules."

"The Inn makes pizza?"

"Good pizza, too. It gets overlooked because the wings are so outstanding."

"Their wings are great. I never had them like that until I moved here."

"That's what chicken wings are supposed to be. Don't get

me wrong. I like Buffalo wings. But a chicken wing is the whole wing, breaded and cooked in a deep fryer."

Boston pulled a piece of pepperoni from his slice, ate it solo. "You lived here all your life, didn't you?"

"Except when I was in the Army."

"How long was that?"

"Nine years."

Boston took a healthy swig. "In that long, why didn't you stay for twenty?"

"It was time."

"You didn't like it?"

"Liked it fine. Loved it most of the time." Saw Boston's confusion. "I did two tours in Iraq. I'd have to stay another eleven years for a pension, which might mean as many as four or five more paid vacations either there, or in Afghanistan. I couldn't see going back and not accomplishing the same things we already hadn't accomplished, risk getting my ass shot off in the bargain."

The words fell out of Boston's mouth like panicked moviegoers from a burning theater. "You ever kill anyone?" Dipped his head. "Don't answer that. I'm sorry."

"It's okay. Once." Doc held up an index finger. "The funny thing is, it was right here in Penns River, and I was off duty. I shot a guy coming up the stairs into my parents' kitchen."

"Sounds like your back was against the wall."

Doc made a dismissive gesture. "It was nothing like your situation, not that we're going to talk about that. My guy was part of a crew that didn't close quick enough after they started shooting up my parents' house, so I had a few seconds to prepare. My cousin had my wing, and he doesn't fool around. I knew every inch of a place they'd never seen before. I put three center of mass from maybe eight feet away. Guy didn't even know I was there until I went down the stairs to talk to him."

"He wasn't dead?"

"Might as well have been." Doc took a second. "We exchanged a few words. He didn't wait for the ambulance."

"How'd it make you feel?"

"At the time? Pretty goddamn good. Bear in mind, we're talking about a firefight where over a hundred rounds were expended and my parents were in jeopardy. I had enough adrenaline to launch that house into orbit." Doc stopped without tapering off.

"What about later?"

This answer didn't come as easy. "I dream about it once in a while. Sometimes it pops into my head when I'm running errands or watching TV. Not the shooting. Kneeling by my parents' front steps watching his candle go out."

"How do you feel about it now?"

Doc set down a slice of pizza. "I try not to think about it much."

Boston chewed. Took a drink. "Did you talk to anyone? About how you feel?"

"You mean like a counselor?"

"Yeah."

Doc shook his head. "You have a bad time last night? Get any sleep at all?"

"I came home and took a shower until the hot water ran out. Then I crashed on the couch and channel surfed until ten this morning. Took another shower, did some laundry, gave my statement, then came back here and did household chores until I went back to surfing an hour before you showed up." Rigidity came to Boston's posture. "I *know* I saw a gun. Some kind of weapon. He had something in his hand."

Doc raised his palms shoulder height, facing out. "We can't talk about that. You need to talk, tell your lawyer. He's a good guy. See a counselor or a clergyman. Someone with privilege. Anything you say to me, any of the cops you know, they can make us tell."

"My parents want me to see a counselor. Said they'd pay for it."

"The department will pay for it. It's in the contract."

"Going to see a counselor is kind of a career-limiting move, isn't it?"

"Not like it used to be. We have one of those Employee Assistance Programs. They'll never know."

"But you didn't use them."

"I'm not saying I did the right thing." Boston's expression invited explanation. "I saw a lot in Iraq. Get to sites ten minutes after a suicide bomb or an IED not knowing if that explosion was the decoy to draw Americans into the open for something worse. Got pinned down by small arms fire and IEDs and mortars on the way to what was supposed to be a routine meeting in Fallujah once. We had to call in an Apache helicopter. Minigun rounds zipping in not twenty feet overhead. If I could put all that in a box, whatever happened on a warm summer night in my hometown is no big deal." Paused to let the familiar images run through his mind. "I don't know how those Eleven-Bravos did it, being their job every fucking day."

"Eleven-Bravo?"

"Infantry. Eleven-Bravo—eleven B—is what's called a Military Occupation Specialty."

Boston allowed Doc to remain wherever he was for a moment. "You miss it?"

"Not really. The camaraderie and the ball breaking with friends, sure, though there's plenty of that here without the fear of getting your dick blown off every day. Don't let anyone kid you about the military. They're very good at what they do. Never been anything like it in the world. It's also a large hierarchy, so it's fucked up, almost by definition. That might be the best thing about working in a department like ours. The fewer the layers, the lower the level of fuckupedness."

"It helped you, though? Not letting things get to you? Like killing that guy off duty?"

Doc set down his glass. Looked at Boston with intensity. "I'm not saying I handled it right. I don't know. Everything I talked about just now, the things I had to do, none of them are

79

anything like your situation. I was always with people I knew would die for me. You were alone in a dark and unfamiliar location, looking for someone who had already shown he didn't give a fuck about your authority.

"I knew that Russian had a gun and that he and his buddies had already thrown maybe a couple hundred rounds at us. I had time to pick my spot and let him get so close I couldn't miss and all he'd ever see was the muzzle flash of the round that killed him. Even if I fucked it up, it was even money my cousin would take care of him. No doubt in my mind." Reflected on the kinds of things he'd learned about his cousin the past few years. "I'll listen anytime you want when this is all over, and I'll muster as much empathy as I can, but I have never been in the situation you were in last night."

Boston looked like he wanted to say something, but didn't. Doc filled the void. "You said you talked with your parents?"

"Yeah. Big mistake." Doc let his expression give Boston the option to proceed. "They never wanted me to be a cop in the first place. They were supportive when I called, but I could feel the 'I told you so' back there somewhere." Looked at Doc for something. Must have found it. "My mom's a teacher. My dad was a prosecutor, teaches college now. He would've been okay with me becoming a lawyer, but when I got to hang around or listen to stories, it always sounded like the cops had more fun. I liked the idea of locking up bad guys. The lawyers could do what they do. I would've done my part."

"That attitude will serve you well."

"I also thought we'd get more appreciation than lawyers do. Most people hear about a trial where the guy gets off or pleads out, they blame the DA. You know, the cops brought him in on a silver platter and you let him get away."

"You haven't spent enough time working with DAs yet. Someone beats a charge or gets a plea, it's always because of the shitty case we brought them. I can't remember the last time I heard a DA admit to blowing a trial."

"It's the people I'm talking about. The citizens. They don't seem to appreciate us much, either. At least not from what I've seen."

"Cops see people in dire circumstances. Even when we catch the guy who did them dirt, we can't undo the damage. They're too caught up in the hurt to remember we're not responsible, but we're the face they see when they have to deal with it. Detectives have it a little easier."

"Why is that?"

"We're generally better people. Nicer looking, too." Took a second for Boston's expression to lighten. "We spend time with them after they've had a chance to process what happened. You see them when things are still raw. The people you help most are the ones you never come across."

"What do you mean?"

Doc's hands moved as if forming the answer out of the air. "Take that robbery you solved at Mroczka's last summer."

"He still got robbed. Come to think of it, he wasn't all that appreciative, either."

"You got there right after it happened, when he was still spun up. Remember I said he asked about you tonight? Jake Mroczka isn't the kind to make overt shows of appreciation. For him, that was like giving you a hug. What I mean by helping the people you don't see is all the people who might've been robbed—or worse—if you hadn't caught those two. They'll never know what you spared them, whether from those guys or two other assholes who got the word we solve robberies here and didn't try themselves. There are people walking around today with lives intact because you took those two down. The fact that they don't know it and you don't know who they are doesn't change anything."

Boston had stopped listening a while ago. "What if there is no gun? What if I was wrong?"

"You weren't wrong." Doc waited for eye contact. "It doesn't matter if the troopers decide it was a good shoot. You acted in good faith on the information you had at the time. That's never wrong. You do need to be prepared to accept the fact you might not've been right enough."

# 13.

The Steel City Disciples rode into town eleven o'clock Friday morning. Not much of an MC yet—six patched members—but President Robert "The Robber" Barron had plans and Penns River might figure into them. The town was too close to qualify as a recreational run but once everyone got wind of the potential for mayhem, they were all over it.

Being racist wasn't a precondition for Disciples' membership; for sure not a disqualification. The Robber liked to think his crew welcomed the opportunity to fuck with straights, rednecks, crackers, spooks, spics, chinks, gooks, faggots, queers, dykes, trannies, Jews, other one-percenters, or cops. Especially cops. Any group the Disciples could rationalize as looking down on them was fair game, which included just about everyone.

No need to spend the whole weekend in Penns River on the off chance of busting heads. The Robber had more on his mind. Eviction loomed on their current clubhouse in Aliquippa. The Disciples' occasional racist provocations didn't go over well with the local Blacks, who made up a third of the town and had gangs of their own who were not bashful about expressing their own opinions by breaking windows or setting fires. The landlord had had enough, and the Disciples lacked the cash to buy the place outright. The Robber decided to leave that shithole to the Tootsie Rolls and set out to look for greener pastures.

They rolled into the Comfort Inn parking lot and asked for

three adjacent rooms. The clerk or manager or whatever she was said the rooms wouldn't be ready until three, come back then. The Robber didn't appreciate some twenty-something, overweight, acne-scarred bitch whose dye job needed a tune-up telling his men what to do. They'd be relaxing in their rooms by now if they rode in wearing Hells Angels or Warlocks patches.

It was what it was. The Angels had been small once. Respect had to be earned. This might be the place to start.

The people at Denny's didn't know what to make of six guys with questionable hygiene wearing leather cuts and Terminator boots. The hostess seated the club at a round table in an open part of the restaurant, where the Disciples set about taking as much space as possible.

The early lunch buzz died when the MC entered and became the center of attention. That was cool, but it wasn't cool for it to seem cool. The Robber nodded to the Sergeant-at-Arms.

Chad "Chonker" Connor made a point to scrape his chair across the floor as he pushed it back. Spoke loud enough to be heard in the kitchen, the parking lot, and the Papa John's across the way. "What the fuck're yinz all looking at? You never seen a motorcycle club eat before? You might want to start getting used to it."

Meals slammed, the waitress brought the check. Treasurer Bruce "Brute" Prohaska did a quick calculation. "Sixteen bucks each."

Knucks Marhefka said, "Fuck that. Alls I had was coffee and toast."

Brute said, "What? Are you all of a sudden Mr. Pink?"

Chonker: "I think Mr. Pink was bitching about leaving a tip. You're not talking about stiffing the waitress, are you, Knucks?"

Pete "Pike" Bishop said, "That's a hilarious scene. How they go from talking about Madonna and big cocks to tipping waitresses. Great fucking movie."

Knucks said, "I'll leave a tip. What's ten percent of two and a quarter?"

Chonker said, "Tips ain't been ten percent since your mother was getting them for hand jobs. Everyplace is fifteen now."

"Fifteen then. But based on two and a quarter, which is all I ate."

Brute was about to speak when The Robber stepped in. "Knock off this *Reservoir Dogs* shit. We ride together, we don't sit around with calculators figuring who pays how much tax like a bunch of cunts. We split the check. You knew that going in. It's not on us you didn't eat more. Now throw in sixteen bucks like Brute said and I'll let you stream the movie next time you come over." Knucks dug out a ten, four ones, and eight quarters. Dropped them on the table.

Denny's manager, skinny guy wearing a tie with a short-sleeve shirt, ran up to Chonker, who was last in line as the Disciples filed out. "Excuse me, gentlemen. We pay at the counter here."

Chonker took it well. "Good for you. We don't." Nodded for the rest of the club to keep walking.

"Sir, we need to settle the check. It's for the bookkeeping."

Chonker gave the pencil neck his full attention. "You saying we shorted you?"

"No no no. If anything, we want to make sure we didn't overcharge you."

"I'll chance it. Unless you want me to call everyone back so we can sort out the money. We could all stand right here where it blocks anyone else trying to get in."

The manager cast desperate eyes at their waitress. "Did they get separate checks?" She shook her head. "It's a single check. Just one of you has to do it."

"*Has* to?"

The manager would need a shower by the time Chonker finished with him. "I don't mean 'has to' as in we'd force you to do it."

"Fucking A to that."

"I just mean, I mean, it's just, we're all set up to do it that way. Everyone does it."

By now the rest of the MC had come back to invade the manager's space. "We look like everyone to you?" The Robber let out a small smile at Chonker marking their territory.

"No no no. Absolutely not."

"So...what, then? We look different from regular people? Like we're not good enough to eat in some fucking Denny's?"

"Please watch your language. This is a family restaurant."

Chonker's gesture included all the Disciples. "*This* is *my* family. And this is the language we use. If you don't think we're fit to spend money in this shithole, say so, and I'll send Knucks back to pick it up."

Knucks took a step in that direction. The Robber put out a hand to stop him. Not the time to inform Knucks his name was short for "Knucklehead." Agreed to by unanimous consent after Knucks missed a major social function because he spent the night in jail for running a light while driving with an expired registration. Completed the knucklehead hat trick by mouthing off to the cop. "Obey all traffic laws" and "Keep all registrations current" were two of the Disciples' Ten Commandments. No reason to give some half-wit with a badge an excuse to cause problems.

A busboy—bus*man*, guy had to be at least fifty—brought the money from their table. "Let's just settle the check, Dave. There's enough here." Another commandment: Never stiff on a bill. Unless circumstances demand it.

Chonker stepped forward, grabbed the manager by his love handles, and set him on the counter without effort. Took the cash from the busboy and stuffed it in the manager's shirt pocket. "There. We paid at the counter. You happy now?"

The manager sat opening and closing his mouth like a fish. Chonker raised an eyebrow. The Robber said, "Let's go."

Kathy Burrows pulled her unit into Denny's parking lot. All she knew was there was some kind of disturbance, see the manager, though someone else called it in. She found half a dozen motor-cycles spread across the handicapped spaces, put two and two together, and parked as close behind them as she could.

Settling her hat when six men with hygiene so dubious she sensed it from this distance walked out laughing. All wore leather vests with patches. They stopped when they saw she left them no way to leave. She tipped her hat coming around the car to greet them. "Good afternoon, gentlemen."

The one in front said, "Officer." Close enough for Burrows to read the rockers on their vests now. His said, "President," "First Six," "Live to Ride," and "Men of Mayhem." Outnumbered six-to-one and outweighed at least fifteen-to-one, Burrows knew she had one advantage: a club stealing patch ideas from *Sons of Anarchy* wasn't operating at a Hells Angels' level. Large assholes lacking creativity could still cause a lot of damage. At least Denny's didn't serve alcohol.

She spoke to President. "You wouldn't know anything about some guys causing trouble in there, would you?"

President looked around to the others. All shook their heads and made sounds of denial. "We were up front paying, Officer. Must've been someone in the back."

A voice behind President said: "Yeah. In the back."

They wanted to play? Burrows could oblige them. "Did you happen to see a motorcycle gang in there? That's the description we got."

President said, "Must've been someone else. We're a club of Harley-Davidson enthusiasts who like to ride together on week-ends. Hardly a gang."

The same voice as before came from the second row. "Yeah. We're Harley enthusiasts."

Burrows knew this could blow up in a Pittsburgh minute and she had no good options if it did. Numbers were always helpful in such situations, but reaching for her shoulder mike to call for backup might be interpreted as weakness and cause an escala-tion before the cavalry could arrive. Hesitation could be just as bad. "Are you the only two who've seen *Sons of Anarchy*, or does anyone else want to throw a few lines at me?"

The voice in the second row said, "*The Wild Bunch*, too."

The man next to him elbowed the speaker. "Dumb fuck."

President said, "He means *The Wild One*. We've seen them all."

"Good to know. I'm going inside to find out what's what. Be here when I get back."

"Are we under arrest?"

"I guess there's nothing that says you *can't* leave. Assuming you can find a way to get your bikes around my car. No way will you be able to do that without me seeing you, which will make me wonder why you didn't want to stick around for a few minutes. That may call for an investigation that requires all of you at the station."

"You're going to take us all to the station? Even if we don't want to go?"

"You'd be surprised at what I'm capable of."

Someone in the second row made a cat screeching noise. Another hissed. Burrows ignored them and went into Denny's. She found a thin, middle-aged man surrounded by employees. He began to speak until she held up a finger for him to wait. Keyed her microphone. "This is PR-Six."

"Go ahead, Six."

"Requesting passive backup at 209 Tarentum Bridge Road to keep an eye on some bikers until I sort things out inside."

"Copy, Kathy. A unit is on the way."

"Kay. Thanks." Burros spoke to the man she presumed was the manager. "Officer Burrows, sir. Penns River police. Did you call us?"

He seemed surprised until another, older man spoke up. "I called, but he's the one you should talk to. He's the manager."

She returned her attention to the man she'd put on hold. "What's your name, sir?"

"Dave Gilligan."

"What happened, Mr. Gilligan?"

With no enthusiasm, Gilligan said, "They came in an hour or so ago."

"Who came in, Mr. Gilligan?"

Gilligan looked through the glass double doors. Indignation began to show. "Them." He pointed. "The bikers. They took the round table in the center section and...acted like assholes. Loud. Addressing the other customers with foul language. When it came time to pay, they threw money on the table and tried to leave."

"You stopped them?"

"I told them we're set up for people to pay at the counter. They gave me a hard time until Larry here brought their money and suggested I let it go. I was about to when the biggest one lifted me up and put me on the counter. Then he stuffed the money into my pocket and said everyone should be happy now because they paid at the counter."

"The big guy, he put his hands on you?"

Gilligan nodded. "Picked me up like I was a first grader."

"That's battery, Mr. Gilligan. Point him out to me and I can arrest him."

Gilligan gave her comment the same consideration as if she'd suggested shooting all the customers. "I just want them to go."

Burrows shifted her attention to Larry. "Did they leave enough for their bill, sir?"

"Barely. No tip worth mentioning, all they made us run for them."

"How much did they leave?"

"Ninety-six dollars for a ninety-three-dollar check."

"What would be a reasonable tip?"

"Twenty percent of ninety-three is eighteen and a quarter."

"Wait here."

Burrows pushed open the door as Barney McGinniss pulled in behind her car. She walked over to President while everyone else watched Barney get out of the car and extend his baton.

Burrows spoke with what she considered appropriate snark. "Excuse me, Mr. President. They're willing to not press charges if you leave a reasonable tip."

"Charges for what?"

"One of you," she looked at the largest of the six, with "Sergeant-at-Arms" on one rocker, "put hands on the manager. That's battery."

The big guy started to react. President said, "What do they consider a reasonable tip?"

"Twenty bucks will do it."

President handed her a crumpled twenty like he was giving a bum a quarter to go away, "Can we leave now?"

"Soon as I move my car." Took her time delivering the money. Told Gilligan to call back if they ever acted up again. About to leave when she realized this was as good a time as any to pee. Stopped at the counter on the way out to buy some mints. There were ways to deal with assholes that didn't require physical or verbal abuse. In the meantime, they were in good hands with Barney.

# 14.

Doc jotted down license plates in the parking lot of Orville and Norval Hatfield's Moonshine Emporium. One Ohio and a West Virginia. The Pennsylvania had a Confederate flag on the bumper. Always a head-scratcher for Doc, Pennsylvania remaining in the Union and all. He'd run the plates back in the office, see if anything popped that might be of use later in the weekend.

The parking lot belonged to a consignment shop that faced Leechburg Road, to which the Moonshine Emporium clung like a one-car cinder block garage. Norval sometimes referred to it as, "Orville and Norval Hatfield's Moonshine Emporium," but Doc had never seen any paperwork to that effect. Far as he knew, it could be "Orville and Norval's Moonshine Emporium," or "Hatfield's Moonshine Emporium," or plain old "Moonshine Emporium." Also possible "Moonshine Emporium" wasn't even in the name. Signage was no help. Two hung from the door. One showed the business hours; the other told whether they were open or closed.

Doc was about to go inside when a man with *Master Race* written all over him came out. An inch over six feet, no more than a pound under four hundred. Camouflage pants and hunting jacket. Dirty ball cap with *Kick Ass* on it. A Colt Python rested in a holster clipped to his belt.

It had been a rough couple of days and the forecast was for more of the same. Doc became a cop because people told him it would be fun. Time to have some. Said, "Good afternoon," as he slipped his badge into a lanyard and hung it around his neck.

"How's it goin'?" The man noticed Doc's continuing attention as he reached for the door handle on the PA truck. "Is there a problem?"

"There might be if you get in."

"The hell you say." Paused. "What kind of problem?"

"That a Python you're wearing?"

The man beamed as if he'd invented the damn thing. "Yeah. So?"

"That's a fine weapon. We cops carry semi-automatics, but I used a six-inch Anaconda as a backup when I was in Iraq."

"Ain't that kind of heavy for a backup piece?"

Doc shrugged. "I figured if the grunts could carry fifty pounds of shit every time they left the green zone, I could handle an extra fifty ounces."

"What was it chambered for?"

"Forty-four Special."

"Not the mag?"

"I didn't want to worry about dislocating my shoulder if I had to fire in a hurry. About that Python. You have a concealed carry permit for it?"

Camo Man smiled like he'd got one over on this rube cop. "Pennsylvania's an open carry state."

"I know. Did you know that as soon as you get in the truck and shut the door it's legally considered to be concealed? And that carrying a concealed weapon without a proper permit is a third-degree felony subject to three and a half to seven years imprisonment and a fine not to exceed fifteen thousand dollars?"

"My ass."

Doc shrugged again. "Get in. Find out."

"And you're gonna take me to jail? By yourself?"

"If you come peaceably. You try to run, it's not like I wouldn't find you, having the plate number and all. Then we can add resisting arrect, illegal flight, failure to obey a lawful order, assault on a peace officer—"

"How is it assault if I just drive away?"

Doc moved his hands to show his position relative to the pickup. "You start to leave, and I have to move to avoid getting run over, that's assault."

Problem solving did not appear to be Camo Man's super-power. "What the hell am I supposed to do? Walk home?"

"Is the gun loaded?"

"Only a damn fool carries an unloaded gun."

"Unload it." Paused to let the insult sink in, if possible. "Put the gun and the bullets in the toolbox I see back there. Separately. Then you can go on your way perfectly legal."

Camo Man stared fifty-caliber holes through Doc as he emptied and stowed the Python. Opening the door when Doc spoke again. "You live here in town?"

"No."

"Here for the funeral, are you?"

"Right."

"Let me say something so you won't feel like you've been set up. I'm going to tell my good friend the patrol sergeant that you should be pulled over at the slightest provocation, and that there's a strong possibility you'll be armed and that, if so, they are to bring you in. Then I'll add a statement to the arrest report about how I advised you on the concealed carry laws no more than two or three days earlier. Do you understand what I'm telling you?"

"Fuck you." Camo Man got in the truck. Started it and lowered the window. "Fuck you."

Doc, under his breath. "And fuck *you*, sir." To Camo Man: "You have a nice rest of your day." Waved as the truck drove away.

Inside the Moonshine Emporium, the four customers already there were pressed ass to elbow. Doc had no idea how Camo Man had squeezed in. Norval Hatfield said, "Howdy, Doc. What can I do you for?"

"I just come in to shoot the shit. Take care of your paying customers first."

The paying customers turned to look at the newcomer. Two saw the badge around his neck and left as if being pulled by a locomotive-sized magnet. Another concluded his purchase, took his change, and told his friend it was too crowded; he'd wait in the car.

The last man standing looked hard at Doc's badge, then his face, "Cop, huh?"

"That's right."

"My brother used to be a cop."

"Whereabouts?"

"Ohio."

"State trooper?"

"Miami."

"Campus or town?"

"You ask a lot of questions."

"It's what cops do when we're not eating donuts. You said your brother used to be a cop. Looking at you, my guess is he didn't retire."

"What's that supposed to mean?"

"Means you look too young to retire, so I figured your brother was, too." Doc turned to the Hatfields. "Is everyone from Ohio this touchy?" The brothers recognized a rhetorical question and did not reply.

"He quit."

"How come?"

"Too many assholes asking questions he didn't feel like he should have to answer."

"You're the one volunteered he was a cop. I was just making conversation."

The man stared at Doc as if deciding how to continue the discussion, came to a decision, and started out the door.

Doc called him back. Pointed to a small poke on the counter. "Forgot your shine."

The man picked up his package. Muttered something under his breath on the way out.

No one spoke until the bell above the door stopped jingling, when Orville said, "Ain't there no whorehouses in town you can clear just by walking in? That's the most business we had in weeks."

"I can't believe those peckerwoods were buying your good stuff in quantity."

"They was assholes, anyway. Tried to Jew us down on a quart. Can I interest you in a taste of the private stock?"

Doc considered. He was on duty and, as a sergeant, part of his job was to set an example. On the other hand, he'd eaten lunch, so the chances of the private reserve dissolving through his intestines to drop out his ass like blood from one of those movie aliens was reduced. "Just one."

Orville took three sample cups from under the counter while Norval went into a cabinet for an unmarked bottle. Orville poured. Raised his cup for a toast. "I would rather be with the people in this room than with the finest people I know."

Doc said, "Back atcha," and everyone drank.

After his eyes stopped watering, Doc said, "That's a pretty smooth batch. What's that I taste?"

Orville said, "Plums."

"Where the hell'd you get plums this time of year?"

"We put some up in Mason jars in the fall. Noticed last week one of the seals didn't look too good, so I figured I better use it before it went altogether bad."

Doc making a mental note to stop for Imodium on the way home when Norval said, "Where's that pretty lady cop you come in here with that time? She can clear the room whenever she wants and I won't fuss."

"She's helping the state police with that shooting down Fat Jimmy's the other night. I'll tell her you asked after her. How's your Uncle Hillard since we run off that Dixie Mafia asshole? Any repercussions?" The brothers grew subdued. "What?

McCord and his pet gun monkey didn't go down there looking for payback, did they?"

Norval said, "I don't think the Dixie Mafia'll be bothering with Uncle Hillard no more. No profit in it for them."

There hadn't been much profit in bothering Uncle Hillard in the first place. Hadn't stopped McCord before.

Orville said, "Uncle Hillard's not at home in his mind no more."

Doc felt himself sag. Never met Uncle Hillard; never even seen a picture. He knew the effects of dementia from seeing it worsen every time he visited his mother and wouldn't wish it on the vilest criminal. "I'm sorry to hear that, boys. Honest to God I am."

Norval broke the uncomfortable silence. "What brings you in, Doc? Not that we're not glad to see you."

Orville said, "Maybe he has another way to fuck up our day," though Doc knew he didn't mean it.

Doc nodded toward the door. "Those guys that were just in here. You seeing many of them the past day or so?"

Orville said, "You mean customers?"

"White supremacists. Neo-Nazis. Like that. We hear a bunch of them are coming for that funeral and we're trying to get a handle on what to expect."

The brothers looked at each other. Norval said, "Far as I know, they's the only ones. Everyone else I seen today we already knowed." Orville nodded. "That just happened the other night, right?" Doc's turn to nod. "When's the funeral?"

"Sunday."

"It's Friday still. Most of whoever's coming in from out of town won't show up until later tonight or tomorrow, after they get off work."

Doc flicked a thumb across his lower lip. "Don't take this the wrong way, but do you see much of that? The white hate, I mean."

Orville said, "How do you mean, 'do *we* see much of it'?"

"No offense, but your business, your background. People of a certain disposition might be more open to saying things around you than around me."

Norval said, "It ain't like that's a normal topic of conversation" faster than Doc liked.

Orville said, "We sell shine. A little artsy-craftsy shit from the hills. Folks come in here, that's mostly what we talk about."

Norval said, "It ain't like we're keeping the coloreds out, Doc. Where we are, and shine not being their beverage of choice, they don't come this way too often. They do, and they want something, we'll sell it to them same as we would anyone else. Just like we done for those was here when you come in."

Doc said, "That's real white of you," not sure how much insult he intended.

"Come on, Doc. Don't be that way. White people got things they like, and Blacks got theirs. Some things everybody likes. The Steelers. Sidney Crosby. That weather girl with the nipples you can see through her top."

Doc rested a hand on the doorknob. "You have many Blacks in the hollers?"

"Ours? None to speak of. Few families over the way."

"Families, though. Mothers and fathers and kids."

"That don't make them special. Everyone's like that."

Doc raised a finger. "Exactly. I like to tell people the best thing the Army taught me was how to be a cop. That's not true. The *best* thing the Army taught me is that everyone is pretty much the same. People want to go to work, come home for something to eat, watch a little television. Have better lives for their kids."

Orville said, "Being a cop must've taught you better by now."

"You know what being a cop taught me?" No answer. Doc hadn't expected one. "All the bad shit we see, all we have to deal with and try to make right? No one owns the franchise on that. I've seen things in white people's houses and families that'd give you night sweats."

Quiet as a church at three a.m. in the small room now. "I

think back to things I said when I was growing up here and I'm ashamed. I get over it. I was a kid and didn't know any better, and my old man wouldn't put up with anything too extreme around the house. Now that I think back…"

Doc felt color in his cheeks. "There's people coming to town this weekend looking to break the place up. Bust some heads if they get the chance and the heads aren't the right color. Fuck that and fuck them. Not in my town and not on my watch. You catch a whiff of anything that might go sideways, I expect to hear about it."

Norval said, "You deputizing us, Doc?"

Maybe Norval meant it as a joke. Maybe not. "I like you both, I do, and I enjoy coming in here to taste the product and break balls. You make a decent living and I'm glad to see it. I don't even want to know what you pull down from selling the illegal stuff every cop in town turns a blind eye to. Well, boys, that costs, and the bill is due. I'm gonna take it personal if I find out any of these peckerwood cocksuckers ran their mouths about something bad in here and you didn't tell me about it. Business will suffer."

Doc let that hang so the brothers would know he was serious. About to walk out the door when Orville spoke. "We hear you. You want to listen for a spell?"

"It's only fair."

"Tip another before you go. You and us have different ideas about some things. We been acquainted a long time and always got along. Have a drink and let's let this dog sleep instead of waking it up to piss on a friendship. We'll hold up our end. We don't want the town broke up any more'n you do."

# 15.

Rick Neuschwander opened the door to the storage room he used as for evidence preparation to find the two state cops. One of them—Rick not sure which was who—asked for a few minutes to go over the physical evidence in the Boston shooting.

Rick pointed to the two chairs not currently supporting files or boxes. "Let me see what's back." Tapped keys. Read a screen. "What do you want to know?"

"Anything from ballistics?"

"This is a quick turnaround, but they know its's a cop shooting." Taps and clicks. "Nothing we didn't expect. Three casings were found, all of which match Boston's gun."

"Bullets?"

"One went through and through and we haven't found it. The others hit bone, so they're too badly fragmented to match. Not that there's any question where they came from."

"Where was he hit?"

"One flush in the sternum. Another rattled off a rib and clipped his aorta and heart on the way out. One ricocheted off a collarbone and tore out the bottom of his left lung."

"Three rounds, three hits. Your boy can shoot. Anything noteworthy in the angles?"

"The ME is careful to note this is conjecture, but it's also consistent with what she found at autopsy. They probably hit him in the order I gave you. First one staggered him, second one

99

dropped him, and the third one hit him on the way down. Like this." Rick touched his neck near the collarbone and traced a route along his chest.

"Distance?"

"No powder burns or stippling."

"No residue or burns on the clothes?"

"Not that I've found. They're pretty cruddy, him falling in all the crap back there. I don't think he put them on fresh out of the laundry, either." Pointed to a pair of jeans and a jacket on a workbench across the room.

Thornton—Rick assumed it was Thornton; he did all the talking—moved toward the table. "Please don't touch anything." Thornton shot him a look. "There's a reason that door is locked even when I'm in here. No one handles anything in an active investigation except me. Holds down the chance of contamination or something going missing or misplaced."

Thornton pulled a face. Stepped away. "What's your estimate of the distance?"

"Position of the body relative to the casings, I'd say fifteen to twenty feet. Half that far by the time Johnson hit the ground. We took pictures of the footprints in the snow soon as we could. They're jumbled up right where the body was, but they should give a pretty good idea who did what."

"Any blood anywhere except on or under the body?"

"Not worth mentioning. There's a little spatter that appears to have come from the round that went through."

Rothermel made a contribution. "Tox screens back yet?"

Rick tapped and clicked and read again. "Just came in. Johnson had a blood alcohol of point one three. Traces of methamphetamine, but he wasn't high. Just drunk."

Thornton: "What about Boston?"

"Above average on caffeine. Nothing dramatic."

"Either have any injuries other than the victim's gunshot wounds?"

Rick wondered if they'd like him to go back to the hotel and read the whole report aloud while he tucked them in. "Boston has none. Johnson has light bruising on his face consistent with a scuffle such as the one Boston came in to break up. Cuts on his hands that appear to have come from falling on broken glass after being shot."

"Any evidence of physical interaction between the two?"

"We know from witness statements they made contact with each other. Johnson slapped Boston's hand and face and Boston grabbed Johnson to cuff him."

Rothermel's turn. "Anything to indicate Johnson had a gun? Oil in a pocket, maybe?"

Rick shook his head. "I found crumbs, lint, hair, all kinds of trace material, including blood. Nothing to indicate a gun."

Thornton: "You found blood? Where?"

"In a pants pocket. It was old. Probably cut himself and put the hand in his pocket while the blood was still fresh. Not related to our case."

The troopers conferred. Thornton said, "We'll go over the new information tonight. Did anything stick out to you?"

Rick scanned the screen while scrolling. "What strikes me most is how consistent it is with what I'd expect based on what we already know."

"How so?"

"Johnson ran, Boston chased him around back, a confrontation, then shooting."

"No gun, though."

"Uh-uh. No gun."

Thornton said, "Do you mind if we ask you something off the record?"

Rick saw no reason for Thornton to treat him like a skel. *Nothing* he said would be off the record. "Go ahead."

"You work with Boston?"

"We have forty cops here. Everyone works with everyone."

"What's he like to work with?"

"Young. Still learning. Shows a lot of potential."

Thornton tired of waiting for more. "That's it?"

"What else do you want me to say? He likes mushrooms on his pizza. Drinks Yuengling. Sandwiches from Bob's." Spoke over Thornton's attempted interruptions. "No offense, but we both know anything good I say will be ignored because you figure we're friends. Anything bad, or not good enough to suit you, you'll grab like a duck on a June bug, wondering why I didn't stand up for him better. This isn't my first internal homicide investigation. I know how things work. If you want my opinion on the evidence, ask me. Leave me out of the rest."

The atmosphere was cold enough to freeze salt water. Rothermel at least made an effort. "Fair enough."

Thornton had a stronger opinion. "That's fine, Detective. Have you collected all the evidence from the scene? Sent everything to Harrisburg?" Rick had. "Then we won't be needing you anymore. We'll get our information straight from the lab, which means you won't need to access it. We'll know if you do."

Rick stared at the closed door while the troopers' footfalls faded away. Turned to his workbench and the gravel, shreds of paper, shards of glass, and other debris spread across it the troopers didn't feel merited their attention. Looked like he'd emptied a Shop-Vac there, which, come to think of it, is about what he'd done. Everything he brought from the crime scene came for a reason. Some things he knew he wanted a closer look at. Some he thought he might. For others, maybe he'd get lucky.

Pulled a stool next to the table and repositioned the overhanging high-intensity lamp. Adjusted a dentist's loupe on his forehead. Used tweezers to pick up a single piece of detritus and examine it. Set that piece aside and chose another. He'd already told Hildy not to expect him home for dinner, though he'd be there to tuck in the kids. He hadn't told her he half expected to come back here after.

# 16.

Doc and Daniel Rollison met in the lobby of The Allegheny Casino. Shook hands, then pretended they didn't want to sanitize them. Doc said, "Dan," because he knew Rollison hated it, "Is this the weekend for the big do?"

Rollison's expression showed how little he thought of Doc's feigned ignorance. "You know damn well it is. Sunday at seven."

The two had a relationship equal parts loathing and grudging respect. Rollison, reputed to be a retired spook, carried himself as if his cloak still hung in the closet, dagger in pocket. Acted as if all information was *need to know* and you didn't need to. Their paths first crossed when Rollison was a private investigator playing an angle on one of Doc's homicide cases. Rollison had since become head of security for the casino. Treated the local law as if the joint were a sovereign entity.

The grudging respect emerged when Doc solved a homicide in the casino's parking lot and learned how good Rollison could be. Doc made at least a courtesy visit every time he came to the casino, which was as little as he could get away with.

"Just double checking the date and time. You requested two cops and a couple of vehicles."

"Both requests were approved. Six weeks ago."

"There might be a problem."

Rollison showed as much of his only facial expression—disgust—as he ever did. "What's wrong this time? Someone's kid having a birthday party? Tell him we'll comp the whole operation here. We do swell parties. Little hats and everything."

"For a guy as alert for potential issues as you are, you don't pay much attention to the news, do you?"

"Anything in particular?"

"How about a group of alt-right douche bags wants to make Penns River the Rust Belt version of Sturgis this weekend? Except these guys' idea of a party is to bust the place up and maybe start a race riot while they're at it."

"Not my problem. We made arrangements with coppers who are off duty Sunday night. We're paying the city to rent a couple of cars."

"Sullivan has everyone on standby until twenty-four hours after the funeral. No vacation, no lost time, no days off."

"Sullivan can work his people twenty-four-hours a day so long as we get what was agreed to. This will be the biggest event this hole ever had."

Credit where it's due: Rollison's ego wouldn't fit in Heinz Field, but the man had no delusions of grandeur. The Allegheny Casino—always *The* Allegheny Casino, like *The* Ohio State University—was a well-lighted dump. A true grind joint. Get 'em in, get their money, get 'em the fuck out.

Rollison continued. "There will be actual money here. A hundred degenerate gamblers, each bringing a hundred hundreds to buy in. It's in the rules: cash only. Daniel Hecker himself will present whoever wins with ten thousand hundred-dollar bills. We promised a police escort out of town, sirens and lights. The mayor signed off. I want the escort here at seven o'clock sharp."

Doc came instead of Sullivan because he owned what little rhythm the department had with Rollison. Doc could also get away with saying he'd have to go back to the boss for a ruling if things went bad. "Humor me a minute. Do you really think, if ice cream turns to shit this weekend, we're going to disengage bodies and units for your dog-and-pony show?"

"You will unless Sullivan wants to explain it to the mayor,

who we both know does not want to explain it to Dan Hecker."

"Call a private company. You can afford it."

Rollison spat out a laugh. "You kill me, Dougherty. Have you ever known Hecker to spend a nickel on anything he can get Chet Hensarling to deliver for free? Chet didn't buy the boat he docks at Brady's Bend with loose change he found in his couch cushions. The advertising and all the promotional materials specifically call for real cops, not rentals."

"Call Tarentum."

"You call Tarentum. Call the state police. Mobilize the National Guard for all I care. This is not my problem. Don't come in here to piss in my ear and tell me it is."

"We might be able to call the state police if the same guy responsible for this extravaganza hadn't burned every bridge between here and Harrisburg."

Rollison opened his hands. *So what?*

Doc said, "I'll talk to Sully, but I'm making no promises. I'm sure he'll do everything he can to honor the agreement, but if we have a riot down the Allegheny Estates and public safety is threatened, that's where we'll be. Whether he can spare the bodies for you will be a game-time decision."

Rollison made sure no one else was within earshot. "I get it, I do. I'd look elsewhere if I had time, but the deal is the day after tomorrow. All my people are already working. I called the armored car company. All they're willing to provide is a car, a driver, and a guard. No escorts. And they want double their usual rate. Besides, Hecker doesn't want this to look like an armored car kind of thing."

"This is *exactly* an armored car kind of thing. Armed guards in Kevlar. Make a show of loading the winner in with the cash. Give him a big send-off and a ride off-site where they can safely transfer the cash. Even better, show the money and slip him a ringer. Exchange the actual cash later."

Rollison started nodding halfway through. "You ever work with thirty-year-old marketing people? If that? They're moist at the thought of the crowd seeing a guy walk out of here with a million dollars in a briefcase."

"Do it right and no one will know any different."

"Hecker will know, and he's worse than any of the kids. I suggested we make a big show, stash the money in the vault, drive the guy around under escort for an hour, then bring him back here and cut him a check."

"What'd he say?"

Rollison looked like he'd spit if they weren't standing on carpet. "He's in love with the romance of a police escort whisking the champion away—that's the word he used, 'whisking'—free as a bird in his own vehicle, cash in hand."

"To be ambushed five minutes after he crosses the town line."

Rollison nodded. "We did make arrangements with Tarentum, Plum Borough, Allegheny Township, all the adjacent departments, to pretend our little convoy has jurisdiction as it goes screaming through their streets."

"Because you have no way of knowing which direction the winner will go."

"More than likely the airport. Hecker's pulling suckers from all over the country for this."

Doc thought of all the things that could go wrong. Stopped when he remembered he had places to be. "Does Hecker realize he could be setting up his champion to be robbed and possibly killed on what this poor jerk thinks is the greatest night of his life?"

Rollison made the spitting face again. "It's not his money and it's not his ass."

"How's he plan to keep the stink off him if it goes bad?"

"Do you really think Dan Hecker looks that far down the road? All he sees is what's shiny and right in front of him."

Doc had made Sullivan's point and Rollison received it better than expected. Time to declare victory and get out. Doc couldn't help himself. "Dan—sorry, Daniel—can I ask you a question?" Rollison didn't say no. "You have skills, you have experience, and you have contacts out the ass. Why do you put up with this tinhorn bullshit?"

"Can you keep this to yourself?"

"You know I can."

Another check for eavesdroppers. "Not for much longer. Hecker threw money at me. Promised points. I vest next year, then I'm out. He can mail me a check every quarter."

"That bad?"

"Have you ever spent time with him?"

"Not worth mentioning. One meeting during those Russian problems when the casino first opened."

"Do you remember the line that woman politician had about Bush Forty-one? How he was born on third base and thinks he hit a triple? I loved the old man, but that's still a great line. Dan Hecker was born on third base and thinks he invented baseball. Keep me posted as well as you can, all right?"

"Will do."

Doc walked toward the exit shaking his head. Never seen Daniel Rollison so forthcoming. Almost felt sorry for him. Pushed the thought aside as he held the door for a young woman coming in from the employees' parking lot.

"Thank you, Detective Dougherty."

Late twenties, five foot ten, high cheekbones, blond hair, and ice blue eyes. Doc knew her. Interviewed her for a case a few years ago. She tended bar near the blackjack tables and put him wise to a guy selling dope on the casino grounds. She'd confided that looks like hers were not always a blessing, depending on who took what kind of interest. Worked four to one Tuesdays through Saturdays. He remembered all this, though the lead went nowhere. Drew a complete blank on her name. "Hi. How's it going?"

"Good, thanks. Haven't seen you around."

"I'm no kind of gambler."

"Don't like the atmosphere?"

"It's a little garish for me."

She hesitated. "I kind of hoped I'd hear from you after that case was over. You know, off duty."

"It's awkward, getting in touch with someone you met as part of an investigation. There are ethical considerations, possible conflicts of interest. Those kinds of things."

"That was three years ago. Didn't that case—what's the term cops use?—go down?"

"Yeah. It's down."

She spoke before the silence got too awkward. "You don't remember my name, do you?"

Doc felt himself blush. "I'm sorry. I remember the interview. We were in Dan Rollison's office. I remember who I talked to before you, and after. What you told me and what we did about it. I'm sorry about your name. Cops' memories get kind of focused sometimes."

He wasn't sure what to make of her glimmer of a smile. "Even though you wrote it down? Along with my phone number?"

"I don't go back to my notes for personal stuff. I'm on duty right now, but I can turn my badge to the wall if you felt like giving me your information again."

"Do you want it?"

"Yes, if by giving it to me you're saying you want me to call. Otherwise it just clogs up my contacts list."

"Get your phone out." She waited for him to get to the *Add a contact* screen. "Judy Abram—"

"Abramowicz. See? I did remember."

"Eventually." Watched Doc enter her name. "You even spelled it right."

"I grew up here. Abramowicz is no challenge."

She told him her number. "I work four to one most nights, but I'm off Sundays and Mondays."

"You're not working the festivities this weekend?"

Judy made a pout. "*Everybody* is working this Sunday. It's a *big event*."

"So I hear." Considered. "You know about the shooting the

other night down the Flats?"

"You never think something like that can happen in a town like this."

"You hear about the white supremacists coming in for the funeral?"

"A little."

"Don't worry yourself over it, but with that kind of crew in town and so much loose cash here Sunday evening, be aware of your surroundings. Think of how you'd get out if you had to in a hurry, or where you'd shelter if you couldn't."

Concern showed on her face. "Are you expecting trouble?"

"Not here, specifically. It's just that, if something does break bad...well, not to sound like your dad, but it's better to be safe than sorry."

Judy said, "Okay." Didn't sound happy about it.

"Don't worry. I probably shouldn't have said anything. Ninety percent chance things will be fine."

"But I should be ready for the ten percent."

"Always."

Judy turned to pass. "Time to get to work. You'll call me? Now that you have my name and number and all?"

"It might not be for a few days, till we see how this neo-Nazi business shakes out, but I will definitely call."

Judy curled her fingers to wave—*French Connection* wave, Doc thought—and started inside. Doc let her go about ten feet. "Hey?"

She turned, eyebrows arched in question.

"You could've called me any time in the past three years, too, you know. You had my card."

Judy tossed her comment over her shoulder as she turned away. "Where's the fun in that?"

# 17.

Doc pulled up his parents' steep driveway as his brother stood in the stoop saying goodbye. Parked so Drew could get past and waited for him at the bottom of the stairs. "You off work already?"

"I took a sick day and jammed in a couple doctor's appointments. Took Elizabeth down to UPMC this morning and saw my mechanic this afternoon." Drew always referred to his orthopedic surgeon as a mechanic. No offense meant; the doctor did it himself, where Drew picked it up. Total knee reconstruction was on the horizon as soon as ski season ended. Elizabeth had type one diabetes and lived her life at the forefront of advancements in insulin delivery technology. "Tomorrow starts my long weekend, so I made it a four-day job."

"Any plans to leave town? Like to be a shit storm here."

"I doubt anything will happen where I live. If it does, I have great confidence local law enforcement will protect my family and our possessions. All else fails, I have Mr. Hillerich and Mr. Bradsby by the front door."

"You'll be fine at home. I'd get the groceries in early, though."

Drew winked. "Already done. I have some honey-dos and yard work for the weekend. Pens tomorrow night and Pitt on Sunday."

Doc nodded toward the house. "What brings you over?"

"Beth Lutz made some of her nut rolls and I brought one for

Mom and Dad."

"Tony's a great guy, but the way Beth bakes, he's not worthy."

"Stop by the house. I'll give you one. We got plenty. She made them for the church sale and got carried away. Dropped off the three we paid for and one more."

Doc shook his head. "Those are for you guys. I'll come over for a couple slices when I get a chance. Tell you what: when what she baked is gone, I'll make an Oakmont Bakery run and bring some back for everyone."

"Don't wait for me to talk you out of it. You'll freeze."

Drew in the process of stepping past when Doc took his arm. "How are they?"

"About the usual."

*About the usual* was no longer good news when checking on Tom and Ellen Dougherty. Doc and Drew shook and Doc went up the stairs.

Ellen was in the kitchen going through the cabinets. "Vegetable? Tomato? You want some tomato soup with milk and a little butter in it?"

Tom, from the living room. "Whatever you want, El."

Doc closed the door. Stepped in. "Hey, guys. What's up?"

"Benny! Did you see Drew? He just left." Ellen shuffled over for a hug and a peck on the cheek.

Tom said, "Hey, Bud. I thought Friday was your Legion night."

"Not this week. Having dinner with Eve and her friend Ronnie."

Ellen said, "You want some supper? We're having soup. I can heat you up another can."

"No thanks, Mom. I have plans. Soup's all you two are having tonight?"

"Neither one of us has much appetite lately. We'll split a can. Maybe your dad will make popcorn later."

Canned soup, cold cereal, and fast food had become staples of his parents' diet. Drew and his wife Paula had them up to the house once a month for Sunday dinner. Paula made enough for ten people and sent Tom and Ellen home with leftovers sufficient for a week, half of which went bad. Doc came down the other Sundays and handled more of the cooking each time. Ellen's failing eyesight made measuring ingredients less than precise; her failing memory turned any meal made from scratch into potluck. Doc tried to hook them up with Meals on Wheels. Might as well have subscribed them to the Larvae of the Month Club.

Doc knew deviations from routine were crises to Ellen. "Don't let me hold you up." Feigned indifference while keeping an eye on his mother as she lit a burner and set the soup pot on it. "I mostly come by to let you know I can't make it on Sunday." That was sufficient deviation to require explanation. "There may be trouble over that guy one of our officers shot Wednesday night. Everyone's working this weekend."

Tom said, "You're a detective, though, right? You come around after things quiet down."

"Not this weekend. It's all hands on deck."

Ellen took the pot from the stove. Soup came near to slopping over the side. "Here, Mom. How about you sit down and I'll get that for you. What are you drinking?"

"There's Mello Yello in the ice box." Doc introduced her to his favorite beverage a few years ago. Now no meal was complete without it.

Ellen started for the refrigerator. Doc kept the soup pot level while tossing a hip into her path. "I got this. You go ahead and sit. Dad? What are you drinking?"

"I got water here I'll bring in."

Doc got his mother situated quick as he could to leave time to watch his father get out of the recliner. Or try to, success never a foregone conclusion of late, even with the stand assist gadget. Stepped in after two failed attempts. Kept his voice low, downplaying everything. "Here, Dad." Took the old man's elbow and guided him up without effort, his father thirty pounds lighter than what he would have called his fighting weight when he was Doc's age.

Tom reached back for his water. Doc said, "Go ahead, Dad. I'll bring it."

His parents seated and eating, Doc checked his watch. "I think I have time for a quick Mello Yello if there's another in the fridge. So you won't feel uncomfortable eating in front of me." Winked.

Ellen said, "Are you hungry, Benny? We have plenty of soup."

"No thanks, Mom. I'm meeting people for dinner in a couple hours."

"Do you have a date?" Ellen lived in eternal hope.

Doc shook his head while sipping from a can. "It's my monthly dinner with Eve Stepler and her friend Ronnie."

Tom said, "How is Eve?"

"Busier than a one-armed paperhanger in an ass-kicking contest." Eve ran a small home improvement and handyman—handywoman—business. Tom took a liking to her when she and Doc were kids and Eve always wanted to watch Tom work in his shop. Asked plenty of questions and still credited him with a lot of what she knew. Tom and Drew could build anything. Doc could tie his own shoes.

"Tell her to leave time to have some fun. Old age creeps up on you when you're not paying attention. Sneaky bastard."

"No worries there. She never works weekends or holidays and takes two two-week vacations every year. The beach in the summer and skiing the in winter. Went to Telluride last month."

Ellen said, "How can she afford that?"

"She makes good money. Gets so much work she farms some out."

"She should still save for retirement." Ellen remained steadfast in her belief economic ruin lurked beyond every corner, even though she and Tom had had no financial concerns since the boys moved out and stopped going through groceries like arrows through toilet paper. "Is this Friday? Why aren't you at the VFW? You always go there on Fridays."

"The Legion, Mom. Not this week." Always a tough choice, whether to correct her. Doc tried never to make a big deal of it, also believed keeping her accurate helped to tether her to the reality everyone else experienced. "I'm having dinner with Eve. Remember?"

"You told me that already, didn't you? I guess I wasn't paying attention."

"You were busy making supper. You two go anywhere since Sunday?"

Tom spoke between slurps. "Light week for us. Saw Raghuveer on...Tuesday. Routine blood work."

"How is Dr. Raghuveer?" The doctor had reached out to Doc the previous summer to suggest Tom and Ellen shouldn't stay in the house. Doc and Drew agreed and did their best. Tom and Ellen were still in the house.

"About the same, I guess. He's young."

"What's he say about you?"

"The usual."

*The usual* was still not good news. Whether it was bad because nothing changed, or worse because Tom had a condition where anything a doctor said that he didn't want to hear went unheard. It was a real thing. Doc looked it up.

Tom continued. "I hope this weather clears up. Your mother needs to go to the eye doctor in Monroeville next week."

"What day?"

Tom pointed his left thumb behind him, sipping from the spoon in his right. "Look on the calendar. Wednesday, I think."

Doc stood to open a high cabinet. A free calendar from the World Wildlife Federation hung inside the door, dedicated to medical appointments. Heart. Eyes. Primary care. Arthritis. Pain. Prescriptions and over-the-counter medications filled the bottom shelf. None had caps attached; neither Tom nor Ellen had the grip to open them. A spill was second on Doc's list of fears, right behind falls, neither parent having an idea of which pills went into which bottles. Doc used to replace the caps when they weren't looking until Tom caught him one day and raised billy hell.

Doc pointed to a date on the calendar. "Conrad, right?"

"That's him."

"Two thirty Thursday."

"Roads'll be clear by then. If it don't snow again."

"I can take her."

Doc knew what came next before either parent had a chance to say it. This time Tom got there first. "I hate to see you take any more time off work for us than you have to."

"They owe me so much time now I could retire next year if they'd let me cash it all in at once. Can probably use a day off after the weekend we're expecting. I'll work the morning and bring you guys lunch so we can eat before we go."

Doc closed the cabinet door. Turned toward the table in time to see Ellen drop her half-full can of pop onto the handle of the spoon resting on the edge of her soup bowl. The can tipped over to spill on the floor. The spoon described a lazy arc as it spun end-over-end to clatter against the oven door.

Ellen pushed away from the table to stand. *"Son of a bitching bastard! Goddamnit!"* Reached for a dish towel hanging off the sink behind her.

*Broken hip* flashed through Doc's mind as he imagined his mother tipping the chair over in her haste. "I got this, Mom." Resituated Ellen and reached for the towel.

*"No! No! Look at the mess on the goddamn floor!"*

Doc already on his knees sopping up said mess. "I got it, Mom. It's all right."

"And the stove."

"One crisis at a time, okay?" Doc worked to keep humor in his voice—it was a borderline Marx brothers routine—found it difficult to hide his fear and frustration. "The stove'll wait for me."

"It's in my shoes. My foot's wet. Goddamnit, I'm soaked."

That killed the humor for Doc. "It's just pop, Mom. Let me dry up this puddle so you don't slip, and I'll get you dry socks before I clean off the stove."

"My shoes are soaked through."

"I'll hang them over the vent in your bedroom. Bring your slippers out so you can wear them till they dry."

Doc was running late by the time he got the situation under control to his mother's satisfaction. No idea why being wet panicked her; a recent phenomenon. She wouldn't have reacted half that much if armed men broke into the house to rob and kill her.

What bothered Doc more was Tom's reaction. Or lack thereof. He sat and accepted the situation as if it were commonplace. Maybe it was. The deterioration in Tom's and Ellen's conditions became noticeable a few years ago and was picking up speed. They refused to live anywhere safer, and Doc couldn't remember the last time he came through the door without worrying he'd find them both dead at the base of the cellar stairs.

Tom liked to say that growing old was no fun. Neither was having parents who refused to do anything about the consequences. Doc knew such thoughts were selfish. That didn't make them any less true.

# 18.

Doc's monthly dinners with Eve Stepler and Veronica Cavanaugh were...weird. In a nonthreatening and often entertaining sense, but definitely off-kilter.

There was history. Ronnie—she loathed "Veronica" as much as Doc hated "Benny"—was Eve's partner. And bisexual. Eve wanted to keep Ronnie from wandering too far on the rare occasions she "just wanted some dick." No one was closer to Eve than Doc; each was the opposite gender sibling the other never had. Setting up Ronnie with Doc seemed the most logical thing in the world to Eve.

Doc and Ronnie were game. Problems arose when things heated up and what Eve began to refer to, with considerable disgust, as Doc's "Incest by Proxy" rule kicked in. Doc couldn't help imagining Eve exploring parts of Ronnie as he vacationed in them. This brought Eve to mind—naked—which shriveled Doc's inspiration into a week-old kid's balloon.

February was Doc's turn to select the restaurant. He chose the Oakmont Tavern so he could indulge his jones for bar food while Eve and Ronnie ate like responsible adults. Doc ordered the Philly cheesesteak—no mushrooms—with onion rings. Eve had a turkey melt, Ronnie the pub chicken salad.

The women watched Doc perform the ritual such a sandwich required. Ronnie spoke as he took his first bite. "No offense, Dougherty, but do you always eat like this? Except when we pick places that don't serve deep-fried arterial plaque, I mean."

Doc flipped a strand of cheese into his mouth. "I'm a sworn defender of the public safety. I have to keep my strength up."

"Your cholesterol, too?"

"Nothing I can do about it. High cholesterol runs in my family."

"Quadruple digits?"

Doc swallowed beer. Shook his head. "I don't know my latest number off the top of my head. It's under control, though. I'd rather skip a meal than have to watch every goddamn thing I eat. I didn't get lunch today and breakfast was a donut. I also see plenty of opportunity to miss meals over the weekend. My conscience is clear."

Eve said, "You think it's gonna be bad?"

"Let's put it this way: the Chamber of Commerce isn't sending a photographer."

"Are you worried?"

"We're as prepared as we can be."

"That doesn't answer my question."

"Sure it does. Think about it." Gave her a few seconds. "Relax. I see a potential insurance bonanza on the horizon for your contracting services."

"I'm serious."

"So am I. Remember, I did two tours in Iraq. At least here I'm not worried about IEDs or suicide bombers. What might happen this weekend will be more along the lines of a pain in the ass. Not that it can't get dangerous. We're expecting a bunch of easily manipulated mouth breathers, and a lot of them will be armed. And drunk. Could get interesting."

Eve said, "And you're not scared? At all? No bullshit, Doc. Remember who you're talking to."

Doc dabbed his mouth with a napkin. "You mean scared now? Are you and Ronnie planning something?"

"You know what I mean."

"I've learned not to be afraid of what *might* happen. I'll worry some tomorrow when I'm out there with my vest and helmet and riot shield. Depending on how things go I might even get a little scared. Best way to deal with that is to have a plan and work it. Concentrate on what needs to be done and not on what some asshole might do. Tell the truth, I think things are as likely as not to be peaceful. A little tense, maybe, but I'm not assuming violence." Saw both women wanted to speak; neither felt like going first. "If it comes to it, I'll be ready. *We'll* be ready."

Ronnie deflected the conversation to a gastroenterologist convention she'd attended at Disney. Eve had a reno she thought Mike Holmes could do a whole month of shows about. Finishing their meals when Ronnie sparked and said, "I almost forgot. I saw you on television today."

Doc hung his head. "They got me, huh?"

Eve said, "You were on television? When?"

Doc refused to say. Ronnie had no qualms. "I half-watched MSNBC while I was getting ready to come over. I don't know which show was on—Ali Velshi was hosting, but he's on like twenty hours a day—and I heard someone mention Penns River. I looked up and there you were."

"He gave an interview?"

"I did *not* give an interview." Snapped both women's heads back with his vehemence. "Not a word. Right, Ronnie?"

"He was good, Evie. It was just video of him standing off to the side of the police station. I think they only took it because his badge was hanging around his neck, so they knew he was a cop and not some lookey-loo."

"I forgot I had it on or I never would've gone out."

Eve asked why he was there, anyway, given his opinions on TV news, especially cable. "They were all over the place. MSNBC, Fox, CNN. Even a couple of those right-wing fringe operations. Talking to people, doing stand-ups—"

"Listen to Mr. Media Jargon," Eve said. "Stand-ups."

"They're all still trying to figure out their positions so they can report their version of the story."

Ronnie said, "What do you mean, 'their positions'?"

"Most cable news channels have what they're going to say pretty well staked out before they cover a story. Not that they'll ignore anything that doesn't suit them, but they're sure as hell not looking for it.

"Take our situation. Cop shoots an allegedly unarmed man." Saw the women's eyebrows go up. "No, we haven't found a weapon. Anyway, in a typical police shooting, Fox will side with the cop, MSNBC with the victim, and they'll build their coverage around that."

Ronnie interrupted. "To be fair, when an unarmed man is shot by a cop, it's reasonable to assume a Black man was shot by a white cop."

"No argument. I'm sure the newsrooms heard 'unarmed man shot by cop in redneck town' and their first thought was to get someone out here and book the usual suspects for panels.

"But this Black cop shot a white supremacist. Take MSNBC. If they come in with their usual position, lamenting the shooting of yet another unarmed man, they'll look like white nationalist apologists. If they support the Black guy, they're subject to criticism for siding with an abusive cop who shoots unarmed victims.

"Fox has the opposite problem. Their default position is 'he had it coming.' They can't very well say that if the victim is part of their core audience. Backing up the cop is going to be tough, him being one of those people they usually say had it coming. Cable news is not designed for this kind of nuance. With any luck they'll both leave us alone."

Doc finished his drink. Waved for the check. "Then again, they might not. Fox could use this to claim it's now open season on whites. Or to show the only color they care about is blue. I wouldn't be surprised to see them try to split the baby and argue both sides."

Eve said, "Split the baby?"

"You never heard that before?" She had not. "It's a Bible

story. Two women are arguing over who a baby belongs to and they appeal to Solomon or Abraham or David, I forget which. One of those Biblical wise guys." Saw Eve's look. "All right. Wise *men.* Anyway, his solution is to ask for a knife. He's gonna cut the baby in half and give each woman a piece. It was the only fair way."

Eve was horrified. "Honest to God?"

"Exactly. He knew the real mother would run away from that solution in a heartbeat and when she did, he gave her the baby."

Ronnie said, "How does that apply to the Fox situation?"

Doc pondered. "Now that I think about it, not so much. I guess I hear it on the news often enough in these situations I figured it must. Anyway, MSNBC will have Chris Hayes here in a down jacket looking like a malnourished Michelin Man doing live stand-ups from anyplace three mopes are hanging around a light pole, asking if they feel safer now that we have Black cops. Which we always did, except they hadn't shot any white guys before. Rachel Maddow will do a twenty-five-minute sentence on what hypocrites Fox is and Tucker Carlson will talk about the war on people like you and me until some asshole in Washington fucks up even worse than usual and they forget all about us."

No one spoke until Ronnie said, "I never heard you talk that long at one time before."

"I try to keep from intimidating others with my imposing intellect."

Eve said, "What about CNN?"

"What about them?"

"Where do they fit in on the cops shooting unarmed people spectrum?"

Doc tapped his teeth with a fingernail. "Good question. They bend over backward to try to be fair to everybody. Maybe Boston noticed Richie left without his coat and brought it out for him. Richie saw this and wanted Trevor to know he was okay. But, in his haste to put Trevor at ease, Richie slipped in what could reasonably appear to be a threatening manner. Trevor fired a warning shot that struck the building—light pole, cloud, what-ever—and killed poor Richie dead. A tragic accident that points out the need for better outdoor lighting and coat check facilities in places of public entertainment."

"Three times?" Eve said.

"Three times what?"

"Wasn't he shot three times?"

Doc pulled on his coat. "Boston was warning the hell out of him. Shit like this is why I don't watch much cable news anymore."

"With that attitude, why do you watch it at all?"

Doc let his chin dip, trying to decide whether to tell them. "Once in a while, after a shitty day, I like to turn on Brian Williams to see if he has Ashley Parker on."

Both women look confused. Eve said, "Why her? She's smart and a good reporter, and kind of cute in her way, but how does that fix your day?"

"Because she smiles every time Brian introduces her and it is impossible for me to feel down when I see her smile. It's almost as good as a laughing baby."

"Why don't you just keep a picture handy? Then every day can be a good day."

"Because that would be creepy. I'm a grown-ass man." Doc shook his head. "Women can be so clueless. The joy comes from watching the smile grow on her face. The anticipation. I don't know why I even bother trying to explain things to the two of you sometimes."

Eve punched his arm as Doc's cell rang. "Dougherty...yeah..." His eyes closed. "Fuck. All right. Who's there now?...You want me to take command?...A couple beers with dinner." Sigh. "I'm on the way. Twelve to fifteen minutes." Broke the connection.

Ronnie said, "What's wrong?"

"Fat Jimmy's? The bar where Richie Johnson was shot out back of?" Both women nodded. "Looks like the wake started."

# 19.

Doc surveyed the damage inside Fat Jimmy's, one butt cheek on a stool. "Jesus, Jimmy. Your insurance cover this?"

Jimmy set two boilermakers on the bar, pushed one across to Doc. "I doubt I'll file a claim. A few broken chairs. Busted window. The bar signs I get free from the vendors. I doubt the actual damage will be more than my deductible." Raised his shot glass to touch Doc's. They swallowed whisky.

Doc let the warmth crawl into his belly. At least tonight's action had been indoors. "Now that we're just two guys talking, let me ask you as a friend of many years, what the fuck happened?"

"Word must've got out we'd been cleared to open because there was a crowd when I got here at six. Some came because of what happened Wednesday night, but most were at least semi-regulars who wanted to show support. Happy crowd.

"About nine thirty, quarter to ten, Big Gay Al took some trash out to the dumpster." Jimmy's backup bartender was neither big, nor gay, nor even named Al. Years ago he did something that reminded a patron of the South Park character; probably some kindness to an animal. Whatever John Hrykowian had done—not even he was sure—the nickname stuck. The guy who hung it on him was doing three-to-five in Fayette and no one felt like driving all the way to La Belle to ask, as he likely didn't remember himself, drunk as he'd usually been. "Al drops the shit in the dumpster and someone gives him hell. He looks around and sees about ten guys gathered around where Richie Johnson got shot. Al asks what they're doing back there, and the guy shushes him again. Says their paying respects to their murdered friend."

Jimmy quaffed half the glass of beer. Wiped his lips with the back of one hand. "Al and Richie had history, none of it good. He tells these guys to clear off and they come after him. You know Al. He don't back down. But this was ten against just him and I guess he figured this wasn't the hill to die on, so he run back inside and they followed him in."

"And mayhem ensued?"

"Al's a popular guy. He comes running in with ten strangers chasing him, we got at least twenty-five guys in here already half lit. Opinions got expressed."

"I'm sorry, Jimmy."

"For what?"

"I probably let you reopen too soon. The troopers said they didn't need the scene sequestered anymore and I knew every day closed was costing you money. I should've waited till this blew over before I gave you the high sign."

"Bullshit. It was a good night until these out-of-town leprous dick-tips showed up."

Doc tore a corner off his coaster. "I got here in time to hear some of them say they'd be back. Maybe you should shut down a while. Till this crew leaves town, anyway."

"Like hell. No way do these jagovs get to dictate my business hours."

"We can't protect you. We'll answer any calls soon as we can, but you and I both know, considering everything else that could happen this weekend, we might not get here until after the fan blows shit wall to wall."

Jimmy walked the two pilsner glasses to the tap. Filled them and walked back. "I have to be here, anyway. I might as well make some money."

"Why do you have to be here?"

"These strike me as the kind to burn a man out, they got the opportunity."

"You're putting people at risk if you really are worried about being burned out."

Jimmy shook his head as he drank. "I'll have a man on the door. With a shotgun. I know guys who'd pay for that job. He raises an alarm, we'll have the whole operation outside in thirty seconds."

Doc knew that was how Jimmy would want to play it. It would be his first impulse, as well. Also the last thing Penns River law enforcement needed to have to worry about, private residences across the street on two sides. "I get that, Jimmy, I do. I'm also thinking this is not the time for a dick measuring contest. You don't know what you might be up against. Hell, *we* don't know what *we're* up against."

Jimmy stared at the entry door. He was too smart not to know the risks. "Fuck it. They don't know what they're up against, either."

Doc lowered his voice in the empty room. "Jimmy." Waited for his friend to make eye contact. "How much can you trust whoever will be in this room to stand up?"

Jimmy looked insulted. "What do you mean? This isn't just my bar. It's all our bar."

"Was Richie Johnson a regular?"

"Semi."

"Did you know he was hooked up with Vanilla ISIS?"

Jimmy pulled back his immediate response. "I knew he was an asshole and had some racial problems. That didn't make him special around here."

"My point exactly. You have a full house and the other shoe drops, who can you be absolutely sure about?"

Jimmy gave it thought. "Big Gay Al. Harley Hagenmeyer. Gene Lagoon. Jim Felice." Eyes scanned the room as if seeing people at the bar or a table. "Gerry Wolfe. Reid Paulice." Jimmy almost said a couple of names. Pulled them back. Focused on

125

Doc again. "You."

"And I won't be here." Saw Jimmy's expression. "I'll come running. Or send the cavalry if I'm tied up. We might already engaged, is all I'm saying."

"I won't let those cocksuckers shut me down. Even the threat of them."

"I understand. I only bring it up so I have a clear conscience that we at least discussed it."

"We discussed it. Fuck these guys."

# 20.

The balloon went up at a quarter to two Saturday afternoon. Doc had already endured the inevitable catcalls when he entered the station wearing his uniform with the fresh stripes and was in in the detectives' office drinking coffee and doing paperwork when Brendan Sullivan leaned through the doorway. "I need you to assume command at the shopping center on Ninth Street, there at the foot of the bridge."

Doc stood and pulled on his coat. "I thought things were quiet. Eye Chart's already engaged?" As patrol sergeant, Mike Zywiciel would be the first supervisor up.

Sullivan stepped in so no one could overhear. Said, "I don't like the look in his eyes," and Doc knew his old Little League coach's retirement papers would be in by week's end.

Four units, eight cops, met him at the Fifth Avenue entrance. No one rode alone today except supervisors. Sean Sisler pointed toward the strip club near the end of the row of storefronts. "Looks like a few tourists got frisky in Chubbie's. The bouncer threw them out pretty easy, but reinforcements came."

"They going back in?" Doc not looking forward to busting heads in an enclosed space containing civilians, clothed or otherwise.

"A guy came by—a local, someone I know to see—told us he heard talk of them taking a walk over to the Estates." Allegheny Estates was the majority Black part of Penns River, a few blocks

127

north of where the cops were.

"We can't have that. Whatever happens happens right here."

"I don't know how Shop 'n' Save's going to like that."

"I'm not crazy about it myself, but we can't have them breaking into small groups or we'll be chasing them like cockroaches from a woodpile." Pointed straight down. "Here is where we can deal with them best. Here is where we'll deal with them."

Another unit pulled in as Doc keyed his shoulder microphone. "PR-uh, PR—It's Dougherty. What the hell's my call sign? I'm not used to being in uniform."

Janine Schoepf sounded as professional as could be expected from someone suppressing giggles. "You're PR-Four, Doc."

"We'll discuss your attitude later, Ms. Schoepf. This is PR-Four. Put me through to whatever we're calling the chief today."

"We're calling him 'Chief.' Wait one."

Barney McGinniss walked up looking large and in charge. "That the disturbance?"

Doc nodded as Sullivan came over the air. "What's it look like down there?"

"Like about twenty guys milling around trying to decide if they want to start trouble. At least half already have loads on. Rumor has it they're headed for the Estates."

"No, they're not. What's the plan?"

Doc counted heads. "We have ten bodies here. Eleven, including me. I want to disperse the crowd in the parking lot and push them away from any potential incidents, then increase patrols in the Estates."

"Do you have enough units?"

"I think so. For now, at least."

"All right then. Do it. Keep me posted. Bear in mind, I'd rather you were safe than sorry so far as calling for help goes."

"Copy. 'Safe' is the order of the day. Out."

Doc called his squad together. Pointed. "Pull your shops over there to hem them in. Batons at hand, not in them. Keep your shields close, but don't pull them out yet. The plan is to ease this crowd through the Eighth Street exit. Keep an eye open in case anyone tries to double back on Industrial toward the Estates. The order is Burrows, McGinniss, Augustine, Trettle, Sisler. Leave space so they can make up their own minds to leave. We do *not* want to provoke anything. Questions?" None. Doc made the whirlybird motion. "Saddle up."

The police cars attracted attention halfway across the lot. A couple tourists pointed. One flashed the white power sign, another the finger. A chant started as the cops took their positions. Almost inaudible at first. Out of the car and on his feet, Doc heard, "No more retreats." Not loud. Not a lot of vigor. But growing.

A different vibe from the crew Doc saw at the Moonshine Emporium yesterday. At least half of this group was younger, clean cut, and dressed like models for PreppyAssholes.com. Doc hadn't expected everyone who'd come to town for this clusterfuck to be textbook definitions of irony for thinking of themselves as the Master Race; seeing the other side gave him pause. They wouldn't do anything violent themselves. They would have a talent for provoking others. Doc didn't think it would take much, from the looks of some of these guys.

The cops took their positions, stood at parade rest. Visors up, no batons visible unless you knew where to look. The chant still no more than a murmur. The two groups faced each other about fifteen feet apart.

Doc left a moment for everyone to appraise the situation. Stepped forward and used his drill sergeant voice to project without yelling. "Who's in charge here?"

From the back of the crowd: "It's sure as shit not you."

"Nor do I need to be. I do have to ask you all to move along."

The preppy closest to Doc said, "We have the right to assemble," in a reasonable tone.

Doc suppressed a smirk. People who dedicated their lives to denying the rights of others while insisting on their own were a never-ending source of amusement. He also knew when someone was baiting him. "You absolutely do. Part of the reason we're here is to protect and preserve that right should someone try to deny it to you. What you don't have is a right to disrupt access into and out of these businesses. You want to assemble, we need you to do it elsewhere."

This voice came from the back and had booze in it. "You got the goddamn parking lot blocked off. Where the hell're we supposed to go?"

Doc pointed over his left shoulder. "Gazebo Park is a block and a half that way. We'll even provide an escort. Go over there and you can sing Kumbaya till dark if you want."

"All our cars is in here."

Doc saw the man now. He fit somewhere between the two extremes in the crowd. Wool jacket-shirt, jeans, hat with ear flaps. "Which is it? Do you want to assemble, or do you want to drive?"

This appeared to be above the man's pay grade. He deferred to the preppy, who nodded. The man said, "I guess I'm ready to drive out of here."

"Show me which car is yours and you can go." Doc turned to Chris Trettle. "You hear it in his voice?"

"Uh-huh."

"Starting the car buys him a field sobriety test."

"Right here?"

Doc shook his head. "Who's riding with you?"

"Skippy."

"Leave now and pull him over as soon as both of you are out of sight. Treat it as a felony stop if there's anyone in the car with him. A gun without a concealed carry permit equals a collar. Out-of-state permits don't count today, reciprocity or not. This'll be over by the time the paperwork gets sorted." Trettle nodded and gestured for Skip Speer to join him.

The protester grew impatient. "Well? Can I go? Freezing my balls off out here."

"Sorry. Got distracted. Which car's yours?" The man pointed to a Buick outside the police perimeter. Doc nodded. "Go with God."

"My friends, too?"

Doc made an ushering gesture. "By all means. The last thing we want is for anyone to be here against their wishes."

The man and a couple of camos passed through the line. Doc faced them as they went to the car, his eyes a block away to where Trettle and Speer pulled into position. Chris Trettle was an asshole and often insubordinate, but he was a solid patrol officer who knew how to get things done.

Doc waited until he saw Trettle pull behind the Buick. "Anyone else ready to drive away? Same deal applies."

The preppy spoke. "What we'd like to do is see what else is in this shopping center."

"Sorry. Can't allow it."

"Why not?"

"While you do have an uncontested right to assemble, you do not have a parade permit. We haven't blocked the streets or redirected traffic to protect you."

"We're not on the streets. This is a parking lot."

"It's also private property. The owners have asked us to disperse you." A reach. Chubbie's asked for help with the rowdies. Dan Hecker owned the strip mall and hadn't said dick.

"Which owner?"

Doc pointed to include the entire complex. "Not just any owner. *The* owner."

"He doesn't want his tenants to do any business?" Doc shrugged. "You realize that, even if you disperse us, we can come back here and shop."

"As individuals. Another large group forms and we'll be back." Saw the preppy working on his next argument. "I don't want to be a prick and it's too cold for us to butt heads all day. How's this? Chubbie's over there is off limits. The manager already said he doesn't want you. You can all wander the other stores and shop, but there'll be a cop outside. First sign of trouble, and I mean if someone wipes a booger under a counter, we go in."

A corner of Preppy's mouth ticked up. No smile in his eyes. Nodded a thirty-second of an inch. "That's all we want. No one is looking for trouble. May we pass?"

Doc made the ushering gesture again. Turned to his cops. "Burrows and Augustine. Who's riding with you?" They told him. "You have store duty. Keep an eye on things the best you can. Anyone acts up, at all, and they go." Nods all around. "Everyone else, on me."

The remaining four coppers followed Doc twenty feet away. "Block the Ninth Street entrance. No one goes up Third Avenue." The Allegheny Estates began two blocks up Third.

McGinniss said, "What about Fourth Avenue?"

"Leave it alone for now. They can't move that way without us seeing them. My big concern is they don't work their way to the end of the strip and keep right on going into the Estates. They want to go up on Fourth, they have to either get their cars or walk across the lot. We'll worry about that if it happens."

Reinforcements for the tourists arrived within minutes. Camos and preppies got out and went into various stores. The general flow was to the north end of the strip.

Sisler said, "You see what I see?"

"If what you see looks like critical mass gathering in front of Family Dollar, then yeah."

"Uh-huh."

"How many you figure are in there?"

"Family Dollar? Or altogether?"

"Both."

Sisler calculated. "Fifteen or twenty in front of the store. At least that many more circulating."

"And we have eight—scratch that—nine bodies until Trettle and Speer get back." A moment's hesitation. "I hate to make an 'all units' call not knowing what else might be going on."

Sisler said, "Get a report from Sully," just as Chris Trettle's voice came over the radio.

"Base, this is PR-Six."

"Go ahead, Six."

"Request a wagon to the eight hundred block of Fifth Avenue. We have three to transport."

Doc waited for Trettle to clear. Called him on his cell. "What'd you get?"

"Driver blew a point one-oh on the machine. Two of his passengers had concealed weapons with out-of-state permits. There was also a loaded weapon no one claimed responsibility for, so Skip and I took them all."

"Nice work. Get over here as soon as you can and tell whoever's driving the wagon to drop that load off and come back. We might need him."

# 21.

The cops watched the crowd come together near the center of the parking lot. The wagon returned in half an hour with an extra cop in it. That brought the complement of officers to thirteen. Against a crowd of fifty. And growing.

Sisler and McGinniss flanked Doc. "Don't make a big deal of it, but get everyone ready to move. These guys start walking north on Fourth Avenue, Ninth Street is as far as they go."

Ten minutes passed before the first contingent left the lot through the Fourth Avenue exit. Four camos. Doc's worst-case scenario, the group splitting up, no good way for his cops to ride herd on all of them.

"Augie. Go up Third and parallel this group without being obvious. Call if you see anything you don't like." Augustine nodded and left.

Doc addressed his remaining officers. "No one else gets free passage. Another group starts that way, McGinniss and Burrows will intercept them at Ninth Street until we see what the rest decide to do. Keep things as low profile as you can, but they don't get by."

Augustine's unit rolled out on Third as the first group crossed Ninth Street. After they went out of sight behind the candle store, another half dozen stepped off. Doc nodded and McGinniss and Burrows paced themselves to reach the intersection ahead of the marchers.

Doc could see but not hear what went on. Discussion appeared to be civil as Mac talked to a preppy. Then a camo said something McGinniss seemed to ignore but sent Burrows's hands creeping toward her baton and pepper spray.

Doc gestured Sisler and Wohleber closer. "If that business on the corner gets messy, or if any more of the big cluster looks like it's ready to join, we're going to haul ass to the Fourth Avenue exit and cut them off. Dave, pull the wagon onto Fourth and keep us between you and the crowd. If we have to start loading people, I want it to be quick."

Status quo for another minute. Then someone on the corner said something that sent McGinniss rigid. The crowd began to tighten and become agitated. Doc said, "Let's go. Code Two."

A string of walkers had started to move when the police cars blocked their way. Doc stepped to the front, officers trailing like a V of geese in flight. "Gentlemen. Where are you off to?"

From somewhere in the crowd: "None of your fucking business."

A preppy, not the one Doc spoke with before, stepped up. Early thirties, short dark hair, khakis, L.L. Bean anorak. "Are you blocking our way?"

"Depends on which way you're going. Kind of a cold day for a stroll and, much as I hate to say this about my hometown, there's not much of interest around here."

"Why does it matter which way we go, or why we want to go there?"

Doc stepped closer. Lowered his voice. "So far everyone's been reasonable. We know why you're here—"

"Why's that?"

Doc paused a beat. "For the funeral, I presume." Went on when Preppy didn't answer. "That's tomorrow. Till then, we'd be delighted for you to patronize our businesses, have a good meal, buy some souvenirs. We want everyone to have fond memories of their trip to Penns River."

"Then why are you stopping us?"

"Because the only thing in that direction is a residential area full of people who don't want to be bothered on a freezing Saturday any more than you do when you're at home."

"You're assuming we'd go there to cause trouble. Is that it?"

"'Assume' is too strong a word. Let's say I have reason to believe you would not get along with the folks who live over there."

"That would be their problem. We just want to walk through."

"That's my concern, Mr.—what's your name, anyway?"

No challenge in the preppy's voice. "What's yours?" The smugness was suffocating.

"Sergeant Dougherty, Penns River police." No response. "And you are…"

"A natural-born citizen of the United States of America with European ancestry."

Doc enjoyed this kind of banter with self-important assholes much more when the stakes weren't as high. "What we have over there is Penns River's largest contingent of natural-born citizens of the United States of America with African ancestry. They're entitled to our protection and they're going to get it."

"By restricting our rights?"

"By ensuring your rights don't infringe on theirs. You want to see the town? Go the other way and turn left on Eighth Street. There's a little park up there you can hang in, or you can walk through the business district, though not much is open on Saturdays. You do that, keep to yourselves, and it'll be our job to make sure no one infringes on your rights. Right now my priority is the people living in the Allegheny Estates."

Preppy made a show of counting the cops with his eyes. Looked over his shoulder at the rest of his cohort, at least sixty now, more coming in on the Eighth Street side. "We can go right over you."

"You can try."

Preppy made calculations. Doc wondered how much water

he drew in the hierarchy. Not Richards nor Tucker, he also didn't show up here by accident.

Commotion behind Doc, where McGinniss, Burrows, and two others faced down the splinter group. Doc kept his eyes forward. His team was far more outnumbered. Heard Sisler say "Mac's arresting at least two" and nodded.

Preppy noticed. "It looks like a couple of our friends are in handcuffs up there on the corner. Are they under arrest?"

"Most likely, if they're cuffed."

"If we agree to leave, may we take them with us?"

"Depends on what they were arrested for." Over his shoulder to Sisler: "Raise Burrows. What's their status?"

A minute passed. Radios crackled. Sisler said, "Two arrests. One for carrying concealed and one for failure to obey."

"The concealed carry is a collar. Tell them to cut loose the failure to obey and send him and the rest of his merry band over here." Turned to Preppy. "There you go. They come back, you all drive away, and we're done."

"I want them both to come with us."

"We're not releasing a felony arrest into a volatile situation. Take the rest and go."

"Or what?"

This condescending Chad was beginning to get on Doc's nerves. "You'd be surprised at the resources we have at our disposal, even in a small town like this."

Preppy kept his vision over Doc's shoulder. "All right. We're not here to cause trouble. We didn't expect such a hostile reception."

"Small town like this, large group comes in without notice, sometimes there's friction. We roll out the red carpet for softball tournaments."

The group detained at the intersection came back through the police line, shouting at McGinniss as he loaded his arrestee into the wagon. Dave Wohleber asked if he should take the van back to the house. Doc shook his head. "We might not be done with it yet."

It took twenty minutes to get all the cars into more or less of a line. The parade turned right out the Eighth Street exit. Doc couldn't see which way they turned on Industrial Boulevard, the next street down, where Eighth ended in a T. Asked Sisler if his freakish vision could. "Uh-uh. Building's in the way."

Burrows came over the radio as the last cars left the lot. "PR-Four, there's a line of vehicles crossing Ninth Street onto Second Avenue at the bridge."

Toward the Estates. Doc cursed under his breath. "Let's roll. Fan out in the Estates and find these assholes quick as you can. Latch on and make sure they know you're tailing them."

# 22.

Doc held his position in the parking lot as police cars criss-crossed the Allegheny Estates looking for incidents. A few units right on the bumpers of suspicious cars, lacking probable cause for a stop but not wanting the out-of-town guests to feel ignored. Doc's consideration of cutting some units loose was interrupted by Chris Trettle's voice over the radio. "This is PR-Six. I have visual on half a dozen number two males on the edge of the basketball courts at the JFK Playground."

Doc keyed his mike. "What are they doing?"

"Right now they're watching a basketball game."

"Today? It's freezing."

Sisler's voice, measured and even: "They play every Saturday, weather be damned. I've seen them shovel off both courts to play."

Doc: "How many today, Chris?"

"At least ten. Another carload of whites just pulled up."

"I'm on the way. Sisler, McGinniss, get over there. Augustine, Burrows, keep patrolling."

Dave Wohleber's voice: "You want the wagon?"

"Yeah, but keep it up the street a ways. Who's riding with you?"

"Mazza."

"Take your position and send her down."

Doc arrived on Pine Court to find at least twenty tourists of all descriptions lined up alongside the basketball court closest to the street. Three units already on scene.

Leaning against his car, Chris Trettle answered the obvious question before Doc could ask. "They're talking some shit. Nothing too bad."

"Who's doing the talking?"

"White guys, mostly. The homies are trying to play ball. I see a few getting the red ass, though."

McGinniss, Sisler, and their partners walked up to make a squad of seven as the wagon pulled in to block the Fourth Avenue entrance to Pine Court. Pam Mazza got out and started down the street. Eight. "Let's get between them. Remember, we're here to defuse a situation, not create one."

Two kinds of insults came from the white crowd. The preppies' commented on how the ballers had free time because they had no jobs, or discussed what percentage of a player's income went into his sneakers.

The camos were more direct. "Look at that boy jump."

"Think how high he'd get if his lips didn't have so much wind resistance."

"Waste of good breeding stock out there."

The cops' arrival opened a third avenue of comment. "Nigger-loving pigs." "Sno Balls." "Fucking fascists," which Doc couldn't keep from smiling at.

The officers walked single file between the hecklers and the game. A few tourists provided minor resistance when nudged aside, not enough to start an incident. The game went on, though breaks in the action provided opportunities for hard looks. Some players made comments among themselves.

A camo with a Confederate battle flag on his cap said, "What're you looking at, yoyo? Ain't no white women over here. Yeah, you. I *know* you're a ghost riding motherfucker."

Doc pointed at the man. "You. Over here." Pointed straight down. "Now."

The man didn't move. The racial insults stopped, replaced by general hubbub.

"You're here in front of me in five seconds or you're going in."

"For what?"

"Inciting a riot. Disobeying a lawful order. At least."

More hubbub, "Race traitor" floated out of the crowd.

"Fuck you. Last I heard we still got free speech in this country."

"Your public defender can explain the concept of fighting words to you in lockup if you don't get your fat ass over here."

A few in the crowd goaded Camo Man as he struggled to make up his mind. Before he could do anything, a Kentucky Fried Chicken bucket flew from the crowd and struck a basketball player in the chest. Bones and Styrofoam containers fell out. The man brushed the debris from his clothes and it was on.

About as many agitators as there were Blacks and cops combined. Once the dam broke there was no choosing sides. The cops were caught in the middle, and would be until things settled down.

The one Doc threatened with arrest stepped up and pushed him hard with both hands. Doc surprised himself with how fast he could extend a baton after eight years as a detective. Hit the guy once across the hamstring to drop him to one knee. Thought about hauling him to the wagon, but the situation was going downhill in a hurry, and he couldn't be spared. Looked up the street and waved for Dave Wohleber to bring down the wagon. Cars and men on foot kept arriving, leaving Doc no choice but to make the call. "This is PR-Four requesting all available units to the playground on Pine Court. Code Three. Repeat: Code Three." Sirens and lights and speed. He needed a show.

A quick look to recapture his bearings. The cops were doing a decent job of keeping the two sides apart. Interceding and pushing for the most part, though Doc's wasn't the only baton in action. Saw what looked like a motorcycle chain connect across the shoulder and neck of a basketball player. Moved toward it. Grabbed an arm as the chain wielder cocked it for another swing. Pulled back hard and fast into a wrist lock in time for the baller to connect with a solid punch to Mr. Chain's jaw. He tried to break free. Doc tightened the hold.

"The fuck're you doing? Let me defend myself."

"You had that one coming. You're going to jail." To the local: "Back off or you can join him."

Dave Wohleber met Doc ten feet short of the wagon. "We're about full up in there already."

"Chain them to the fence or light poles if you have to. Everyone we bring over goes to jail."

Sirens were audible and getting closer as Doc surveyed the scene. The line of coppers had about disappeared as individuals and pairs of police tried to keep things under control. The situation teetered near a tipping point, each spot as bad as the next. About to wade in to see where the flow took him when a roar erupted. "Yeah! Hit him! Hit him! Beat that nigger's ass!"

Doc pushed his way through combatants of all three allegiances to find Barney McGinniss beating living hell out of a Black man already on the ground. "Officer McGinniss!" Another whack. "*McGinniss!*" No response. Doc swam between a camo and a preppy. Grabbed McGinniss by the arm as he raised the baton for another go. "Goddamnit, that's enough."

McGinniss broke free. Stood to face Doc. Held up his left forearm. The sleeve was torn. Blood dripped to the ground. "That motherfucker cut me!"

"I see. Take him to the wagon and call for an ambulance."

"Fuck the ambulance. I'm taking mine out in trade."

"Not with this one you're not. We'll settle up later." Doc did a quick scan of the area. "Where's the knife?"

The basketball player worked his way to his feet. Blood streamed from his forehead. "Ain't no fucking knife. I tried to tell him it weren't me. Who brings a knife to a basketball game?"

McGinniss said, "Down here? You're all safe bets for at least a knife."

"Enough. Sort it out at the house. And call for a goddamn

ambulance. You both need stitches." Gave an encouraging push toward the wagon as something hit the back of his head. Knocked him forward, not down.

Clearing the cobwebs, Doc saw half a dozen fresh cops working through the melee swinging batons. The reinforcements appeared to weaken the resolve of the combatants, though the outcome was still in doubt.

Caught motion in the corner of an eye and saw a camo swing what appeared to be a small pipe. Doc turned to absorb the blow with his right shoulder. Numbness shot down his arm to the fingers. Found himself in a virtual sword fight, holding off the pipe with the baton left-handed. Losing ground until Camo telegraphed a swing and Doc rammed his stick into the tourist's belly through to the backbone. Feeling returning to his right arm, he switched the baton to that hand and brought it down on his assailant's wrist to knock loose the pipe. Heard the bone break before the man screamed.

"You broke my fucking arm, you son of a bitch!" Reached for the pipe with his other hand.

Doc stepped on it to remove the threat. "Your balls are next unless you come along with me right now. An ambulance is on the way."

The man shook free as Doc took him by the sleeve to guide him to the ambo. "I'll get there myself, you nigger-loving son of a bitch."

Doc continued the escort, hands free. Kept his head on a swivel to see if a more general alarm needed to go out, but the latest batch of coppers appeared to have turned the tide. An unbroken line of blue was forcing the two sides apart. Doc stepped back to look for remaining hot spots.

Sean Sisler sidled up, a bruise on his left cheek. "Glad to see you're getting the hang of being a sergeant. Stand back and watch other guys fight, not do it yourself."

Doc nodded toward what remained of the scrum. "Why are you out here?"

"I just hooked a couple to the fence for Dave to collect later." Nudged Doc's arm. "See that one? Cuffed to the no parking sign?"

"What about him?"

"Her."

Doc looked again. "Really?"

Sisler nodded. "Called me everything but a child of god when I hauled her over. Said she'd swear out a complaint for sexual assault if I tried to frisk her. It would almost have been worth coming out just to see the look on her face."

"What did you do?"

"I got Mazza to take care of it."

Doc couldn't look away. "That's a woman."

"Only because of the plumbing. I have never been so happy to be gay in my life."

Doc remembered he was a sergeant. "Coffee break's over. Get back in there and keep things moving in the right direction so I don't get this brand-new uniform dirty."

Sisler smiled. Walked up to a camo running his mouth as close as any to the remaining basketball players. Took hold of one arm. "Do you want to go to jail?" Doc couldn't hear the reply. Sisler put the sole of one boot against the man's ass and pushed as he let go of the arm. "Then get the fuck out. I see you again today, even just blowing your nose, and you go to jail."

The man regained his balance and faced Sisler. "Fuck you. I'll blow my nose on your shirt if I want to." Sisler took a step forward and the man left.

Doc flexed his fingers as he walked toward the wagon. The arm had loosened up enough to hurt. Ten camos inside. Eight more people shackled to the fence or light poles: four camos, a preppy, and three basketball players, the man McGinniss beat among them. Spoke to Dave Wohleber. "Go ahead and take this load back while we clean up. You'll have at least two more runs to make for us and who knows what else is going on."

"I think I can get all the rest in one trip."

"Uh-uh. One run for the whites and another for the Blacks. I'll let you know which goes first when you get back."

Doc's mind not yet made up about who to send in when. Did he want the tourists to freeze, or rather allow the Blacks a little time to let tempers cool and maybe get a pass, considering they'd been minding their own business playing ball when things broke bad? Of course, the man McGinniss claimed cut him had to go in. Maybe, maybe, he could go alone with a patrol unit. Decisions, decisions.

About to speak to the restrained baller when McGinniss came up, arm still leaking blood. Doc pointed toward the ambulance. "Let the EMTs take a look at that arm. I don't know if you'll need stitches, but you might want a tetanus shot."

McGinniss stared through the man alleged to have cut him. "My shots are current. Besides, they're busy working on the guy whose arm you broke."

Doc kept his voice down. "You sure this is the guy that cut you?"

"Goddamn right I am. How can you ask me that?"

"It was a clusterfuck, everything going on at once. All I'm thinking is, these guys came here to play ball. This other crew came looking for trouble, and they didn't care who they gave it to. Of the two, which is more likely to bring a knife?"

"You don't think half these guys been carrying knives since they could walk? Remember, they see the news, too. Maybe that's why they were out here, looking for something more interesting than a game."

"I have it on good authority they're here every Saturday afternoon."

"He had a fucking knife and he cut me with it. End of story. Okay?"

"Okay, Barney. I got there late. We'll sort it out."

"About getting there late. You ever put hands on me again, I'll lay you down."

Doc couldn't allow such a comment to pass. Turned so

McGinniss could see the stripes. "Officer McGinniss, we have a busy couple of days ahead of us. When they're over, you and I are going to have a discussion about respecting rank. Get your goddamn arm looked at. That's an order."

McGinniss shot Doc a look that would buckle a lesser man's knees. Turned on his heel and walked to the ambulance.

Doc wiped sweat from his forehead. The hand came away bloody. Trying to remember what cut him when a familiar voice spoke at his side. "Detective Dougherty. A moment, please."

# 23.

The Reverend Doctor Christian Love—birth name Alfonsus Tate—was a large man, tall as Doc with the heavyset gravitas that plays so well for televangelists, which is what Love was. He had a small TV studio in Pittsburgh he'd hoped to move to Penns River as the anchor of a religious-themed shopping center he called Resurrection Mall. Love paid more attention to fundraising than hiring practices, resulting in five murders and a fire.

He sold the site to Dan Hecker for what Doc heard was twenty cents on the dollar. Hecker cleared the purchase through the town by promising to build a riverside park, which struck Doc as odd because there were two blocks between the site and the river, and the intervening land was owned by others with going businesses.

In the end, Hecker did away with the enclosed mall and religious businesses that had already been built—bookstore, thrift shop, counseling service, daycare center—and replaced them with a strip mall containing

 A beer distributor
 A vape shop
 A gun store
 A strip club

Added a supermarket and a discount store when the locals

protested the loss of what had been there before. No question in Doc's mind a liquor store would have gone in if the Commonwealth didn't monopolize the sale of anything stronger than beer.

Doc and Love had a respectful relationship, not close. Love's tone had not requested Doc's time; it informed him the time was no longer his own. Given the situation, Doc tried to keep his impatience from showing. "What can I do for you, Dr. Love?"

"A bit more brusque than usual today, Detective Dougherty. Does that come with the uniform? Or the stripes on it?"

"It comes with today's activity, which I know you had nothing to do with. I apologize for my tone. No offense intended."

Love waited to speak, as if he wanted to be sure he had Doc's full attention. "None taken. I know you weren't responsible, either. It is a shame that young men can't play a friendly game of basketball without being harassed."

"I agree." Doc didn't mention that these friendly games required police intervention two or three times a year.

"Things seem to have gotten out of hand today."

"We would've been here sooner, but no one made an appointment for us to referee."

"Are you injured, sir? You're bleeding."

"I'll live. I don't want to be rude, Doctor, but I expect to be needed elsewhere before long."

"I understand and will be brief. I see you're already aware of the beating Devon Dandridge took at the hands of one of your officers."

"That's correct."

"Devon did not cut that officer."

"Did you see who did? A witness, particularly one of your standing, would be a big help."

Love shook his head. "The first thing I noticed was the officer reaching for Devon. I only say he didn't cut him because I know the young man."

"When you say he reached for Devon, do you mean he had to go and get him?"

Love considered his answer. "It didn't appear to me there was a chase involved, but no, they were not standing right next to each other."

"Can we call you for a statement?"

"Are you telling me there will be an investigation?"

"Yes, sir. A police officer was injured, as was a citizen. There will be an investigation."

"I will be happy to give a statement so long as I am satisfied the investigation is fair and impartial."

"I won't be the lead detective because I was personally involved, but the detectives work under my supervision. I give you my word we will investigate fully to the best of our ability and jurisdiction."

"Penns River is not part of your jurisdiction?"

"Beyond a certain point we have to call in the state police. Or if a citizen requests state intervention."

"Who requested the state police in the matter of Trevor Boston's situation?"

"That's an officer-involved homicide. State police action is automatic."

"You've already decided it's a homicide?"

"The law defines a homicide as one person causing the death of another. Could be an accident. Murder, or even anything unlawful, is not implied and should not be inferred."

"I doubt Mr. Boston's situation will be considered an accident."

"There are levels of justifiable, or excusable, homicide. Self-defense comes to mind."

"Do you believe Mr. Boston acted in self-defense?"

"I never 'believe' anything about investigations. I draw conclusions based on the evidence."

"Have you drawn any conclusions from the evidence here?"

"It's not my case. No offense, but even if it was, I couldn't discuss an open investigation with you."

"You have no involvement at all?"

"Not since the state police took over."

"Have you heard Mr. Boston's statement?"

"No." There were people Doc enjoyed lying to under the right circumstances. Christian Love was not one of them, and this was not among those circumstances.

"Read it?"

"No."

"Have you spoken with him at all?"

"Officially? No."

"Unofficially, then."

"My private conversations are my own. I'm sure that as a man of the cloth you appreciate that."

Love groped for a new tactic. "Should I infer anything from the fact the state police are taking longer to investigate this shooting than they did a few years ago when a white officer shot a Black man?"

"It's apples and oranges, Dr. Love. Sean Sisler shot an armed man who was about to shoot another police officer, namely me, in front of three African American witnesses. Said man had, within the previous hour, threatened you with great bodily injury and set fire to your mall. The only controversy was how Sisler could have been so accurate from such a distance, which he put to rest at the range by showing what kind of shooting he's capable of.

"Officer Boston has no witnesses. No weapon was found on or near the dead man. This one is going to take a while."

Doc knew Love better than to think he'd argue for the sake of it. Still, an argument was brewing. "Mr. Dougherty, you and I came to a position of mutual respect when our paths crossed before. We're not going to see eye to eye on a lot of things, but I believe we each respect the other's integrity. I'm trusting you to see that Mr. Boston isn't railroaded here."

"Like I said, I'm no longer involved in the investigation, so I'm not in a position to make broad assurances. We have a detective acting as liaison and she has given no indication anything is amiss. Trevor has a lawyer with him any time he's questioned." Paused while deciding whether to go on. "You of all people are well aware cops don't like to lock up other cops. I know that's a problem for someone in your position a lot of the time and I understand why. Right now it might work in your favor. Take your good fortune where you find it and don't anticipate an undesirable outcome."

"We're going to look closely at this."

"As you should."

"If we sense Mr. Boston is being treated unfairly, or unjustly punished, we will express our displeasure."

"Understood. May I make a suggestion?"

"Of course." Sounded more like *How dare you.*

"Nothing is going to come out of the Boston investigation for at least a few days. In the meantime, if you feel the need to take to the streets, all I ask is that you wait until this bunch leaves." Pointed over his shoulder at the departing tourists. "There are too many on both sides for us to handle if things break bad. People will get hurt. People may die. Let us get these jackholes out of town. We can give you a lot more leeway then."

Love's tone was colder than the wind off the river. "Thank you, Detective Sergeant Dougherty. I was hoping for an opportunity to ask how you thought the Black community should respond to yet another injustice."

Doc was about to reply when his cell went off. Orville Hatfield.

"You said you wanted a call if we heard anything might go sideways."

"You have something?"

"Couple guys left here talking about getting down to Fat Jimmy's before they missed all the fun. Thought you'd want to know."

"Thanks, Orville. I'm on the way."

Doc closed the call and spoke to Christian Love. "I'm sorry if I offended you. Let's hash it out when things calm down. Right now I'm needed elsewhere."

# 24.

Doc wanted to stay off the air, so he called Janine Schoepf on his cell. "Who's patrolling the Flats?"

"Nobody. Everyone responded to your ten-thirteen. What's wrong?"

"Maybe nothing. I'm going over to check a tip I got about a possible incident at Fat Jimmy's. I'll get on the air if I need anyone."

Two and a half minutes to Fat Jimmy's with lights, no siren. Doc saw the situation in the parking lot and let go with two whoops as he eased in behind a cluster of men facing the building. Out of the car before it stopped rocking.

Fat Jimmy stood shoulder to shoulder with Harley Hagenmeyer. Harley held a shotgun level but not pointed at anyone. The image set Doc back a little. He'd seen Harley with shotguns before. Couldn't remember the last time he saw Jimmy outside twice in as many days.

Half a dozen of what appeared to be patrons flanked Jimmy and Harley. At least twenty others faced them, a cross-section of the various types of tourists in town. No fighting. No hollering. Everyone tense as a bow string at full draw.

Heads turned at the sound of the siren. Followed Doc as he positioned himself halfway between Jimmy and the tourists. He already had their attention, so he got right to it. "What's the deal here? You giving away free beer, Jimmy?"

Not a sound. His humor unappreciated, Doc tried Plan B. "Anyone care to tell me what's going on?"

Jimmy said, "They ain't coming in."

From somewhere on the other side: "The hell we ain't."

That provoked a shouting match along the lines of *are too are not are too are not*. Doc could have worked as school security if he'd wanted. "Enough!" Turned to Jimmy. "Why can't they come in?"

"This is the same asshole busted up the place last night. Let them drink down Earls or one of the colored places in the Estates. See how welcome they are there."

The last thing Doc wanted was to give ideas on where to raise maximum hell. "Understood. I don't blame you." Turned toward the crowd. "Who speaks for your group?"

A man wearing jeans, Red Wing boots, and a plaid overshirt stepped forward. Neither a Chad nor a Bubba, he looked like someone Doc might expect to see inside Jimmy's on a Saturday afternoon, though he didn't recognize the man. "I guess I can." No guessing about it. Everyone deferred to him.

"What are your intentions here?"

"We just want to come in for a drink."

Jimmy: "What else is he going to say? Asshole."

Doc raised his hands in a placating gesture. "Why here? One thing we don't lack for in this town is drinking establishments."

"You trying to tell us where we can or can't drink?"

*Everything is a Supreme Court case with these guys.* "You understand why Jimmy might be reluctant to let you back in after what happened last night."

"That wasn't us."

Jimmy: "Bullshit."

"It could've been guys in town for the funeral like we are. It wasn't us."

Jimmy: "Lying sack of shit."

Doc lowered his voice to speak to Jimmy, "You want to cool it? You're not helping." Jimmy looked like he might have a response. Chose to hold onto it.

Doc scanned the crowd. "I was here last night. A couple of you do look familiar." Pointed to a man near the back. "What about you?"

The man looked around as if Doc might mean someone else. "Me? Uh-uh, I was nowhere near here last night."

"I know you from somewhere. Come up front where I can get a good look."

The man shuffled his feet. Gave every appearance of someone trying to come up with an argument until his peers lost patience. "Come on. We're freezing our asses off out here." "Show him you weren't here so we can get on with it."

He bowed to the pressure and stepped forward. Doc gave him a twice over. "Jimmy? Was he here last night?"

Jimmy stared a laser through the man. "I don't think so. He looks familiar, though."

Doc, to the man: "Are you local?" No comment. "Answer the question. Are you from around here?"

"Yeah, okay? I live out past the old dairy farm over by Allegheny Township."

Doc's hard drive spun up. "What's your name?"

"Ted Abbott."

Doc was pretty sure Abbott had an outstanding warrant. Domestic violence, maybe. Kept it to himself for the time being. "You ever drink in here before?"

"Couple times."

To Jimmy: "Might that be where you recognize him from?"

Jimmy gave Abbott a hostile inspection. "You ain't Kenny Paxton's cousin, are you?"

"Nephew."

"Your uncle know you hang with these douche bags?"

Doc, without moving his lips: "Do you *want* them to bust the place up? Work with me here."

"Sorry. I'm still touchy about last night." Jimmy raised his voice to address the crowd. "Sorry about the douche bag comment." Under his breath: "Douche bags."

Ringleader had grown more fidgety as time went on. His bladder could turn out to be the deciding factor. "Well? Can we go in? It's freezing out here."

Doc, to Jimmy: "I can't really run them off. How about we let in a few? Not so many you and who's already on hand can't handle them."

"You mind if I call a few regulars? Increase my odds a little?"

"Mind? I encourage it. Follow my lead." Doc spoke so all could hear. "Jimmy, what's the fire marshal say is your maximum capacity? Thirty? Thirty-five?" Knew it was at least fifty.

"Thirty-five."

"Isn't today the day you have that private party? What time are they due in?"

Jimmy made a show of looking at his watch. "About half an hour. Forty-five minutes, maybe."

"How many you got in there now? Including employees."

"The six of us out here and a couple more working inside."

"How big's that party?"

"Twenty. Maybe more."

Doc made a show of doing math in his head. "I can let seven of you in. The rest either have to go elsewhere or wait for someone to come out."

Ringleader was not impressed. "You expect us to wait out here because twenty people *might* show up?"

"We can't expect them to wait; they have reservations."

"He's not allowed to discriminate."

"Who's he discriminating against?"

"Us."

"It's private property. He's free to deny entrance to anyone so long as they're not part of a demographic group."

"We're a group."

The comebacks wrote themselves in Doc's head. He was on duty, so, "A group of what?"

This answer didn't come right away. "We're, uh, we're from

out of town."

Doc spoke over his shoulder to Jimmy. "This function. It's a twenty-first birthday party, isn't it? People coming from all over?"

"Absolutely."

To Ringleader: "See? He's okay with people from out of town. The irony here is that it's because he's so welcoming to strangers, there's no room for you. Now, do you want to pick seven, or do you want to drink someplace else?"

A minute's milling about produced a decision to drink elsewhere. Doc called out as the crowd dispersed. "Mr. Abbott! Ted Abbott! Can I see you a minute?"

Abbott trudged over. Doc asked for his license and parked him a few feet away where he'd be in sight without overhearing what Doc and Jimmy said. "That's the best I could do under the circumstances, Jimmy. I'll do what I can to have a car keep an eye on the place, but we both know we're all on call."

"It's okay. They know they're on your radar now. I'll keep someone on the door, just in case."

"The doorman probably doesn't need a shotgun."

"Maybe not. Or maybe so. I'm still not sold on the idea they won't come back serving Molotov cocktails."

"Fair enough. Just keep it low profile, okay?"

"Before you ask, I don't think I'm gonna open tomorrow. Supposed to snow like a bastard, anyway. I might come in myself and watch TV. Keep an eye on the place."

"Thanks, buddy. I know that wasn't your preference and I appreciate it. Now, if you'll excuse me, I have pending business with this character."

Doc keyed his mike. "Base, this is PR-Four. Requesting a warrant check on Theodore Abbott." Read the address and number off the license.

"PR-Four, I was just about to call you. Chief Sullivan wants you back at the house forthwith."

"Copy. On the way." Surveyed the parking lot. The tourists were gone. "Jimmy, you mind if Mr. Abbott there comes inside?

I want him handy while we check him for outstanding warrants, but I can't stay myself. If no one comes for him in the next twenty minutes, cut him loose. I'll tell him myself on my way out."

Jimmy nodded. "What's with that 'forthwith' business?"

"It's Sully-speak for 'right the fuck now.' I'll call you later."

# 25.

The chief's office was already full. Sullivan sat behind his desk. Deputy Chief Nancy Snyder and Patrol Sergeant slash walking dead man Mike Zywiciel occupied visitors' chairs. Deputy United States Marshal James Hensley leaned against the wall in a corner.

Doc slid into the vacant chair. "What'd I miss?"

Sullivan nodded toward the television. Fiddled with his computer. Spencer Richards appeared on the screen. Appeared to be in a hotel room, though not the Comfort Inn, unless substantial remodeling had been done. "A dozen of our brothers were illegally arrested by Penns River police this afternoon while peaceably exercising their Constitutional rights of assembly and free speech. This police action came at the behest of those who allowed a buffalo soldier to shoot and kill an unarmed white man without fear of consequence. This was not unexpected. The forces of the Deep State that undermine our freedoms and deny the work white Americans have done to build this country are not limited to the federal government. Even Pennsylvania, where the Declaration of Independence and Constitution were written, is not immune to enclaves of Socialist, anti-American conspirators.

"Their superior numbers and armaments required us to leave the field. Our heroic brothers did not retreat. A tactical decision was made to regroup and consider options while awaiting the return of our brothers from jail and the hospital where they currently languish. I invite all those who cherish the Fourteen Words to join me in the ballroom of the Penns River Comfort Inn at six thirty tonight—"

Zywiciel muttered, "Cocksucker Hecker," Dan Hecker having bought the former Quality Inn two months earlier.

"—where we will discuss our next action. We must secure the existence of our people and a future for white children. With your courage and sacrifice, we will."

Sullivan killed the picture. Asked Doc how many were in the hospital. "Only one that I know of."

"He hurt bad?"

"I think I broke his wrist." Sullivan's expression invited details. "He come at me with a pipe. That's how I got this." Pointed to the cut on his forehead. "We fenced around some until I disarmed him with a blow to the wrist."

"But nothing like you had him down on the ground and were beating him."

"Nothing like that." Not the time to bring up the McGinniss situation.

Sullivan turned to Nancy Snyder. "How many arrests?"

"Fourteen downstairs, plus the one Dougherty put in the hospital." A wink toward Doc. "No arraignments until Monday, so they're not going anywhere unless we decide not to charge them. It is getting crowded down there, though."

"That's the sheriff's problem. I'll let him know there may be more on the way." Sullivan leaned forward onto his elbows. Pointed a finger toward the dark television. "We need to know what goes on in this meeting."

Snyder said, "Can we wire the room?"

"Even if we could get a warrant, I doubt there's time to do it and not be seen."

Doc said, "What if we got someone in undercover?" Zywiciel asked if he was volunteering. Doc shrugged. "Sure. What the hell."

Sullivan spoke up. "I hear you had a pretty high profile at

Chubbie's and the playground. You might be too memorable."
Zywiciel's head dipped an inch. He had to know it should have
been him out there today.

Everyone thought until Snyder broke the silence. "What about
Sisler?"

Zywiciel said, "What about him?"

"Early thirties, blond hair, blue eyes, fair complexion, has
some size on him. He looks like a recruiting poster for these
assholes."

Sullivan said to Doc, "How engaged was he downtown?
Might he be recognized?"

"It's hard to say. Everything going on there, things tend to
run together, with a few exceptions." McGinniss came to mind
again. "We all had helmets and vests on. How recognizable he'd
be out of uniform? I don't know."

Zywiciel said, "Maybe we should see how he feels about it
first. It's a volunteer thing, right?"

Sullivan said, "Not if you mean he has to walk in here and
offer his services unsolicited. We'll ask him and he can decline
without prejudice."

"He won't decline. How safe it is won't enter into it."

Sullivan looked to Doc. "You two are close. What do you
think?"

"I agree with Eye Chart. No way Sisler turns this down. He's
a Marine."

"Was a Marine."

"All due respect, but I have them on both sides of my family.
There's no such thing as a former Marine."

Sullivan spoke with rueful humor. "I knew while I was still
saying it someone would call me on that. I should've known it
would be you. Point taken. We'll decide among ourselves if it's
safe before we ask. Agreed?"

Nods all around. No comment for at least a minute, when
Sullivan said, "Let's see who else we might use. What about
Barney McGinniss? Lots of experience. Knows his way around.

Reliable man."

Doc said, "He'll be recognized. I can't vouch for what Sisler got into at the Estates today, but Barney was too high profile for us to expect someone won't pick him out." Doc also not one hundred percent sure Barney wasn't a potential collaborator.

For a second Sullivan looked like he might ask what Doc meant by that. "Okay, Barney's out. What about the rookies? Obidowski or Holtzclaw?"

Zywiciel took his time before saying, "They're awful green."

"That could be an advantage. They don't have that cop smell to them yet."

"Maybe. I'm more worried either one might end up sweating like a whore in church. Be either too nervous or too eager. Besides, they're town cops and some of these guys are local. They could've come in contact anywhere."

Snyder said, "Good point. That applies to all the patrol officers."

Hensley spoke for the first time. "I can do it."

That shut everyone up until Sullivan said, "The Marshals Service won't mind you taking an active role in a local matter?"

"I have good reason to believe my fugitive will be there."

"You're not worried about being recognized?"

"Tucker and I have never laid eyes on each other. I'm only after him because we have intelligence that says he's in this district. I haven't done much with white nationals, so it's safe to assume I haven't encountered any of these people."

Sullivan appeared reluctant. Hensley went for the close. "Richards is doing me a favor, gathering his chickens in the same coop like this. I can look for Tucker—I *will* recognize him—and see what else I can find out. Anything relevant to your situation I'll pass along right away in the name of interagency cooperation and all that good stuff."

"You willing to wear a wire?"

"Don't need one." Hensley held up his smartphone. "It records. The Marshals Service has software that filters out extraneous noise. I can even email you the file if you need it for probable cause or evidence."

Doc said, "You feds have all the cool toys."

Hensley wasn't finished. "The only thing I want in return—"

"Here it comes."

"—is that whoever picks Tucker up, he's my prisoner. The reason I'm available to provide assistance is to capture him, so I want him. You can file local charges, but they'll have to wait until Uncle has a crack at him."

Sullivan said, "Deal," so fast he sounded like he'd been about to volunteer Hensley's request had the marshal not brought it up first. Fine with Doc. It would take months—years, even—to sort out the legal ramifications of this weekend. Lawyers made a lot more money than he did. Let them earn it.

Hensley looked at his watch. "If no one objects, I'd like to go back to my room and change clothes. With luck I'll get back this way for something to eat, maybe make a new friend to walk in with."

Sullivan said, "Where will we hook up with you after?"

"Right here. Unless something urgent breaks. Then I'll call."

"We'll have people right outside. You need help, call me and we'll come running."

Doc said, "This won't void your membership in the Secret Society of Disciples of Bass Reeves, will it?"

Hensley gave an up from under glare. "You're a piece of work, Dougherty. It may delay my entry into the inner circle, but it'll be worth it to save you some paperwork."

# 26.

Hensley took a shower and stretched out damp on the bedspread for five minutes of eyes closed. He chose the Springhill Suites at Pittsburgh Mills because it was the closest to Penns River without actually being in town where the chances were high he'd interact with too many of the protesters.

He dressed in a flannel shirt worn open over a tee he pulled from his laundry bag. Jeans and Timberlands he'd brought just in case he needed them. Checked himself in the mirror. Made adjustments so he wouldn't look too stereotypical. Walked down the hall and stepped into an elevator already occupied by Spencer Richards, Karl Tucker, and a third man who looked familiar.

Hensley could arrest Tucker right here and frog-march him to the car. He'd be locked up in Pittsburgh before anyone who might want to do anything about it even knew the arrest had been made. On the other hand, a lot of outstanding warrants could be cleared and intel gathered based on what Hensley learned tonight.

He went for the gusto. "Hey, aren't you Spencer Richards?"

Richards lit up like a teen in his first whorehouse. Tucker nudged him. "See? What'd I tell you?" Pay dirt.

"I saw you on the internet the other day. That's why I'm here." Turned toward Tucker, hand extended. "Sorry. I didn't mean to ignore you. Jay Hensley."

"Karl Tucker." They shook.

Hensley extended a hand to the third man. "Jay Hensley."

"I...uh...I'm not with them."

Richards redirected Hensley's attention. "Did you see the post this afternoon? About the rally?"

"I've been on the road all day. No internet. What'd I miss?"

"The police broke up a peaceful demonstration this afternoon. Arrested over twenty and sent half a dozen to the hospital. We're meeting at six thirty in the Penns River Comfort Inn to decide what to do about it."

"Fucking cops. Can I come?"

"Absolutely. Where are you from?"

The elevator stopped at the lobby. The unidentified man detached himself from the group as everyone stepped off.

"Woodridge, Illinois." Near where Hensley lived a couple of assignments ago.

"Don't know it."

"It's a little fart of a bedroom community outside Chicago. Most people think of the whole area as Downers Grove."

"That I heard of."

"See what I mean?"

Richards's expression implied the start of an erection. "You drove here all the way from Illinois?"

"This is a big deal. They start getting away with killing white people and it's all over for us. Gotta draw the line somewhere."

The three stopped near the lobby doors. Tucker said, "What do you do for a living?"

"I'm the dairy manager at Jewel-Osco." No sign of recognition. "It's the big supermarket-pharmacy chain." Hensley had worked his way through college at a supermarket, but not Jewel and not in Illinois.

"You married?"

"Wife's a schoolteacher."

"She didn't mind you coming all this way alone?"

Hensley hemmed. Stopped short of hawing. "We're separated."

"I'm sorry to hear that."

"Don't be." Hensley tried for a combination of bile and remorse. "She wants to live in a bubble and ignore the truth. It's her choice."

"Kids?"

"Two."

"Give it time. She might come around. We have more women in the cause than most people think." Tucker and Richards made eye contact. "We're about to get some dinner before the meeting."

"Sorry. I didn't mean to keep you. You said the Comfort Inn at six thirty, right?"

Tucker said, "Why don't you join us for dinner?"

Hensley's car had U.S. Government plates. "No, thanks. I'd just be a third wheel."

"Wouldn't you like to learn a little inside baseball?"

*Even more than the fantasy with Charlize Theron and the chocolate fountain.* "Sure, but can I meet you there? My car's running on fumes. I can't even get to Penns River until I hit a gas station."

"We have room. Ride with us."

Hensley's brain on overdrive trying to think if there was any way they could know who he was. "You're sure you don't mind?"

They didn't. Drove across the mall parking lot to Longhorn Steakhouse, where they cut the line when a bartender recognized Richards, who hadn't finished getting his rocks off over the extraordinary measures Hensley had taken to join the fun. "What time did you get in?"

"Three, three thirty. That's why I'm staying out of town. The Comfort Inn was full. This is a little pricey for me, but I forgot to make a reservation before I left."

"What time did you leave Illinois?"

"Around five thirty Chicago time."

Small talk until the steaks arrived and the waiter left them alone. Tucker cut into his steak, nodded. "The police think they got over on us today, like what happened at that basketball court was a planned demonstration. What it was, was a handful of assholes going off on their own."

Richards, chewing: "Still, perception is everything."

Tucker nodded. Swallowed. "The perception that's out there now is that the cops sent us running. We can't allow it to stand. Do you know how many we have in town, Spence?"

Richards chewed and thought. "Hard to say. According to Jay the Comfort Inn is full and I can't believe there's that much call for rooms in a town like Penns River this time of year. Could be more in the hotel we're at and the other ones we saw getting off the Turnpike. Who knows how many are local enough to stay at home? We'll have a better idea once we see who shows up this evening, but I don't think five hundred is out of the question. Maybe more."

Tucker took a map from his pocket. Refolded it to show the Allegheny Estates and surrounding area. "I drove around down there after things cleared up this afternoon." Pointed to a spot. "Here's the basketball court. This street—Fourth Avenue—runs right through what they call the Allegheny Estates. Might as well call it the jungle for all the more different skin tones live there. Our problem is finding parking close to where we want to demonstrate. It's too far to walk from the hotel."

Richards said, "What about the parking lot where things jumped off this afternoon?"

"That's not bad, but it's still a few blocks and we have to assume the police will be keeping an eye on the place. They could pen us into the lot. It would be better if we parked closer. Legally, though. The last thing we need is a bunch of cars towed."

"We could get people to ride together as much as possible."

Hensley ate and listened like a child allowed to sit at the adults' table who knew his place. Suppressed a smile at the idea of the Master Race carpooling to a riot.

Tucker said, "That'll help. The less cars we have the easier it'll be to get them in that parking lot if need be. We can rally here," pointed, "at Fourth Avenue and Pine Court, and here, where Pine Court empties onto Eleventh Street. Converge on the playground from both ends. Say a few words, then go back out one way or the other to march through the neighborhood with the torches, spreading the good word."

Richards nodded and chewed. Swallowed. "My only concern is we don't have a permit. Without it we'll have no police protection to keep the natives off us."

"Remember what happened this afternoon. Do you really think the police are going to stand up for us, permit or not?"

"No, but still. We're walking along these streets half blind from the torches screwing with our night vision—"

"It's not like we'd see anything but teeth and eyeballs."

"They know the terrain and we'll all have to go back to our cars wherever. It's prime for an ambush."

"Is that a bad thing?" Richards didn't follow. "We're marching peacefully, well within our First Amendment rights, and a bunch of niggers swing down on vines or however they'll come at us and start something. Any scars from that engagement are badges of honor. We could make patches or pins: *I was at Penns River.*"

"It's okay if they come unarmed. Can we count on that?"

Tucker shrugged. "It's not like none of us will be carrying. Besides, a martyr or two can only help the cause. I don't think too many of our brothers will lose sleep over the prospect of pushing some roaches back into the walls, even if there's a little risk to it."

Hensley said, "Do you really think it will come to that? Martyrs?"

Tucker eyed him. "You getting cold feet?"

"I'm just thinking. No one has ever heard of this place. What kind of attention will it draw?"

"No one heard of Gettysburg, either, until there was a battle there."

Hensley showed his palms. "Okay, I understand. I'm just thinking it's better to have a martyr than be one."

Richards dismissed his concerns with a hand wave. "The fact you're thinking about it means you won't have to be one. A movement like ours, most of the people in it aren't good for much except fodder. They're like infantry in the Army, casualties go with the job. Remember that half-wit drove his car into those people at Charlottesville? Killed that woman? I don't mind taking an occasional scalp, especially if it's a race traitor, but that asshole would've done the movement a favor if he'd have let them drag him out of the car and kill him. Stay close to us and you'll be fine."

Tucker said, "Tomorrow, too. We're pulling this together on the fly tonight. We have plans to run their asses ragged tomorrow."

Hensley said, "How can I catch up?"

"I'll connect you with a guy. He'll have something worthwhile for you."

"What about tomorrow?"

Tucker chewed his lip. "Spence will be at the command post. I have a thing going, but the team's already picked. Alf will take care of you. What kind of involvement do you have in mind?"

"I don't mind busting heads. Like you said, a point has to be made."

"That'll increase the chance of martyrdom."

"No offense, but I'm not talking about leading the charge."

Tucker smiled. "Smart man. Things work out this weekend, we might have future plans for you."

The check came. Hensley took care not to let anyone see his government credit card as he drew out cash. Richards waved him off. "We got this."

"You sure? I didn't contribute anything to the planning."

"Just having you around reminded us who we're in this for and what kinds of risks are acceptable." Laid enough cash on the table to cover the check and a respectable tip.

Hensley wanted to give Penns River as much of a heads up as he could. Stood next to the table as Richards and Tucker got into their coats. "Do I have time to hit the can before we go? I have to piss like a racehorse." Hoping for good cell service in the men's room.

Tucker said, "I could use a good draining myself." Richards concurred.

All three went to the john, which created a new problem for Hensley: he didn't need to pee.

# 27.

Chonker Connor didn't know what to make of the crowd. Not like they were rattling around in what the Comfort Inn described as The Grand Ballroom, all the dividers folded back for maximum space; not jammed in ass to crotch, either. Maybe two hundred altogether.

Chonker was here because of the potential to kick ass. He had no special dislike for Blacks. For sure not a racist like these other peckerwoods. He wouldn't let one date his sister—not that it had come up—and he wasn't sure how he'd feel if one tried to join the MC. No use for Black doctors, but that was okay because they were either Equal Oppor-coonity or went to medical school in Jamaica or Grenada or Haiti or some other shithole country. A man had to be careful about his health.

What Chonker liked to do was drink beer and kick ass. This group seemed up for both. If kicking Black ass was on the menu, Chonker was game. Any Asians or spics or faggots wanted to serve as either appetizers or dessert, well, the more the merrier.

The trip to Penns River was going better than expected. Chonker and The Robber and Brute ditched Knucks and the others Saturday morning and rode around to get a feel for potential opportunities. Skirted a midafternoon disturbance, two or three o'clock, sirens and lights and ambulances. Against the Disciples' nature to skip a fight, but the heat was already involved; half the point of this trip was to stay under the radar.

What they learned:

- The spooks had a pretty good handle on the heroin trade in what the locals called the Allegheny Estates. They'd be hell to push out and had no need of a partner, as their contacts, distribution, and muscle were already better than what the Disciples could offer.
- The distribution network for pills and grass was irregular. Running off the current dealers shouldn't be too tough if the MC picked its spots. Others could be partnered with.
- The meth situation was a disorganized mess. No one filled the void after the primary lab blew up last summer. Even Chonker knew nature absolves a vacuum; the first group in with sufficient energy and will could run everything.

The best news might have been Knucks, bless his dumb ass, coming across a foreclosed service station to serve as a clubhouse. Every Disciple tuned and repaired their own bikes; Chonker and The Robber built theirs from parts. A shop would be an excellent source of revenue and even better cover when profits from the side hustles showed up.

Nothing they could do about any of that until next week, so Chonker turned his attention to the show. See if anyone else here had class.


James Hensley had information the Penns River Police Department needed. The problem was Richards and Tucker kept him closer than a nun's knees since they went to dinner. They went to the bathroom with him. Put him in the front seat of the car with Tucker for the drive to Penns River; Richards alone in back like Miss Daisy. They even brought him up on the ballroom platform to introduce him as the person who'd traveled farthest. Confident they hadn't made him as a federal agent, he still provided no benefit to the police outside hoping for some insight.

Richards had no written remarks. He and Tucker discussed the talking points while Hensley made mental notes, their conversation too soft to record. Next to Tucker, Richards seemed almost diminutive, like someone who would make inflammatory videos in a basement, possibly his mother's.

Until he stepped to the microphone.

The Comfort Inn had been a respected venue in its day. The ballroom held upward of five hundred people with the dividers pulled back as they were tonight. Richards didn't let the fact fewer than half that many were here bother him. He didn't bask in their applause; he grew in it.

"This country has lost its way. It was white people who endured the hardship of travel across an intemperate sea to a new world. It was white people of European ancestry who settled a hostile land. It was white people who conquered a vast continent. White people subdued the savages. White people built the railways and the highways to connect two distant coasts. White people made this country an economic and military power unlike anything the world has ever seen.

"And then, like Greece, like Rome, we grew complacent. We listened to the weak, the inferior, and the deservedly poor. Allowed them to turn our kindness against us. It was slow at first, as all insidious ideas are. A thought that integration could take place without leading to mongrolization. An idea that Blacks and whites could live side by side, eat at the same table, and treat each other as equals without recognizing their inherent inequality. We forgot, or took for granted, that what made us great was the drive and intellect and strength possessed by white people, and allowed ourselves to believe that greatness, once earned, was perpetual."

Hensley didn't know what to make of Richards. He didn't seem to be someone who would turn on a dime the instant

172

white nationalism became unfashionable and become a preacher or a right-wing politician or a Fox News host. He believed what he said, but after dinner together, Hensley wondered if Richards believed it with as much vigor as he displayed.

"So we let them sit at the table we built with toil and sacrifice, and we fed them. Not the leftovers, but the full meal, just as if they had worked all day in the sun along with us. We knew they'd steal the silver. We knew they'd fornicate with our women. We believed it was more important to be magnanimous, so we let it slide. We ignored the truth that was right before our eyes if only we had cared to look."

Tucker was different. His hate had no orientation of its own; he used it to provide energy to propel himself in which-ever direction he chose. Hensley felt it radiate off him like a microwave as they sat next to each other discussing options for this evening. Tucker was a true believer, and what he believed in was himself. He hated, so a hate movement suited him, but he was no more a follower of this group than lightning follows thunder.

"Now they come after us directly. It's not bad enough we let them have guns. We compound the error by giving them badges and a license to kill. What did we think was going to happen? They started coming after us, claiming the law is on their side. Like what happened here the other night. The media wants us to believe this—I hate to use the word 'cop'—this lawn jockey..."

Laughter from the crowd.

"This cargo with a badge..."

Encouraging shouts.

"The media wants us to believe that even if he was wrong—like it's ever not wrong for one of *those* to shoot a white man—they tell us that even if it was a wrong shooting, we should overlook it. It's an isolated incident in a small, backward town. It's not representative of society. That's what the media wants us to believe. And who runs the media?" Cupped an ear toward the crowd.

"Jews!"

173

"Who?"

"*Jews!*"

"Come on, give it up. I can't hear you."

"*JEWS!*"


Chonker wouldn't go out of his way looking for cotton pickers to beat up, but he had to admit this Richards guy had game. The connection between Jews and niggers had never occurred to Chonker until Richards laid it out; then Chonker couldn't believe he'd missed it all this time.

"You know how it works. You don't want to admit it, well, that's what I'm here for, to speak the truth only you'll understand. It's the Jews that position the darks against whites. People ask why they would do that? So they can continue their scheme. They already own the media. They've always owned the banks. They want to own you. And they will, if their partners continue to be the white man's burden as they have for so long. Why would they stop? They've perfected it.

"So no, Mr. Mediastein, Mr. Newsberg, this isn't an isolated incident. Not unless the people in this room, white people, make it one by stopping things right here. Right here and right now."

Chonker felt himself caught up in the excitement. Taking action was always more satisfying than lying in the cut. He knew The Robber was smarter and could play the long game, and The Robber wanted them to stay under the radar until the MC established a foothold in Penns River. This wasn't club business. All Chonker needed was for someone to tell him where to take the resentment and anger he'd stored up in the months since he was laid off and that bitch he was married to moved out with the kids and asked for a restraining order. This could be his chance to make someone pay.

"The basketball courts where the police tried to take us down today are in JFK Park. That's appropriate. Every ghetto in the country has things named after two people: John F. Kennedy and

Martin Luther Coon. They started all this integration nonsense, the Rev in his relentless hunt for white pussy and Kennedy's thirst for Black whores. The media are making a symbol out of where this supposed police victory took place. They think it's the start of a new energy in their perverted cause. We're going to let them know it's the end. Right now. Right here. Partner up because there's not much parking, but we're going from here to the parking lot near the bridge where the storm troopers first came after us. You're not sure where it is, come on up and get a map. Be sure to bring your torches. Are you with me?"

"Yes!"

"Are you with me?"

"*Yes!*"

"Why are we going?"

"Fourteen words!"

"Why are we going?"

"*Fourteen words!*"

"Let's hear them!"

"We must secure the existence of our people and a future for white children!"

Chonker didn't know the words. He followed along the best he could.

Hensley used the tumult to hop off the dais and punched a number into the phone. Dougherty answered just as Karl Tucker approached.

"I can't talk right now, we're going to a rally. Don't worry, everything is fine. We're just going down to the parking lot where some stuff happened earlier today and finish our demonstration." Showed Tucker an index finger to ask for a minute. "I have to go. Hug your sister for me and I'll see you both next weekend." Hung up as Tucker stepped in front of him, glaring.

# 28.

"Here they come. Take your positions."

Nancy Snyder had half a dozen uniformed officers with her at the edge of the Comfort Inn parking lot, where a two-lane stem emptied onto a side street that led to Tarentum Bridge Road. A natural bottleneck the cops had blocked to regulate who came and went.

Brendan Sullivan hadn't needed a call from James Hensley to tell him trouble was brewing and the logical place for it to erupt was either the JFK Playground or Fat Jimmy's. Sullivan didn't have enough cops to cover both, so his best option was to delay departures from the Comfort Inn.

The first vehicle rolled toward the checkpoint; others lined up behind. Snyder stood in front of her car blocking the incoming side of the stem and nodded to Holtzclaw, who stepped into the right-of-way, arm extended. The car stopped. Obidowski approached the driver while Burrows took a position on the passenger side.

Obidowski twirled a finger in the classic *roll down the window* gesture. "License and registration, please."

"What's going on?"

"License and registration."

"What did I do?"

Obidowski looked less sure of himself. "License and registration, please."

Snyder gestured to Augustine, who sauntered over. "Is there a problem?"

"I want to know what the hell you're stopping me for."

Augie turned to Obidowski. "Did you ask for his license and registration?" The rookie nodded. Augie turned back to the driver. "Did you hear him ask for your license and registration?"

"Yeah. I want to know why he's asking."

"Because he wants to see it. We have reports of heavy drinking going on in the Comfort Inn. The last thing we need is a couple hundred impaired drivers hitting the road at the same time, so we set up a sobriety roadblock. Have you been drinking, sir?"

"No."

Augie asked Obidowski, "Anything give you reason to think there's been drinking going on?"

Obidowski gave an impression of a deer in the headlights. Burrows said from across the car, "Someone has. I can smell it from over here."

"Step out of the car, sir." Augie moved back to make room.

"You're shitting me."

Augie's expression remained friendly, his body posture relaxed. His voice had steel in it. "Get out of the car."

Someone in the back seat said, "You better get out, Steve."

Steve got out. Handed Augie his license and registration. Obidowski checked for outstanding warrants while Augie administered the test.

"Stand with your feet together. Extend your arms to the side. Close your eyes. Touch your nose with the index finger of your right hand. Touch your nose with the index finger of your left hand. Count to a hundred by sevens. Recite the alphabet in reverse." This was Snyder's favorite. She doubted some of these guys could recite the alphabet in regular order.

Steven Dawson of Bruceton Mills, West Virginia had no outstanding warrants. Counting by sevens proved difficult and the reverse alphabet was beyond him, though his failures appeared more attributable to IQ than to blood alcohol. Augie returned

Dawson's documents and allowed him to proceed. Elapsed time: not quite six minutes. Snyder turned so the next driver couldn't see the small smile she allowed herself. At this rate at least half would give up and she had no doubts Dougherty could handle one car every six minutes.

Sean Sisler rolled his unit through and around the Allegheny Estates. Tonight five cops worked a sector typically patrolled by one, though on Fridays and Saturdays a rover moved between the Estates and the Flats as needed. Driving west on Thirteenth Street when Barney McGinniss approached and flashed his headlights. Sisler rolled down his window and coasted to a stop.

McGinniss stopped abreast of Sisler's car. Leaned his elbow on the open window ledge. "Is this bullshit or what?"

"I was in the Corps. A lot of what we did was showing the flag so no one started anything we'd have to clean up later. That's all this is."

"It's still bullshit." McGinniss spat into the street. "What do you figure the chances are anyone comes down here tonight with bad intent?"

"We'll see a few. Their intent may be negotiable once they see a half dozen cops down here. Maybe they'll tell their friends to stay away, those badasses in the PRPD have this wrapped up tighter than skin on a pepperoni."

McGinniss gave Sisler an ambiguous look. "Well, at least the natives are staying in. I guess I should be grateful for that." Drove off before Sisler could decide whether to respond.

Doc stood bullshitting with Skip Speer and Dave Wohleber in the parking lot where things got dicey earlier in the day when a godawful orange Dodge Challenger entered from Eighth Street and departed on Fourth Avenue. "That's the third time around for those guys. You'd think they'd drive a less obvious car if they're trying to be sneaky."

Keyed his mike. "All units. Be on the lookout for an orange Dodge Challenger, West Virginia plates Foxtrot Uniform Charlie Five Eight Seven. Vehicle has four occupants and may be moving toward the Estates." Wohleber touched Doc's arm and pointed. "Correction. Vehicle is definitely moving toward the Estates. Occupants are potentially armed. Approach with caution."

Chris Trettle saw them first, moving north on Fifth Avenue. Pulled in behind and made no effort to hide the tail. "This is PR-Five following suspect vehicle northbound on Fifth Avenue. We're passing the Estates now. I'll follow and will advise if anything changes. Five out." Dougherty copied.

The Dodge stayed on Fifth Avenue till it ended at the old glass house. Trettle had already decided to turn them loose if they made a right and went up the hill. The car turned left. Only two things in that direction:

1. The river.

2. Streets that led back to the Estates.

Trettle stayed tight on the Dodge's ass. Opened the channel when the car turned left again, this time onto Fourth Avenue. "This is PR-Five. Be advised, subject vehicle is now moving south on Fourth Avenue."

Dougherty's voice: "What's your twenty?"

"Passing Sixteenth Street."

A pause before Dougherty came back. "PR-uh...shit. Sisler and McGinniss, move to intercept subject vehicle. First one there pull in front and make him ride your bumper. Second unit, parallel along Third Avenue and be prepared to intercept if he veers off. I'm handy if you need me."

Trettle didn't care much for Dougherty, even less for a detective masquerading as patrol sergeant implying three units might not be able to handle a car full of hillbillies. Had to admit, if Dougherty did get a call, he'd come running and pitch right in.

He'd shown well this afternoon.

A police car pulled onto Fourth to lead the parade. Trettle guessed it was Sisler. He was always first to respond. Fucking guy was fearless. Of course, he could afford to be, no wife or kids. Whoever it was, he slowed to not much more than idling speed, forcing the Challenger to match him.

Dougherty: "PR-Five, what's your location?"

Trettle: "Still southbound on Fourth approaching Pine Court."

"Who's leading the parade?"

Sisler: "PR-Nine. I'm making them crawl."

Dougherty: "Pull over and block any turn onto Pine Court. Barney, what's your twenty?"

McGinniss: "Driving parallel on Third Avenue."

Dougherty: "Hang a left on Eleventh and cover the other entrance to Pine Court. Chris, if they pass through the Estates and go to cross the bridge, let them. Any turns into the Estates buys them a stop. Copy?" Everyone did.

The Challenger slowed abreast of Sisler's car when he pulled over at Pine Court. Turned right on Eleventh, McGinniss approaching from the opposite direction.

Trettle: "This is PR-Five. Subject has turned right on Eleventh."

Dougherty: "Take him. Sisler, come on down to block Pine Court. They are not to leave Eleventh Street. I'm on the way."

Trettle hit the roof lights, no siren. The Challenger veered as if turning onto Pine Court until McGinniss pulled over to cut off that option. The Dodge didn't stop until Trettle gave one whoop on the siren as McGinniss turned on his roof lights. The backup lights didn't flash after the car stopped. It was still in drive.

Trettle got out. Clicked on his flash. Sisler had not made an appearance, though his lights ricocheted around Pine Court. Trettle had microphone in hand to activate his bullhorn when Sisler's voice came over the air: "This is PR-Nine, requesting backup at the JFK Playground on Pine Court."

Trettle switched to radio. "This is PR-Five requesting backup at the intersection of Pine Court and Eleventh Street. I have the subject West Virginia Challenger stopped."

McGinniss: "This is PR-Eleven, responding to...Dougherty, which call do you want me to take?"

Dougherty: "Assist Nine. Five and Nine, hold your positions and await backup. I'm less than a minute away."


Doc turned onto Eleventh as McGinniss darted into Pine Court. Trettle stood next to his unit, flashlight glaring off the Challenger's driver mirror. Doc parked to block Pine Court and saw two police units with a civilian vehicle between them. Took a support position on the opposite side of Trettle's hood. "How's it look, Chris?"

"They haven't done anything except take the scenic route to get here and try to turn onto Pine Court two different times."

"We may have crashed a party. Sisler and McGinniss have someone stopped by the playground. Treat it as a felony stop. I'm on your wing."

Trettle nodded. Switched the mike back to bullhorn mode. "Driver of the Challenger with West Virginia plates. Turn off your vehicle and toss the keys into the street."

A tense twenty seconds, then backup lights flickered as the car went into park. The engine stopped and a few seconds later Doc heard keys clatter on the pavement.

Trettle moved forward. Projected his voice as if talking to someone a block away. He could be an asshole but he knew how to handle a stop. "Everyone reach your hands through the windows, fingers extended."

The driver's door opened. Doc's and Trettle's sidearms appeared in their hands as if by magic. "Stay right there! Do *not* exit the vehicle."

From the car: "I need the keys to turn the car on so we can wind down the windows, asshole."

Trettle spoke before Doc could make a suggestion. "Everyone

out one at a time, driver first. Keep your arms extended in front of you with the palms of your hands open and facing us."

The driver's door opened. Hands appeared, then a face. "Don't shoot me, goddamnit. Trigger-happy motherfuckers in this town."

"Lean against the roof and spread your legs." The man took his time, but complied. Another long minute and all four had assumed the position.

Doc and Trettle patted everyone down and found nothing. Sent them all to lean on the hood. Doc said, for everyone to hear, "Officer Trettle, keep an eye on this bunch while I make a plain sight search of the car."

The driver said, "Don't you need a warrant or permission or something?"

Doc and Trettle exchanged head shakes. "We're allowed to look for anything in plain sight. You know, what the average citizen walking by might notice." Shined his light into the car and rummaged around with his eyes. About to tell Trettle he could cut them lose when Sisler's voice came over the radio. "Sergeant Dougherty, are you still with PR-Five?"

"I am."

"Can you come over to Pine Court when you have a minute. Something here you need to see."

Doc turned to Trettle. "Hang onto this crew for a minute, just in case." Walked up Pine Court to where Sisler, McGinniss, and two men Doc didn't know stood next to a middle-aged Impala. The car's doors were open, as was the trunk.

Sisler pointed to the trunk. "Take a look in there."

Doc stopped three feet from the car. Scrunched his face. "Yeah," Sisler said. "That's what we thought, too."

Inside the trunk was a case of whisky, the bottles separated by cardboard inserts. Each had what appeared to be a piece of torn T-shirt sticking out the neck. "I thought the gas line was broken, bad as it smells back here. Whose car is it?"

Sisler pointed to the man on the right. The tails of a flannel shirt stuck out beneath his down jacket. Already accessorized with handcuffs, as was his companion. "Sitting here like they were waiting for me when I drove by. Based on their reaction, I doubt it was me they were expecting, but I don't know why they're so pissed off. I might've saved their sorry lives."

"How so?"

"You smelled the car."

"Yeah?"

"Jay and Silent Bob here were smoking when I rolled up. I had to explain how it's not the liquid gasoline that explodes, it's the fumes. The inside of the car smells like a refinery. I'd be afraid to start it. Could blow up half the block."

Doc looked at the two men. Shook his head. Keyed his shoulder mike. "Base, this is PR-Four. I need the wagon for half a dozen suspects. A couple of tow trucks would be nice, too."

# 29.

The brain trust convened in the chief's office eight o'clock Sunday morning. Sullivan, Snyder, Zywiciel, Doc, and the man Doc had started calling Deep Throat, Deputy United States Marshal James Hensley. They'd about covered the rally at the Comfort Inn when Doc asked Hensley how he got out of there.

"Richards and Tucker gave me a ride." Expressions directed his way demanded details. "There was no point going anywhere but the hotel by the time we got past the sobriety check. We rode up in the elevator together, I got off at my floor, packed my suitcase, and checked out. Found a place in Harmarville by the Turnpike exit in case either of my new best friends got a peek at the register in the Springhill Suites."

Doc said, "It looks like you got to see them with their guard down, at least a little. Is it too much to ask for them to be poseurs?"

"They're true believers, no question. I got the feeling they want different things out of it, though."

"Such as?"

Hensley came as close to smiling as he ever did. "Let's just say they each have their own agenda for what their hate is used for. I didn't spend enough time with them to get a better feel than that."

Sullivan broke in. "Save that discussion for Homeland Security. We have more urgent problems. Marshal Hensley tells me DHS has informed the Marshals Service the Aryan Brotherhood put out a bounty on Trevor Boston. They didn't say exactly where he lived, but close enough to worry me. Dougherty, you live pretty much across the street. How big is that apartment complex he lives in?"

Doc did calculations in the air. "They're not apartments, they're condos, though I think most of them are rentals. Got to be at least a hundred people living there."

"Bring him in. We can't have a hit squad shooting up the place with that many civilians around. I'll put the word out he's under protective custody."

"Trevor's not going to like that."

"It's just for the day and tonight. Apparently the bounty is only good for one day."

"One day? Really?"

Hensley said, "My guess is the AB sees an opportunity to swing their dicks by offering a bounty but doesn't actually want to pay it."

"Boston's still not going to like it."

Sullivan said, "I wouldn't either, but it's not like we're going to lock him up. If he bitches, tell him it's an order. You're a sergeant. Act like one."

"Will do." Doc stood and something came to mind. "Can I make a suggestion?" Sullivan opened his hands in consent. "Someone should call Christian Love before this goes public. He's on the fence about whether Boston is getting a fair shake. I want him to know this isn't some back door arrest."

Sullivan squeezed his eyes shut. Opened them and blinked twice. "Do it on your way out. Who did I say to take with you?"

"Sisler and Neuschwander."

"Take McGinniss and Burrows, too."

"You think Boston's going to resist?"

"Not if he knows what's good for him. I want eyes around you in case someone already has the place staked out."

\* \* \*

Hensley lingered inside the office as the others left. Waited for Sullivan to notice. "I know how busy you are, Chief, but I need a word."

"Shut the door."

Hensley did. Remained in place. "There was a third man in the elevator with Richards and Tucker last night. He wouldn't shake my hand or give his name. Said he wasn't with them and made tracks when the elevator opened in the lobby. I thought he looked familiar, but I couldn't place him. This morning in the shower it dawned on me he was one of those state troopers here investigating your shooting."

"Which one?"

"The older one. I don't know their names."

"You got a good enough look to be sure?"

"I was closer to him than I am to you right now."

"You tell anyone else?" Hensley shook his head.

Sullivan leaned his elbows on the desk. "Might he be staying there and just happened to be on the elevator?"

"I checked before I came in this morning. He's registered at the Comfort Inn here in town."

"Describe the conversation in the elevator."

"Small talk. Richards and Tucker identified themselves to me, and talked about the rally last night. Did the trooper say anything to you?"

"I haven't seen or heard from either of them since Thursday." Sullivan dipped his head to stare at the desk blotter. "I understand they want to limit interaction with this department. Even if we assume this was an innocent encounter, he should've said something."

"That's why I brought it up. Just in case."

"I appreciate that. Keep it to yourself for now. We have plenty to do today and I want to think about how best to handle this."

\* \* \*

Love's assistant answered Doc's call on the second ring. "He's getting ready for the service, Detective. Can this wait?"

"I know he's busy, Shawntel, but it's urgent. I promise not to take more than a minute."

On hold for longer than expected, Doc considered the irony of how hard it was to find Christian Love on a Sunday morning. The reverend answered with a polite but emphatic reminder of how little time he had, though it wasn't like things would start without him.

Doc described the situation in as few words as possible. "We're going to bring him in to the station for protection. This is a courtesy call so no one who sees him leaving with us thinks he's under arrest."

"Will he be locked up?"

"No. He will be confined to the station until the threat passes."

"Why can't he be protected in his home?"

Doc understood Love's pushback. Still had to fight his own impatience. "Trevor rents a condo in a building with about forty units. Quite a few kids there. The last thing we want is for someone to take a run at him with citizens in the mix. Everyone is safer if we bring him to the house."

"For how long?"

"The AB says the bounty is only open today. We'll probably keep him tomorrow as well so we can check the intel to make sure we're not sending him home to a trap."

"Will he be given means to protect himself?"

"If you're asking if he'll have a weapon, the answer is no. He's still on administrative leave." Doc cut off Love's argument. "It's nonnegotiable. State law." If it wasn't, it should be.

Love was silent so long Doc began to wonder if the call had dropped. "How will it be handled? You bringing him in, I mean."

"Five of us are going over—"

"Five? Are you expecting resistance?"

"Safety in numbers, in case anyone is already watching and might be inclined to make a move while we're in transit. The transfer will also be recorded and released to the media so everyone knows he's not home, and won't be."

"The concerns I expressed to you yesterday are still valid."

"I agree. Bear in mind, we wouldn't be talking now if we were about to arrest him. This is a courtesy call so there are no misunderstandings."

"And so I'll keep the natives from getting restless."

Doc and Love needed a come to Jesus meeting when this was over. "I could bring him to your church."

"Which is already a likely target."

"Which is why I didn't suggest it. No one wants you or your congregation in any more jeopardy than you may already be in. Just like I don't want a building full of families placed in danger if the Proud Boys or Oath Keepers or some mouth-breathing sovereign citizen decides to come for Trevor at his home."

Another uncomfortable silence. "Your point is well made and well taken. I hope you understand my reluctance even though I have no better alternative."

"I do. Please understand I'm not trying to tell you what you should be doing. We are not arresting Trevor Boston. We're protecting him. Do with that information whatever you think is best. I'm sorry to be abrupt, but I have to go."


Boston answered the door wearing jeans and a Temple University sweatshirt. Doc gave it to him straight. "Get dressed. The Aryan Botherhood posted a bounty last night. Sullivan wants you in the station where we can keep an eye on you without having to worry about your neighbors."

This was a lot for Boston to process. "They know where I live?"

"Close enough."

"So you don't think they'll come here, anyway?'

"We're sending a video of you leaving here and arriving at the station to all the local outlets. After you're in the house."

Boston still in catch-up mode. "Can I at least put shoes on?"

Doc released a single snort. "You're not under arrest. Pack a bag. Bring something to read. Assume you'll be there overnight, maybe one or two more. Think of it as a really cheap vacation."

"Overnight? Where will I sleep?"

"In the crib if you want, though I expect those sheets are pretty cruddy by now. Wherever you can find a spot. You're a guest of the city."

Boston nodded. Walked toward the back of the apartment as if in a trance. Doc called after him, "Don't forget a toothbrush."

McGinniss and Burrows led the way a landing at a time. Doc escorted Boston. Sisler covered the rear. Neuschwander and his iPhone waited downstairs.

Doc sent the advance team to clear the lobby, its approaches, and the route to the car. Satisfied, they took positions covering the short distance between the building and Doc's car, passenger door already open, roof lights flashing. Doc walked Boston out at a brisk pace, Sisler backing behind. Neuschwander took care to capture Boston's face as much as he could. Doc hadn't been in a better executed maneuver since he left Iraq. Could have lived without Boston turning to the camera and saying "Bring it on, crackers" as he got in the car.

McGinniss and Burrows on point, Sisler in the rear, Doc and Boston between, Code One all the way. Snow began to fall as McGinniss turned into the station.

# 30.

The brass reconvened over lunch. The Comfort Inn sent enough food to feed twenty, Marla McClure's way of telling the cops she disagreed with Dan Hecker making the ballroom available the night before. Sullivan had the food delivered to the roll call room to be available to all, while the brass filled plates and went to his office. He spoke when everyone was situated. "How's it look?"

Mike Zywiciel nodded for Doc to speak. "Quiet for now, but we never expected it to get hairy until after the funeral." Gestured toward the closed blinds in the office window. "You look outside lately?"

"Still snowing?"

"Like a bastard. Getting colder, too."

"How bad's it supposed to get?"

Nancy Snyder said, "The high for the day was at eight o'clock this morning. Forecast is calling for at least a foot."

Doc said, "I measured four inches when I let the food guys in."

Sullivan: "When did it start?"

"On our way back with Boston. Eight thirty or so."

Sullivan mathed. "At least an inch an hour, then."

"And it looks like it's picking up."

Sullivan leaned into his thinking pose. Doc wondered if the chief would have permanent indentations in his forearms after the weekend. "Is the snow good or bad for us? Obviously, it's

190

bad for the town in general, but what do we think about the possibility it keeps the troublemakers away?"

Eating took place while everyone stayed busy not going first. Hensley picked up the glove. "We have to figure almost everyone who's coming is already in town, and no way will anyone already in town miss the funeral. After? These are white supremacists. Prudence and caution aren't among those fourteen words they think so much of. Besides, you're talking about people who tend to drive four-by-fours. They see a foot of snow as a challenge at worst, recreation if they're lucky."

Grunts of assent all around. Doc thought about saying something, but whatever the Comfort Inn had done with these potatoes was more fascinating than anything he might contribute, so he took another forkful and listened.

Sullivan turned to Zywiciel. "Everyone have their assignments?" Assignments Doc knew Sullivan and Snyder worked out among themselves, Zywiciel so checked out it was hard to say what held his uniform erect in the chair.

"Enhanced funeral escort gathers at the mortuary at one thirty. Once everyone's at the cemetery, all units leave for the Estates except for two that will stay behind to slow departures."

"How are they going to do it?"

"Mostly by directing traffic and limiting left turns. We're also going to take manual control of the light at the bypass."

"Thanks, Mike. Anything they can do to limit traffic coming into town will help."

"In addition to the funeral detail going to the Estates, we're bringing anyone not already working back at two o'clock."

"Outstanding. I'm holding ten officers here to guard the house in case anyone makes a move for Boston. Right now he's in the day room reading. He is not—repeat, not—to be given a weapon or to assist in his own def—I mean the house's defense— in any way. Are we clear?" He was.

"The county side of the complex is locked down. It's Sunday and snowing like hell, so it's not like we're putting too many people out. Sheriff's deputies are covering every ingress point. Furniture and construction barriers are positioned at both ends of the tunnel in case there's a breach. Questions?"

Doc said, "What's the disposition of the units in the Estates?"

"Deputy Chief Snyder has a command post at the community center on Third Avenue and will coordinate the extra units from there. You're the Dutch boy, Dougherty. Be prepared to move wherever you're needed."

Sullivan looked at everyone in turn. "Everyone needs to keep a cool head so we don't escalate a situation unnecessarily. We also don't want to let anything slide that might blow up on us. It'll be a balancing act and I'm not going to second guess decisions that could go either way.

"So we know, Tarentum and Plum Borough will help with routine calls that are close to the borders. Their assistance will be requested through dispatch only. Anything heavy comes up, we're on our own."

Doc called his parents while the car heated up. "How's the weather?"

His father spoke into the speakerphone as if in another room. "We're getting some snow. How is it where you are?" Which was a mile and a half away if crows were flying.

"Snowing like hell. Don't even think about going outside. Drew or I will get by tonight or tomorrow morning to dig you out." Tom and Ellen's driveway ran sixty feet up a steep slope before a ninety-degree left, downhill into the garage. "And remind Mom it's Sunday, so don't go for the mail. I have a few minutes before I have to get busy. Do you need anything?"

Ellen said in the background, "He should stay home in this weather."

"I'm already out, Mom. I'm working today. That's why I didn't come down the house for dinner."

"I thought you had weekends off."

"This weekend I'm in uniform for that funeral. Remember the guy got shot down Fat Jimmy's?" Doc's parents watched the local and national news every night on Channel 11. Tom read the paper front to back every day. Maybe Ellen's mental acuity was slipping faster than Doc and Drew realized.

Tom said, "There's nothing we don't have we can't live without. Pitt's on the TV at two o'clock and that's all I have planned. Maybe watch a movie later. How's the snow laying up on the hill?" Said "up on the hill" like everyplace in Penns River wasn't down one steep hill and up another from the Dougherty house.

"I measured four inches an hour ago but coming out now I see there's at least another inch."

"You be careful. Those assholes want to burn down part of the town, you let them." Tom Dougherty didn't have a mean bone in his body. It also wasn't his part of town that might burn. Move the crisis a couple miles east and he'd be on the phone asking what the hell his taxes bought him.

"It's what they pay me for. I have friends down that way I don't want anything bad to happen to, so I'll mosey on over once the funeral is over."

"Funeral? Today?"

Doc exhaled. "That guy Trevor Boston shot Wednesday night's going in the ground. Might be some trouble after."

"Who the hell protests a funeral?"

"I gotta run, Dad. I'll talk to you later. Stay in till Drew and I can get by."


Snowing so hard Doc couldn't see the casino across the street from Pfeffer's Funeral Home. Bill Pfeffer met him at the door. "Ben, I'm sorry about this." Bill a family friend almost as long as Stush Napierkowski and one of the handful who could call Doc by his given name and live to tell the tale.

"What are you sorry about?"

Bill pointed to the vehicles streaming into the parking lot and the enhanced police presence. "All of it. I had no idea we'd be talking about this kind of trouble."

Doc cocked his head as if Bill were apologizing for his kids having brown eyes. "Everyone's entitled to a decent burial. That's what you're doing, giving him a proper send-off. It's not your fault he was a racist piece of shit, or that his racist piece of shit buddies decided to make a show of it. You did Jack Harriger's funeral when he died in the line of duty and you'll do my whole family, though I hope not for a while yet. Give Johnson the same consideration you'd give anyone else. Whatever else happens is my problem."

Bill hesitated. "A guy come up to me a few minutes ago, wants to hang a Nazi flag behind the coffin. That's not the business we're in. I'll bury anyone, but we don't associate ourselves with political positions. From either side, but I have to admit, this stings. I had ancestors in Sobibor. I don't want anything to get the impression we condone that kind of thinking. Not even a little bit."

Bill's comment reminded Doc "Pfeffer" was a shortened version of a Hebrew name he didn't recall. "Tell him no, then." Saw Bill's reaction. "It's your place, Bill. Your policies. Tell them no, ask them to take it out. If they don't, we can see about a trespassing charge. That will solve your immediate problem, though I doubt it will stick in court. So you know, we'll support any lawful decision you make." Bill's expression implied he'd hoped for more. "You want me to talk to them?"

Relief flowed out of Bill like water from a split hose. "I'd sure appreciate it."

"Point him out."

Bill indicated a preppy surrounded by half a dozen camos. "In the red down jacket."

"Let me see what I can do. Be aware, I can't proactively prohibit him. You may still have to make the request and him ignore it before I can do anything."

"I understand."

Conversation ceased as Doc neared the group. He put on his Officer Friendly face. "Good afternoon, gentlemen. I'm Sergeant Dougherty, Penns River police. Did one of you ask Mr. Pfeffer about placing a flag near the casket?"

The preppy stepped forward. "I did. He said he wanted to wait until the police got here. I see you're here."

"He asked me to tell you he'd prefer it doesn't come in."

"He prefers? Or we can't?"

"He doesn't want the flag in there."

"We're paying for this funeral. We'll decorate however we want."

"You are? Or is it the family? Doesn't matter. Even if you are, you're not purchasing his place of business; you're leasing time and space. He can place restrictions on it as he chooses."

Doc knew what was coming before Buster Brown opened his mouth. "We have rights, you know."

"First Amendment rights, no less. Those rights forbid me, as an agent of government, from preventing your display of that flag in a public space. The First Amendment does not deny Mr. Pfeffer's property rights. I can't stop you from taking it in there, but I can assist in having it removed if he asks. Whether criminal charges would apply would be up to a judge, but the end result for today would be the same."

A smile crossed the preppy's face. "You're telling me a flag can commit a crime?"

Doc let show a smile of his own. "A flag is an inanimate object incapable of conscious thought, independent action, or intent; obviously it can't commit a crime. However, if Mr. Pfeffer tries to remove the flag and anyone lays hands on him to prevent him doing so, that's assault. If he asks us to assist and anyone resists, a number of charges could result. The flag would go free as an unwitting accomplice not acting in concert."

The preppy couldn't stop his eyes from darting, no doubt looking for Richards or Tucker to take the weight here. A novice, not knowing they'd make grand entrances at 1:59 sharp.

Doc lowered his voice. "It's not worth it. You want to fly the flag from a vehicle on the way to the cemetery? We can't stop you. Wouldn't even try. What happens before you leave funeral home property and after you enter the cemetery grounds is up to them. We will enforce their wishes if necessary."

"And what if someone objects to our symbols on the public thoroughfare?" Like that would be an issue, snowing hard as it was.

"Depends on how they do it. They want to call you names, flip you off? They have First Amendment rights, too. They try to get physical, we'll protect you. Just like we'll protect them from any post-funeral activities you might have planned."

# 31.

Doc saw none of the funeral. Sat in his idling shop at the front of the line, running the heater and letting the wipers work on the slowest interval setting. Quiet in there, the engine muffled by accumulating snow. Nothing worth noting on the police frequency—a couple of minor traffic accidents—and Doc never listened to AM or FM unless the Pirates were on.

He liked the quiet to organize his thoughts and still his mind. As a kid he loved to lay on the couch on summer days when the only sound in the house was the refrigerator kicking on. Waited for it to shut off, not a sound out there in the country unless a car went down the road or someone cut their grass. Served him well in the Army, standing posts for hours with nothing but his thoughts and a willingness to bask in stillness where any sound would alert him.

Brushed an inch and a half of snow from the roof and trunk when the first mourners exited the service. Waited for Bill Junior to start the hearse before calling ahead to block all access to Leechburg Road from Alder Street to the 56 bypass. The procession would have clear sailing the first three-fifths of a mile.

Doc despised the idea of giving these evolutionary cul-de-sacs preferential treatment. Hated the idea of them causing any more trouble and potential injury even more. Did the math in his head:

- Three-fifths of a mile to the bypass at fifteen miles per hour was about two and a half minutes.
- Three and a half to four minutes on the bypass to the cemetery.
- Ten minutes, maybe twenty, getting all the mourners' cars situated before the service in the mausoleum.

He'd be a real cop again in half an hour.

The procession went without a hitch except for the Nazi flag. None of the vehicles had a holder big enough, so some Werner von Braun in camouflage decided to hold it out the window with the pole between his legs in the passenger seat foot well. That was fine until the wind kicked up and pulled the flag—big bastard with an eight-foot fly—right out of the cab. The staff hit Werner in the mouth on its way out, and he bit a good half inch of tongue damn near off. Someone farther back in the line rescued the flag, but not before it touched the ground. Doc didn't know the protocol for that situation. Sacrifice a blond, blue-eyed virgin, he supposed. Wondered what Judy Abramowicz was up to. She probably wasn't a virgin, though. At least Doc hoped not.

The drive to the cemetery was uneventful until the inevitable clusterfuck getting that many vehicles into the turnaround and pathways closest to the mausoleum. Doc led the hearse around the loop and watched until the last car pulled in. Gestured to George Augustine this was now his show and drove into town.

Road crews had been working since before the snow started, so the bypass wasn't bad. Slushy as hell, salt everywhere. The wind blew snow across the road to make visibility even worse than when it was snowing harder but coming straight down.

Doc wanted a sense of the conditions off the main highways, so he turned in the direction of the bridge, then up the hill on Freeport Road toward downtown and the Estates. Slid some going up the hill as far as the tennis bubble before things leveled out and the driving got easier. Dropped into Golden Dawn supermarket to talk Cathy Cuglietta into letting him fill a Thermos with coffee if he bought a dozen thumbprint cookies—six chocolate frosted and six butter crème, this week with red Valentine's Day sprinkles—and decided to go down into the Estates on Drey Street.

A decision when he made it. A mistake by the time he got to Alcoa Drive, not halfway down the hill. Frank Bullitt wouldn't chase a car down Drey Street in good weather, steep as it was and quick as the levels for cross streets broke downhill again. Doc called them *whoop-ohs* when he was little and Stush would bring him down the hill to provide a four-year-old's idea of weightlessness. Today Drey Street was snow over ice. Gusts pushed the heavy car to the left at each intersection. Doc considered bailing out at Leishman Avenue but by then he could see the promised land across the tracks and reminded himself any other street he took dead-ended at the crest of a steep drop into the railroad right-of-way.

Three minutes that seemed like a week later he was on level ground, passing the old glass house. Turned left on Third Avenue and parked in front of the community center where Nancy Snyder sat at a desk near the back of the room. Doc stomped snow and ice from his boots as he looked around. "Lonely down here, isn't it?"

Snyder smiled when she saw who it was. "Let's hope it stays that way."

"Amen." Doc crossed the room to stand in front of the desk. "It occurred to me on the way here we'd all be rolling and could stop for coffee and refreshment whenever, but you were kind of stuck here." Held up the Thermos. "You have coffee?"

Snyder held up a Coleman half-gallon cooler that had been on the floor next to her chair.

Doc showed her the bag. "I'll bet you don't have Golden Dawn thumbprint cookies."

"Bless you." She looked like she meant it, too. "I realized

about an hour ago I didn't bring anything to eat. It's embar-
rassing, long as I've been a cop."

Doc pointed toward Third Avenue. "Been like this all day?"

"You're the first car I've seen in half an hour. You'd think
the Steelers were in the Super Bowl. How was the funeral?"

"I didn't go in." Told her the saga of the Nazi flag. "Any
reports of trouble brewing down this way?" Snyder shook her
head. "Watching the Pitt-Duke game, maybe." Doc thought of
his father in the recliner muttering "dumb ass" at every Pitt
turnover. Where Doc would be right now if not for the SS cover
band invading the town. Looked at his watch. "Ten to four.
Game should be over in fifteen, twenty minutes. Where do you
want me?"

"Stick around until something happens. I can't stop myself
thinking of worst-case scenarios with no one to talk to."

Doc liked Nancy Snyder. They didn't hit it off at first, in part
due to a misunderstanding long since resolved. The rest was due
to Doc's perception that she was aloof, a trait he tolerated with
difficulty in bosses and not at all from peers, which they were
when she signed on.

Over time Doc learned Nancy Snyder wasn't aloof; she was
shy. Glad he figured it out before she made deputy, which
caused more than a few rank-and-file officers to dislike her for:

A. Jumping the line.
B. Being a woman.
C. All of the above: Sleeping her way to the front
of the line.
D. None of the above.

The correct answer was D. Nancy Snyder was a good cop,
the best suited for the job of all the available candidates. She
didn't ask for the gig and hadn't wanted it. She also never shirked
a responsibility. Doc felt the same way about his sergeant's
stripes. Their shared discomfort brought them together in a

leadership cadre where Brendan Sullivan was undisputed leader and Mike Zywiciel was on his way out.

Doc sprawled in a chair that had been well-loved for good reason. He and Snyder sipped coffee and ate cookies and watched the snow fall while talking about their parents. Hers in South Bend, Indiana; she didn't see them as much as she'd like. Doc sometimes wished he didn't have to see his as often as he needed to.

Janine Schoepf's voice in stereo on their radios: "PR-Five. Respond to a traffic accident on Drey Street across from Proctor Alley."

Snyder said, "Isn't that Roosevelt Park?"

Doc nodded. "The wake must be about to begin. No local is dumb enough to come down that way in this weather." Left out that he had done exactly that less than an hour before.

Neither moved, though Doc sensed heightened awareness in both of them. Five minutes later Janine was on the air again. "PR-Two, report of a disturbance in the Allegheny Estates."

Snyder responded. "PR-Two, copy. Do we have an address?"

"Negative, PR-Two. We'll send along information as we get it."

Doc stood. "I'll take a look." Zipped his jacket and pulled on his gloves as he walked to the door.

"Thanks for the cookies."

"If only the detectives took such good care of their boss." Placed the back of one hand against his forehead. Made an exaggerated sigh. "Good thing I'm not sensitive, he wept." Winked. "See you later."

# 32.

The logical place for a disturbance was the JFK Playground. Doc let his shop idle along Pine Court, windows down, the only sound his tires crunching on the snow. He drove through the Estates, ears open, head on a swivel. Saw random tire tracks already disappearing. The car's external thermometer showed eighteen degrees, snow coming down like God had ordered a clearance sale.

Made one circuit without seeing anything out of the ordinary. Stopped at the playground to watch the snow fall while he made his mind a blank. He'd do the first thing that came to him, a technique that had served him well in the past.

The first thing that came to him was a flurry of radio calls. Sounded like an invasion after the preceding quiet.

"PR-Eight, respond to the traffic accident on Chester Drive near Harvey Avenue."

"PR-Six, respond to a disturbance at 1361 Fourth Avenue."

"PR-Seven, see the woman at 447 Esther Avenue. Domestic disturbance."

Easy to forget the everyday bullshit wouldn't stop just because the cops were otherwise occupied. The weather subdued most criminal activity, but people cooped up in houses who weren't accustomed to such intimate confinement with loved ones didn't always respond well.

Doc keyed his mike as he put the car in gear. "PR-Seven, this is PR-Four. I'm headed that way in case you need backup."

Kathy Burrows's voice came over the air. "Roger that, Four. Approach Esther from above. Bad as it was driving down that hill half an hour ago, I can't imagine trying to get up it."

"Copy. I'm headed that way. I just want to drive past something first."

The Fourth Avenue call for unit six gnawed at the back of Doc's mind. The address sounded familiar, a place he should know. He turned left on Fourth Avenue. About to cross the railroad tracks when:

- Janine requested any available units for backup at the Fourth Avenue address.
- Doc recognized it as Christian Love's church.

He responded to dispatch, then told Burrows she'd need someone else for backup. Snowing too hard to see the church from a block and a half away. Bumped his speed up to thirty and felt snow sliding under the front bumper. Still nothing out of the ordinary a hundred yards away. Starting to wonder how much trouble the Nazis could cause just calling in false alarms when he passed a house that obstructed his vision and saw what the problem was.

Kids throwing snowballs.

Not little kids. High school, at least. Throwing hard and yelling. Doc gave a quick *whoop-whoop* pulling in as Sean Sisler did the same from the other side. The kids threw what was in their hands and split. Sisler accelerated to a dead run three steps out of the car and took down one of the fleeing kids with a beautiful open field tackle. Sat his prize against a fence. "You want to talk to him, Sarge?"

"Hey! Can I get up? This snow is freezing."

Doc strolled up to take charge. "Sit your ass down while I figure out if you're going to jail." That got the kid's attention. "What were you doing?"

"We was just throwing snowballs."

Doc, to Sisler: "Any damage?"

"I didn't see any, but I just got here myself. Who called for all units? Wasn't me."

"Shit." Doc opened a channel. "Base, this is PR-Four. Cancel the all units call to Fourth Avenue. Sisler and I have the situation under control." Returned his attention to the kid. "What were you yelling?"

The kid turned his face down. "Nothing."

"Lie to me again and you're going to jail for sure."

"I'm not lying."

Doc held back his first response. "Let's say, for the sake of argument, you're telling me the truth. Someone sure as hell was yelling. Who was it and what were they saying?"

"It's not on me what someone else says."

"I'm not saying it is. I just want to know what it was."

"I couldn't hear."

"Bullshit."

The kid seemed put out Doc would speak to him in that manner. "I wasn't paying attention. What's the big deal?"

Doc pointed to Sisler. Swept his fingers to indicate the kid. "Hook him up."

Sisler showed the tiniest smile. "You sure? I mean—"

"Goddamn it, that's an order. Hook his bony ass up." Spoke to the kid while Sisler pretended to have trouble getting his handcuffs from the holder. "Okay, genius. You're going into the system, and you'll have a jacket. How old are you?"

"Seventeen."

"Dumbass. Couple years ago this would be a juvie beef and the record sealed when you turned sixteen. Now it'll follow you the rest of your life. Even if you beat the charge this will show up on background checks. Any job you apply for, college, military, loan application," Doc feeling his oats now, "marriage license. Hell, even Little League runs prospective coaches through the system."

"What are you charging me with?"

Doc turned so he couldn't see Sisler struggling to suppress laughter. Held out a gloved hand to tick off the charges one at a time. "Disturbing the peace, vandalism, destruction of property—"

"He said nothing was broken."

"He said he didn't *see* anything broken. We haven't started looking yet. I find a cracked brick, it goes on your tab." Chanced a look at Sisler. "Where was I?"

"Destruction of property."

"Destruction of property, acting in concert, conspiracy," switched to the other hand, "failure to obey a lawful order, obstruction of justice, making terroristic threats—"

The kid was near tears. "We never threatened nobody."

"There are people in there who won't come out for fear of getting hit with a snowball, or worse. It's all fun and games for you out here, but if you hit some eighty-five-year-old woman and she strokes out, or grandpa loses his balance dodging a snowball and breaks his hip, you're looking at jail time. Not county jail, where Mom and Dad can come by every day and bring you cookies and tell you what a good boy you are. We're talking about felony time at Marienville or Skippack where they keep the big boys." Turned to Sisler. "Why isn't he in handcuffs? I gave an order, goddamnit."

Sisler took hold of one of the kid's hands. "Wait, wait. I can't go to jail."

"Sure you can. You've already done the hard work. We'll take care of the rest."

"You don't understand. My dad—"

Doc put out a hand to delay Sisler. "What were you yelling?"

Took the kid a while and Doc had to lean in to hear. "Niggers. Go back to Africa. Stuff like that."

"Do you know anyone in that church?"

"No."

"Anyone in there ever done you any dirt?"

"No."

205

"Then why would you do that? Throwing snowballs is one thing. What you yelled makes it a hate crime."

Another delay. "A guy paid us."

The cops exchanged looks. "Who paid you?"

"Some guy. We didn't know him."

"How much?"

"Huh?"

"How much did he pay you?"

"Forty bucks."

"Each? Or total?"

"Each."

"Describe the man who paid you." Kid gave a generic description that fell into the preppy camp.

"What's your name?"

"Hunter Marshall."

"Who was with you?" Hunter didn't want to give up his buds. "Listen to me. Two things have to happen in the next ten minutes that will keep you out of jail, but you'll have to do them both. The first is you tell me who was with you."

"Scotty Hartnall, Matt Martin, Brandon Dubinsky."

"There were two more."

"I don't know them. Honest. They're friends of Brandon's."

Doc wondered how cold Hunter's ass was by now. Said, "Get up," and the kid launched himself to his feet like he'd been sitting on a coiled spring. "Come with me."

"Where are we going?"

"Doesn't matter to you, so long as it's not to jail."

Doc led Hunter to the church's side door, Sisler tagging along, curious. "You're going to apologize and you're going to mean it. I catch any whiff of insincerity, or get the idea you're saying what you think I want to hear, you're going in. Understood?" Hunter nodded.

Doc pounded on the heavy wood door with the side of his fist, cop style. A middle-aged Black woman answered. Slender, hair mostly gray, reading glasses suspended around her neck by a string. "Yes?"

"Sergeant Dougherty, ma'am. Penns River police. This young man would like to apologize. I wish we'd caught more than one, but I think he might be sorry enough for all of them."

"I'll get Dr. Love. Why don't you step inside where it's warm?"

Doc looked at Hunter's wet sneakers and jeans. "Thank you, no. We're fine right here."

Christian Love took his time and knew how to make an entrance. "Good afternoon, Sergeant Dougherty, Officer Sisler. I'm sorry, young man, I don't believe we've met."

Doc nudged Hunter. "Tell him your name."

"Hunter Marshall."

"Good afternoon, Mr. Marshall. What can I do for you gentlemen?"

Doc was about to nudge Hunter again when the kid stood up on his own. "Me and some buds was throwing snowballs at your church and yelling stuff. We shouldn't of done that and I'm truly sorry. It was a shitty—a mean thing to do. I shouldn't of had nothing to do with it but this guy give us forty dollars—"

"Someone *paid* you?"

"Forty dollars. Here." Hunter took two twenties from his pocket. "You take it. Put it in the collection or the poor box or whatever."

Love accepted the crisp bills. Put them in a vest pocket. "Thank you. I accept your apology, and I commend you for having the courage to deliver it in person. Ms. Vernice? Are you satisfied with this young man's act of contrition?"

"Yes, Reverend. I am."

"Very well, then. Now, Mr. Marshall, there are a couple of things I'd like you to do for me." Hunter tightened. "They're small things. No trouble at all. Do them for me and we're even."

"What are they?"

"Do you drink coffee?" Hunter did not. "Tea?" Tea, Hunter drank. "I'd like you to come back here next Saturday at two o'clock and have some with me. Won't take half an hour. You can bring your friends from today if you like."

"That's all?"

"And I'd like you to shake my hand." Love extended a meaty paw. Hunter impressed Doc with how he accepted it. "You made a mistake today, Mr. Marshall. I think you know that. We all make mistakes. I myself make many. The way to spot a good person is to see if he or she learns from them. I hope, and I think, you have today."

Doc and Love exchanged small nods. Goodbyes said, the door closed. The cops walked Hunter across the lot. Doc said, "How'd you get here?"

"Rode down with Brandon."

"Who I don't suppose waited for you." No argument. "Where do you live?"

"Keystone Drive. Up past Arby's an' 'at."

About a mile and a half, the last part up a bastard of a hill. "Well, then, you better get going. Be dark soon." Saw Hunter's expression. "You didn't really think staying out of jail would be that easy, did you?"

# 33.

Hard for Kathy Burrows not to feel good about drawing Obidowski as a partner today. Her with three years on the job, him so new his shoes weren't broken in yet. Putting them in the same car on today of all days showed the level of confidence the bosses had in her.

She eased the car to a stop across from the Esther Avenue address, tires crunching in the snow, brakes gripping. Glanced at Obidowski, who looked like, as Sisler would say, he was holding a peach pit between his ass cheeks.

The rookie said, "I hate domestics. It's probably some asshole who figured he could get drunk early because of the snow and is pissed off Pitt lost."

"They lost?"

"Yeah, 85-77. Had it to within three with a minute to play and turned it over twice."

Kathy reached for her hat. "The worst domestics are Saturday afternoons during college football season. Some nineteen-year-old kid no one heard of misses a field goal and his team doesn't cover. Dad's home with his load on and realizes he blew the grocery money. Sometimes it's hard to tell who's beating up on who, mad as some of these wives get."

Obidowski started to get out of the car. Kathy pointed to his hand on the door release. "Put your gloves on. My first year here, a day even colder than this, I slipped and my hand stuck to a downspout when I used it to break my fall. Sean Sisler had tears in his eyes from laughing."

"How'd you get loose?"

"Sisler asked the homeowner to bring out a cup of warm water. Broke up the fight, the couple seeing a cop stuck to their house like that. Okay? Let's go."

A handrail showed where steps led from the sidewalk to the yard, under almost a foot of snow. The two of them maintained a straight line across to the stairs and up onto the porch.

Both cops stomped snow from their boots. Kathy stepped aside and nodded to Obidowski, who pounded on the door with the side of his fist. "Penns River police! Open up!"

She was about to remind Obidowski not to crowd the door when a shotgun blew a hole through it and shattered the glass of the storm door. Knocked Obidowski off-balance to fall down the stairs. Kathy vaulted the porch railing into the snow, scooted as close to the edge as she could. Keyed her shoulder mike. "This is PR-Seven requesting immediate backup to four-four-seven Esther Avenue. Shots fired. Officers need assistance."

Kathy drew her weapon and looked over toward Obidowski as the reassuring "all available units" call went out. "Pete! You all right?" Obidowski groaned and rolled toward her. "Get out of his line of sight. Roll into the driveway if you have to."

Obidowski didn't move. No blood on the snow. Maybe the blast caught all vest and knocked the wind out of him. On one knee as if clearing his head when the front door opened. Kathy didn't wait to see what or who came out. Yelled to Obidowski and darted across the snow to knock him out of the way as the shotgun appeared. No time to aim and fire. Turned to present as much vest as possible and grabbed Obidowski as she flew past to drag him down the slope that led to the driveway just as the shotgun went off again.

Blood on the snow showed their path from the house. Kathy rolled into a prone position. "Penns River Police! Drop your weapon or I will fire!"

The man with the shotgun didn't seem too enthusiastic about following them into the weather. Static and chatter on the radios appeared to confuse him. "Who the hell's out there? Show yourself."

She raised her head only enough to project her voice. "Police! Put down your weapon and step out where I can see with both hands up!"

"Kiss my ass. There's a foot of snow out there and I'm in my slippers."

Kathy took a deep breath. This hunkering down in the snow and yelling was more tiring than it seemed. "You have fired on two police officers. Throw the shotgun and any other weapons out where I can see them and step off so you can show me your hands."

All the yelling roused Obidowski, who tried to stand. Kathy pulled him to the ground. "Stay down. Guy's up there with a shotgun. Where are you hit?"

From the porch: "Fuck you, then. I'm going back in the house. Fucking freezing out here."

Obidowski felt around himself. "I think I'm okay. Must've caught the vest."

"Then where's all that blood coming from?" Followed the trail with her eyes until she saw the pool between her legs. Rolled partway to see her pants torn and bloody. Fought a wave of fear nausea. "This is PR-Seven requesting an ambulance to...four four seven Esther Avenue. Officer is down. Repeat, officer is down. Suspect is on premises and armed."

Sisler came back before Janine in dispatch could respond. "I'm half a mile away, K-Bar. You hang in there."

Kathy assessed the situation. No idea how bad the wound was. Seemed like a lot of blood, but she didn't see any spurting, so the femoral artery might be intact. First aid kit was in the car, no way for Obidowski to get there without exposing himself. She needed to get the wound above her heart to slow the bleeding.

She could ask Obidowski to help her turn around so she'd be

head down on the slope, but then she'd lose sight of the house. "Pete. Pete! Stay out of sight but crawl down below me. Pack as much snow as you can around my legs. Make it nice and snug."

"You'll freeze."

"I'm more worried about bleeding to death before the ambulance gets here. Come on. I need your help."


It took a lot to spin up Sean Sisler. Yet here he was, three blocks from a wounded fellow officer, and the fucking car wouldn't go up the fucking hill because of the fucking snow and the fucking ice, which was bad enough without these white supremacist asshole cocksuckers spreading the department all across town because they felt butthurt over some other white supremacist asshole cocksucker getting himself shot. Sisler was so mad he saw no irony in a gay man using *cocksucker* as an insult. Wished he'd shot the shithead himself.

Put the car in park. Jacked the brake. Turned to Skip Speer: "I'm going up on foot. Give me a minute to grab the rifle then see what you can do about getting this piece of shit up the hill."

Sisler took the AR-15 and a couple of extra magazines from the trunk. First aid kit. Rummaging for anything else that might be useful when he remembered he was a Marine, and a Marine with a rifle was all that was ever needed for a situation. Hoo-rah.


Doc did his service in the Army. Drove a longer route with grades not as steep and approached 447 Esther from above. Encountered George Augustine two blocks away and sent Augie down Walter Street to cover the back. Let the car crawl until he was behind Burrows's unit. Checked his extra magazines and drew his weapon as he exited the car. Took a couple seconds to assess the situation. Blood on the snow led to two cops' heads in a defensive position on the downslope into the driveway. Nothing else.

Motion caught his eye to the right. Turned to see something he'd never seen before, though he knew it should not have surprised him. Sean Sisler, dressed in riot gear, running up the hill as fast as conditions permitted, rifle at port arms. Doc couldn't help but smile. No obstacle was so great it prevented Sisler from coming to the aid of whoever needed it. Doc loved that fucking guy. In a manly, heterosexual way, of course.

Sisler reached Burrows and Obidowski breathing hard, far from winded. "What's the situation?"

Obidowski looked paler than Burrows. She said, "Domestic call. Guy fired a shotgun through the door. Knocked Pete goofy and off the porch. He got me while I was helping Pete over here."

"How bad are you hit?"

Deep breath. "It's my left leg. There's a lot of blood."

"You call for an ambo?"

"On the way."

"Where's the suspect?"

"Last we saw he went back in the house. He hasn't come out this way, but I can't say if he might've gone out the back."

Sisler looked at Obidowski. "Pete. *Pete!*" Slapped the rookie's cheek. Held up a tactical tourniquet. "You know how to use one of these?" No response. "Goddamnit, Pete, panic on your own time. Do you know how to use one of these?" Knowing full well it was part of academy training.

"I...I think so."

"Fuck it. Work your way down the driveway until you can see the front door. Stay low, but I need to know if that door opens, or if you see anything in a window. Do you understand?"

"Yeah. I think so." Obidowski stood. Started walking down the driveway.

Sisler grabbed an arm. Jerked him down hard. "What the fuck is wrong with you? Getting shot once today wasn't enough? Stay low. And draw your weapon, for Christ's sake."

"I'll never hit him, even from here."

"No, but you can keep his head down if he tries anything. I need time to wrap her leg."

"Yeah. Okay." No movement.

Fuck Obidowski. "K-Bar, I'm going to turn you so you're head down on this slope and I have some cover to tie you off. You ready?"

"That'll expose you to the house."

"Not long enough to matter."

Sisler scurried to a spot above her head, presenting as much vest as possible to the house. Heard the shotgun. Felt a few pellets hit the vest, most of the pattern to his right. Grabbed Burrows's shoulders and was in the midst of turning her when he heard another round jacked into the shotgun. Tucked his head to make himself even smaller when five shots sounded in rapid succession from the street. Dragged Burrows to a safer position and glanced to his left to see Ben Dougherty duck-walking along the driveway, his mouth a firm line. "That ought to keep his head down."

Doc watched the house while Sisler finished with the tourniquet and repacked Burrows's injured leg with snow, her head downslope. Sisler put an arm across Obidowski's shoulders and pulled him close so Burrows wouldn't hear. Spoke in a tone that allowed no misunderstanding. "I'd like to keep her warmer, but the bleeding is so high on her leg I can't make the tourniquet as tight as I'd like. If she starts to look shocky, at all, rub her wrists and arms. She stops breathing, start CPR. Do not stop until the ambo gets here, then make sure they don't waste time looking for you. Do you understand?" Obidowski nodded, eyes distant. Sisler lowered his voice another notch. "You'll answer to me if she dies, rookie."

Turned to Doc. "What's our situation?"

"Augie and whoever he's riding with have the back covered.

Ambulance is on the way. Where's Skip?"

"Still trying to get that bastard car up the hill." Sisler keyed his mike. "Skip, what's your twenty?"

"Half a block away, but I don't see me getting any closer."

Doc cut in. "Leave the car and get up here. We need you to help with Burrows and direct the ambulance."

Sisler: "And make sure that fucking rookie doesn't do anything else stupid."

Sisler turned to Doc. "Let's get this asshole." Stood and started for the house without waiting for an answer. Doc followed in tactical formation, the two approaching on either side of the fading footprints.

Sisler halted at the edge of the stairs. "That hole in the door from when he first shot Obidowski?"

"I guess so."

"Then it can't be one of those steel reinforced sons of bitches." Sisler trotted up the stairs, across the porch, and kicked in the door without stopping.

Doc on the top step when he heard, "Police! Put your goddamn hands on your head before I blow the fucking thing off." Saw the big wet footprint just above the knob as he entered. Sisler already had the man on the floor. A shotgun rested against the wall.

The ambulance siren became audible coming down the hill. Doc saw Sisler's knee in the shooter's back. "Watch for anyone coming from upstairs while I clear the rest of the house." Sisler nodded.

Dining room. Clear.

Kitchen. Clear.

Half bath. Clear.

A glance toward Sisler. He nodded and Doc went up the stairs.

Landing. Clear.

Guest bedroom. Clear.

Extra bedroom, used for storage. Clear.

Heard George Augustine open the back door and announce himself. Sisler sent him to clear the cellar.

Upstairs bathroom. Clear.

Master bedroom...

She was a small woman. Falling backward on the bed lifted both feet off the floor where they hung perpendicular to her knees as if posed. Blood spatter on the wall and the hole in her chest showed she'd been standing next to the bed, facing the door. He hadn't been more than a couple of feet away when he pulled the trigger based on the scorch marks and bits of wadding on her clothes. She had a pleasant grandma face, or more likely a favorite aunt. Her eyes stared at the ceiling as if hoping there was something beyond it for her.

Augie shouting, "Cellar's clear," from downstairs returned Doc to detective mode. Stepped back to preserve the crime scene, not that this would be a whodunit.

Downstairs, the suspect was on his feet as Sisler reached for his handcuffs. Said with a smirk, "Find her?"

Doc wiped off the smirk with a left. The right to the man's midsection would have dropped him had not Sisler held him up. Doc saw the other cops' stares. "Wife's upstairs with a hole blown clean through her."

Skip Speer came to the front door. "The ambulance is ready to go."

"Then why aren't they gone already? Send them off and tell Obidowski to get his ass in here."

Sisler's usual demeanor returned. "What's the plan?"

Doc ran through the competing priorities in his mind. "He's your collar, but do you mind if Augie takes him in? I'll still write you up as arresting officer, but I need you on the street."

"Fuck the collar. Tell me what you want me to do."

Doc already making mental notes for what to put on Sisler's commendation. "Augie, take this piece of shit to the house. Leave as much of the paperwork as possible for the detectives so you can get back in service." Augustine left without a word.

Obidowski stood at the front door, uncertainty on his face like a stain. Doc said, "You were responding officer, so it's your crime scene. The body's in an upstairs bedroom. You will secure the scene until Neuschwander processes it. I don't care how long it takes. Under no circumstances are you to leave the house or touch anything that might hold a print or trace evidence. Do you understand me, Patrolman?"

Obidowski squeaked out, "Yes, sir."

Doc looked back up the stairwell as he pulled on his gloves. Thought of the woman in the bedroom and Burrows in the ambulance. "Clusterfuck." Walked out to the car to put himself back in service and see if Sullivan had anything else for him to do.

# 34.

Brendan Sullivan had no lack of things for Dougherty to do. Prioritizing was the problem. Calls came in a steady stream, most of them false alarms. The tourists seemed to have decided there was no need to go out in the weather if they could run the cops ragged from a warm and safe place. Nice to know the town wasn't burning, but Sullivan's cops were braving miserable conditions to arrive at locations with undisturbed snow. Tarentum and Plum helped as much as they could, but both had weather-related concerns of their own.

McGinniss and Wohleber answered a call to find three kids building a snowman. Trettle and Waddell discovered a guy shoveling his driveway so things weren't too bad when he had to go to work in the morning. The false alarms came in such volume Janine Schoepf started recognizing repeating numbers, but the cops still had to answer every call.

The highlight came when Peters and Mattern answered a call to the Flats. The tourists didn't appear to know much about the racial and ethnic makeup of Penns River and had chosen to raise hell at the Dairy Queen on Greensburg Road, which was:

- Closed.
- Adjacent to Penns River's highest concentration of rednecks.

A decent number of those who lived in the Flats were Proud Boys material. Even so, they weren't about to put up with any shit in *their* neighborhood. The cops got there late, so no tourists remained to contest the locals' story and no blood was on the snow. Peters and Mattern filed a report and put themselves back in service.

In case his cops weren't spread thin enough, Sullivan also had an officer down. Procedure dictated her partner and the chief should be at the hospital, but Obidowski was anchored to the crime scene and Sullivan couldn't afford to take himself out of service.

At least this was a problem he could do something about. Called Mike Zywiciel to the office. "I need you to represent command at the hospital with Burrows." It was an important job, but Sullivan couldn't help but be aware Zywiciel might receive the request as an insult, a reminder Sullivan considered him the unessential man. "I'm sorry, Mike. It should be me."

"Don't worry about it. I feel for that girl like she was my niece." Zywiciel stopped at the threshold. "After this blows over and Boston's situation resolves, can we take a little time to work out my exit strategy?"

"Whatever you need."

Sullivan watched his patrol sergeant walk away. Knew it was time for the older man to go; still felt bad it had to be like this. Mike Zywiciel had almost forty years on the job, all of it honorable. His only failing was getting old at the same time the job changed.

His departure would hurt. It wasn't just cops who had soft spots for Zywiciel; citizens knew and respected him. Trusted him. He could walk into places where police weren't welcome, tell people things they didn't want to hear, and they'd accept it. They knew Sergeant Z would play straight, because he always had. That couldn't automatically transfer to a replacement.

The mayor called. He didn't care about snowstorms or riots. All he wanted to know was who Sullivan was sending to the casino that evening. Word of Dougherty's visit had wafted up to Dan Hecker, who called the mayor directly, an almost unheard of action for a man who lived to delegate as a show of power. While Hizzoner made sympathetic noises, Sullivan knew Chet's timeshare in Myrtle Beach wouldn't pay for itself, so Sully had goddamn better get a couple of cops over there.

The detail wasn't supposed to be a big deal. Boston and Burrows—who Dougherty referred to as "The Killer Bees"— were the first choices. Both looked good in uniform and would show the new diversity the department was building.

Then Boston shot Richie Johnson. He was out.

Plan B was Burrows and a rookie. That fell apart when Richards announced the blitzkrieg. Burrows had become a valuable and trusted officer. Sullivan wanted her on the streets if things went bad. So the casino team became Obidowski and Holtzclaw on the premise they'd be missed least in a pinch. Obidowski got himself shot and Burrows almost killed rescuing him. Dougherty now had Obidowski stapled to the crime scene and Sullivan dared not move him.

True, anyone could secure the scene. The rub was Sullivan's reluctance to override Dougherty, who hadn't wanted the stripes in the first place and sure as hell never expected to have to put the bag back on and command troops in the field. It would not do to question the man's authority over a ceremonial function. Besides, early reports were Obidowski had not covered himself in glory while Burrows almost bled out. Not the kind of behavior Sullivan wanted to reward.

The thought crossed his mind to call Zywiciel back from the hospital and send him to the casino. Dismissed the idea out of hand. Zywiciel's ego was already so fragile Sullivan saw no way the assignment wouldn't be thought of as clown duty for someone who was no longer considered a real cop. Not to mention only Dougherty hated Dan Hecker more than the soon to be ex-patrol sergeant. Z was going where he'd do the most good, the first person Burrows saw when she woke up. Assuming she did.

This was supposed to be a retirement job.

He made arrangements for Holtzclaw and Lester Goodfoot to handle the casino event. The phone rang before Sullivan could take his hand off the receiver. Bob McIntyre, Neshannock County sheriff. "Chief, Wally says a dozen men are trying to force entry through the Craigdell Road entrance."

"The door's chained, right?"

"Yeah, but if they break the window, they're in."

"Wally's armed, isn't he?"

"So are they."

Sullivan drummed fingers on the desk. McIntyre was a solid man. Ran a good jail and courthouse. Not accustomed to making tactical decisions, and his deputies weren't trained for this. "Are you there with Wally?"

"Handy."

"Take safe positions, but let them see you're armed and mean business."

McIntyre hesitated. "We're game, Chief, but there's a dozen of them and two of us."

"I'm sending help. Pull back if they breach the door before reinforcements arrive. Hold them up as much as you can. We can live with property damage, but under no circumstances can they be allowed through the tunnel."

Dougherty answered his cell on the second ring. Sullivan spared him any preamble. "We may be about to have a breach at the Craigdell Road entrance. I need a cavalry unit ASAP. Who do you want?"

"I can pick anyone?"

"Anyone."

"Have Sisler, McGinniss, Trettle, and whoever's riding with them meet me in Walgreens's parking lot fast as they can get there."

# 35.

Doc saw Walgreens glowing through the snow as he crested the rise on Freeport Road after closing the call with Sullivan. Hit the siren and lights and zipped through the empty intersection at Tarentum Bridge Road, all right-minded people safe at home. Fishtailed turning into the almost empty lot. Left the lights on.

Walgreens sat at the northwest corner of Craigdell Road and Leechburg Road, across from the county side of the government complex. Doc couldn't see the tourists, but he knew they couldn't miss his lights bouncing off the windows of the old video store the other side of Craigdell. Fine. Let them wonder what he was up to for a change.

Sisler arrived first, of course. McGinniss and Trettle came in one behind the other less than a minute later. Hell of a show. No way the tourists hadn't seen and heard the lights and sirens. Time for shock and awe.

Doc gathered his crew. "We have a potential breach on the county side of the government complex. We'll leave through this exit," pointed toward Craigdell Road, "then go Code Three until we're behind them." Saw an expression. "Yeah, I know it's only a hundred yards. I want them to see we mean business. Assume they're armed, so speed and precision are important. Take your riot guns and make a show of charging them. We'll see how serious they are after that. Any questions?"

Sisler: "I'm tired of chasing these assholes all over town. Is it okay to shoot one? I don't want to kill him. Just make a point."

Someone let out a tight laugh. Doc threw some side eye. "Let's go."

They crashed the intersection of Craigdell and Leechburg roads as the light turned green. Stopped as short as conditions allowed. Killed the sirens, left on the lights. Car doors opened. Cops scrambled out. Shotgun slides made the familiar and ominous *chuh-chuk* sound. Surprise showed on the tourists' faces. Whatever they'd expected from small town cops, this wasn't it.

Doc stepped forward. Put on his drill sergeant voice. "Everyone against the wall and assume the position. I'm sure this is old hat for some of you but for the virgins here, I want your hands on the wall supporting your weight, your legs back and more than shoulder width apart. Spread out in both directions like crabs till you're separated five feet."

Mumbling and bitching. Nothing concrete or challenging. "Close enough. Stay where you are." Aside to Sisler: "Good thing zip ties are cheap. I never arrested eleven guys at once before."

From the line, near to Doc: "We're arrested?"

"Goddamn right."

"For what?"

"Destruction of public property, for starters. Menacing a law enforcement officer. I'm sure others will come to mind. Officer Trettle, will you assist me, please? Everyone else keep watch. If they move," an image of William Holden in *The Wild Bunch* flitted through Doc's mind, "restrain them."

The pat-downs started on the left. Trettle frisked a Chad. "He's clean."

"Cuff him." To the Chad: "Sit your ass down."

"In the snow?"

"Unless you got a blanket in your pocket." Chad looked like he might have more to say until Trettle placed a hand on one shoulder and pressed him to the ground.

Next in line was a Bubba. Trettle stopped halfway through the frisk to take a Taurus Judge from a jacket pocket with two fingers. Bubba said, "I got a permit for that."

Doc: "What state?"

"Ohio."

Doc spoke over his shoulder. "Officer Sisler. Does Pennsylvania have a reciprocal concealed carry agreement with Ohio?" Knowing full well they did.

"Ohio? That's a tough one. There are so many states. I have a hard time keeping track."

"Same here." To Bubba: "We'll look into the legalities when we're inside and warm. For now I'll put it on your tab."

Doc and Trettle worked their way down the line. Third guy from the end, another Bubba, volunteered he had a gun in a pocket of his field jacket.

Trettle asked which pocket. "Lower right."

Trettle lifted out a substantial weapon. "Is that a Desert Eagle?"

"Yeah."

Doc in full drill sergeant mode and enjoying every minute. "A Desert Eagle? You some kind of commando?"

"I'm a patriot."

"You got a permit for that hand cannon, Patriot?"

"Don't need one."

Doc and Trettle exchanged looks. Doc said, "You don't?"

"Pennsylvania's an open carry state, ain't it? I told you where the gun was."

"Where are you from, Patriot? And don't say 'Pennsylvania,' even if you have to lie."

"New York."

"Whereabouts in New York? You don't look like you're from the Bronx." Bubba was five-ten and at least three fifty. "Brooklyn, even. Staten Island? Queens?"

Bubba mumbled something. "What's that again?"

"Attica."

"Inside or outside the wire?"

Doc sensed anger building. Doubted Bubba would act on it

until he was safe with the boys at Adolph's Bar and Grille, where his retelling of events would show him to be a supreme badass. "Outside."

"Well, Mr. Blue State Outside the Wire Attica Patriot, here's a civics lesson, courtesy of the Penns River, Pennsylvania police: open carry means to carry a gun in public where it is visible to a common observer. Do you know what you've done when you place a weapon where such a passerby cannot see it?" Didn't wait for an answer. "You've concealed it, dumbass. You concealed that Desert Eagle the second you put it in your pocket, and now you're going to jail for it. Hook him up, Chris."

The friskings complete, Doc stepped back to survey his collection of miscreants. "You're all under arrest for disturbing the peace, destroying public property, and menacing law enforcement officers. A couple of you also have weapons charges. I'd love to leave you out here all night, but the Supreme Court has an opinion about that, so I'll see about getting you accommodations."

Dialed the sheriff. "Mac, you have room for eleven more?"

"We'll squeeze them in."

"I'll get a couple of detectives who've been sitting in a nice, warm police station eating donuts while their intrepid leader freezes his ass off to help process them while you get mints for their pillows. We'll hold them here until the detectives show up."

Scrolling through his contacts for Sullivan when the chief called. "What's your status?"

"Eleven arrests. I was about to ask for a couple detectives to help Mac process them."

"I'll send two right down. How many uniforms do you have there?"

"Six, not counting me."

"Leave two to guard the prisoners. The rest of you haul ass to the casino. I think it's being robbed."

# 36.

Daniel Rollison's day started before the snow, making sure everything and everyone was where they were supposed to be. The players started rolling in around ten, traipsing through the increasing accumulation with satchels, briefcases, shoulder bags, and purses that all had one thing in common: ten bundles of one hundred hundred-dollar bills. That was the gimmick, bringing the cash in so the posting of the entry fees became part of the coverage. (Hecker wasn't a complete idiot. Each player had signed a contract with remedies for anyone who failed to appear or showed up short.) Counting the bills and enrolling the entrants created a scene not unlike the floor of a commodities exchange, people jammed together waving stacks of money, trying to get someone's attention so they could get on with why they were there.

Rollison had no idea how the casino expected to start a tournament with one hundred players at noon and finish by seven. That was the general manager's headache. Rollison had plenty else to do with so much loose cash in the house.

The snow helped. All of Rollison's alleged security personnel made it in. People with no money at stake who might have come out to see the fun took a look at the weather and picked up the remote to find out what time the Virginia-Wake Forest game came on.

Those benefits were negated by having Hecker around all

day. Bad enough the smaller crowd diminished both the spectacle and the income. What really broke his balls was how many of the invited big shooters didn't bother to have someone drive them to the shelter of the porte cochere, lest a snowflake blow onto their cashmere overcoats. The glitz factor was way down.

Daniel Hecker did not suffer disappointment in silence. No omission was too small to escape his corrective wrath. Chewed a greeter up one side and down the other for an undone shoelace.

Rollison turned aside much of Hecker's ire early in the day by deflecting questions about the police escort to Penns River Mayor Chet Hensarling. Hecker called Chet without going through an intermediary, which was almost unheard of. Instructed the alleged mayor to tell Brendan Sullivan in no uncertain terms that two *real* cops *would* be there at seven o'clock, as promised. Rollison had an idea of how Sullivan's day was going and would loved to have heard that conversation.

The event itself went as well as could be expected. No action to speak of on the other tables as everyone interested in such things watched the tournament, which had no effect on the slots. Rollison concluded long ago that slot players weren't gamblers so much as they were masochists. Seeing someone else win held no interest for them.

As daylight waned, Rollison's sixth sense began to itch the back of his neck. Typical attire at The Allegheny Casino would not allow anyone to confuse it with Monte Carlo, though the out-of-towners classed the joint up a little. A handful of today's spectators looked like they'd come straight from deer hunting.

They first drew his attention around five when he saw a couple wandering through the rows of unattended slot machines like sightseers. The Allegheny Casino didn't draw gawkers like Caesar's Palace or Circus Circus, so the strollers caught his eye. They struck him as people who were together, making a conscious effort not to look like they were together. The grand tour complete, they took positions between the main exit and the tournament tables. Might have seen an SS thunderbolt tattoo peeking out of a shirt collar.

The two cops arrived at 6:51. A rookie who looked like he was still in high school and the old Indian who only worked nights. That almost irritated Rollison until he considered how much it would disturb Hecker. Shook the cops' hands, got them coffee—the best thing about the Allegheny was the coffee—asked them to keep an eye open for anything suspicious. They looked so happy to be out of the weather they might have bussed tables if asked.

By seven thirty only two players remained. Rollison was going over his checklist of post-tournament activities for the hundredth time when a roar signified the crowning of a champion. Rollison gave a quick inspection of the floor before turning for the vault, saw the men he'd been watching move toward the exit.

After returning with the money, Rollison scanned the room as he stood on the dais behind and to the right of Dan Hecker during the ceremony. His security team flanked the exit route, as instructed. Four clustered at the foot of the stairs leading from the dais to escort the champion—a forty-ish man with a receding hairline and the distance vision of a mole if the thickness of his glasses were any indication—from the building to become the cops' responsibility. Once the champion was out of sight Rollison would go to his office for two fingers of Macallan before driving home and taking Monday off.

Hecker was near the end of his speech when Rollison noticed the men he'd thought had left lingered between the main exit and the champion's car, the valet already holding the door. Hecker said, *"One million dollars,"* Rollison's cue to present the cash. Made Hecker reach for the case so as not to lose sight of the men as he pulled his wrist toward his mouth to give the order to move the loiterers out.

Not that he let it show, but Daniel Rollison had mellowed with age. He'd come to the decision that even a million dollars cash wasn't worth the life of a security guard or a cop or, god forbid, a citizen. He'd hand the money over to robbers himself before risking gun play even though it would cost him his job. Let his lawyer work out the vesting.

Rollison's men surrounded the champion as he stepped off the dais. The applause was fuller and more enthusiastic than expected. Hecker seemed to swell, he was so happy at seeing *his* security people and *his* cops ready to escort *his* champion out of *his* casino. He'd be in early tomorrow so as not to miss any of the buzz and goodwill that was sure to flow in.

Rollison knew today's goodwill would be measured in milliliters. Saw no reason to disillusion his boss; that shit would roll downhill soon enough. Right now the chief of security was busy watching for anything that could still go wrong.

The group in the back repositioned themselves. One patted a pocket. Two others reached into theirs. A fourth made the amateur mistake of taking something out so he could look at it.

Rollison never had exceptional eyesight, which was why he'd gone into intelligence; he didn't qualify as a pilot. Pushing sixty, he wished for an instant he had the freakish vision that one cop—Sisler?—was said to possess. Couldn't tell for sure if a cellphone or a gun came out of the man's pocket.

Knowing he might create a major disturbance over someone checking the time, Rollison grabbed the microphone from Hecker's hand in midsentence, the owner still blathering on about what a great experience this had been, how the winner was sure to make a name for himself in Vegas, and if he got as famous as Amarillo Slim Hecker hoped "Penns River" got worked into the nickname somehow; even better, "Allegheny." Hecker turned toward Rollison, his expression equal parts surprise and anger. Rollison spoke into the microphone for all to hear: "Stop. Bring the champion back to the dais." Surprise and indecision on the escorts' faces. "*Now!* Get him back here."

The suspects at the back of the room also looked confused. The younger cop, too. The old Indian had his hand on his weapon and his head on a swivel. Rollison breathed a silent prayer of thanks that he wasn't completely alone and dialed 911 as he came down the stairs.

# 37.

Karl Tucker about shit when the guy who'd handed over the money called for it back. No more than five seconds to choose between:

1. Walking away
2. Waiting to see what shook out
3. Going after the money

Option One was out of the question. An opportunity like this—a million dollars cash in the same room as him—would literally never happen again. He hadn't come this far, in this weather, to walk away empty-handed.

Wait and see crossed his mind. Problem: the longer he hesitated, the more time the casino had to secure the cash. Two cops were already here; they'd call for reinforcements. Tucker had no idea how much his orchestrated disruptions would affect a response, but every second lost lessened the chance of success.

Following the money was his only real option.

It wasn't like he had a team of quasi-terrorists like Robert DeNiro had in the movie *Heat*. Or even the *Ocean* movies, where violence wasn't on the menu, but everyone knew their jobs and could think on their feet. Tucker had six nitwits straight out of a Guy Ritchie flick, whose only job had been to stand outside, out of sight, until the winner—or, as Tucker thought of it, the money—left the building. Then all they had to do was overpower the guards, who were at least as nitwitted as the robbers, and split. The getaway car was a stolen four-by-four and the cops would have their work cut out trying to keep up. Tucker already had a place to lay low while the search broadened, thinning out as it did so.

Except these assholes didn't want to stand in the cold and wind and snow, not even for fifty grand apiece. They'd clustered near the exit, meaning Tucker, who had spent all day not looking like he was with them, had to sacrifice his preferred position to maintain the illusion. He'd worked hard to make the situation in Penns River as much of a clusterfuck as possible. The one place he didn't want mass confusion was here at the casino. Yet here it was.

No time for subtlety. Tucker strode to his team. Kept his voice down as much as possible, but the cat was already clawing its way out of the bag. "Get that fucking money. *Now.*"

The sharpest knife of the six said, "What do you want us to do then?"

"It doesn't matter until we have it, does it? Grab it and look for me while I figure a way out of this."

The six took off down the aisle. Looking for a vantage point, Tucker noticed the older cop—might be an Indian—hand on his weapon, flap open, checking Tucker out. He walked as straight away from his crew as possible without leaving the building to find a place to get the drop on the cop if necessary.


Judy Abramowicz stood behind the bar closest to the award dais, stationed there because she "presented so well." Judy knew it was so Hecker could hit on her using language that would allow him to deny his intent if called on it. Having more fun than she'd expected, what with the million dollars only a few feet away and the anticipation in the room as the presentation approached. Business picked up as those who waited to see the money change hands, most of them tournament losers, lined up to get drinks for the road.

She'd gone over Dougherty's advice as kind of a game, like when watching a movie and thinking what she'd do in a similar situation. Which was almost never what the characters did, who almost always chose to do whatever made the situation worse. Judy was smarter than that.

Her station was close to the door that led to the back offices and staff lockers. She had a card key. Twenty steps, a swipe, and she'd be off the main floor with plenty of time to get to an emergency exit. Worst-case scenario, she could curl up in a ball and lay behind the portable bar. She doubted it would stop a bullet, but she'd be low and out of sight.

It irritated her at first, freezing when she heard Rollison call the winner back. Once she recovered, a quick look showed fifty people between her and the door, which led to the vault, which was where they'd take the money, which was where whoever they were afraid of would go. Looked for the emergency exits off the main room, but the situation was already turning to chaos and the last thing she wanted was to be caught up in a stampeding herd. Dropped to the floor behind the bar and alternated between squeezing her eyes shut and watching the panicked feet of those who had no plan.

Doc led the procession from the City-County Building to the casino. Even with siren and lights, thirty was the most speed he could make. No one was out and the roads had been treated, but the snow was coming down so hard it reflected the headlights back through the windshield. Turned them off and found it easier to see with just the overhead flashers.

Five minutes to the casino. Doc went inside as the others arranged their cars to block traffic while giving themselves quick egress. Saw Lester Goodfoot at the main entrance, gun in his right hand, pointing with his left.

"Everything was going like we expected, then that security guy grabbed the mike and says for the winner to come back to the stage. Everyone's standing around with thumbs up their asses and this big guy walks up to half a dozen who've been hanging by the door and says something. They headed for the stage. He looked at me and went that way." The direction Lester had been pointing.

"What's this guy look like?"

"White guy. Short hair. Looked like his nose was broke pretty bad at least once. Couple scars on his face." Lester showed where on his own.

"How big?"

Lester rested his weight on his back foot. "Your size, anyway. A little bigger."

Doc nodded. "Snyder's on her way to take command. You here alone?"

"I sent Holtzclaw to cover the back."

"You're a good man, Officer Goodfoot." Doc saw his team jogging up. "I'm taking Sisler, Trettle, and McGinniss inside. You take the others and get eyes on all three hundred sixty degrees of this building. No one in or out until Snyder or I say different. You got me?"

"That's a lot of ground to cover, Doc. Sorry. I mean Sergeant."

Doc glared. "You know better than that." Lester raised an apologetic hand. "Do the best you can. It's not like anyone is leaving at high speed. Tell your team if they see something they don't like, call for help. No heroes tonight. You're in charge out here until Snyder shows up." Lester pulled his new team to the side.

Doc gathered his squad under the porte cochere. "We have at least seven subjects. All should be considered armed and dangerous. Lots of civilians in an uncontrolled environment, so no shotguns. Sis, you were here for that anti-terrorist exercise last year. Is there a place you can see the entire gaming floor?"

Sisler nodded. "There's a spot where I should be able to see damn near everything on this side and quite a ways into the restaurant section."

"Good enough. Get the rifle." Sisler departed double-time.

Trettle asked about the casino's security cameras. "They're in a room down this hall. I don't think we've heard anything from them, so something might be wrong. Scoot up that way and see what's what. Let me know soon as you do." Trettle left.

Doc turned to McGinniss. "Barney, you and me are going in to take a look."

"Just the two of us? Seven suspects?"

"We're not going in, in. Just far enough to get a look so we can decide what to do when Sisler can cover us."

Daniel Rollison watched his security team bring the champion back toward the platform. Saw the six subjects come down the aisle behind them. Met his team on the floor as they arrived at the dais. Took the champion by the arm. "Give me the case."

"The case? What? No. That's my money,"

Rollison pointed to the approaching men, guns drawn. "Do you want to hold the money or live to spend it? I'll give it back. They won't."

The champion vapor locked. Made no effort to hand over the case. Didn't resist when Rollison took it. "Disappear into the crowd. We'll find you later."

About to lead his men into the back area when someone grabbed his arm. Dan Hecker said, "Where the fuck are you going with that money?" Gripped Rollison's hand that held the handle.

It took a lot for Rollison to lose his cool. This wasn't even in the neighborhood. "You're being robbed. We have to get this money into the back before they cut us off from the door."

Hecker pointed to the champion, still as a brick an about as responsive. "The only way that money leaves here is with him. Give me the case or you're fired."

Rollison saw the six armed men thirty feet away and closing. Punched Hecker on the top of the biceps and felt his grip on the case slip away. Said, "Follow me," to his detail and made for the door. Felt pinned from behind when he paused for his card key. "Keep them off me and we'll make a stand in the vault."

Rollison's men weren't what he'd consider competent, but they were game. Their barrier held off the robbers' initial surge. Rollison swiped his card and felt himself pushed through the door hard enough to hit the opposite wall. Turned to see a man slam the door, leaving the security detail on the other side with the robbers.

Rollison dropped the case to free his hands. Light showed in the man's eyes. Twenty-five years younger and forty pounds heavier, he parried Rollison's first thrust and buried a fist in the older man's midsection. A cross to the jaw put him down.

The man stood over him. Wasn't even breathing hard. "Now where the actual fuck did you think you were going with my money?"

# 38.

Karl Tucker hadn't wasted time in this shithole town raising hell and calling people names. He hated niggers and Jews as much as anyone here this weekend, but a million dollars was a million dollars. No more religious than he had to pretend to be to maintain his standing in the movement, but, hey, if a tribal policeman killing an Aryan brother the week a million bucks went for a walk in the same burg wasn't a sign from God, Tucker didn't know what was.

He'd found an excuse to cut Spencer Richards loose for a few hours Saturday afternoon when casino preparations were underway. Knew the public spaces well, and where the doors were that led to the employee-only areas. Understood where the money had to go as soon as security started leading the champion back to the platform and made sure to be there in time. Now it was just him and this borderline geezer, alone with the money.

The older man had recovered his wind. Took a beating and kept his voice cool and level. A pro. "You didn't have to hit me. I would have given you the money."

Tucker popped the case latches. Took a look to make sure they hadn't used a ringer. They hadn't. "This way was quicker."

"This way was more fun for you."

"That, too." Tucker looked up and down the hallway. "Security office back here? With the cameras?"

The older guy shook his head. "Other side of the building.

237

This is the general office side. HR, marketing, finance, event management."

"The vault?"

"It's under the gaming floor. Down that corridor and into the elevator." The casino guy must have seen Tucker's surprise. "Don't bother. It takes two keys to open, one on either side of the doorway. One man can't do it."

"You have a key, though."

The man nodded. "Me, the GM, the owner, the comptroller, and the floor manager."

"Any a them around?"

The man pointed to the door they'd come through. "Out there." Anticipated Tucker's next question. "I don't know off the top of my head how much is in the vault. Probably at least as much as you're holding. Even if you had another key, you wouldn't be able to carry it all out of here."

"I'll bet I can get you to help me." Tucker pulled back his coat to show the gun on his hip.

"Where would we take it? If the police don't have the building surrounded already, they will soon."

"Assuming any a them dipshits working for you thought to call them."

"*I* called them."

"Bullshit. I been watching you."

"Check my phone."

"Slide it over. Nice and easy, but I expect you know how this works."

The man made a show of unlocking the phone. Pushed it across the corridor with a foot. Tucker brought up the log. 911 showed as the last outgoing call.

Tucker put the phone in his pocket. "Now what'd you have to go and do that for? I was thinking we might get along."


James Hensley was pissed. Tucker's profile described an ardent racist and provocateur, but the full file noted he also liked to steal money. The Allegheny Casino had a million dollars on the hoof today, so Hensley thought this might be where they could get together. What pissed him off was being in the men's room with his dick in his hand—literally—when the balloon went up. Zipped himself and ran toward the commotion in time to see Tucker push someone through a door and out of sight.

Hensley reached the doors too late. Looked for a casino employee to let him in and found at least a dozen men going at it. Several wore casino security uniforms. Another six he'd been keeping an eye on as suspicious. The rest looked like locals who hated to miss a brawl and might not know whose side they were fighting on.

About to cull a security guard from the cluster when someone in that mess remembered he had a gun. Two shots followed by even more yelling and frantic activity. People ran in whichever direction came to mind. Bumping into each other, tripping, falling, screaming, crying. More shooting. A bleeding man went down. Hensley was armed, but this resembled Bloody Lane at Antietam more than law enforcement. No battle lines, no clear sides except for the uniformed men, who were all in the mix. Any round he'd fire was as likely as not to hit a civilian.

Drew his weapon and stepped behind a pillar to look for an opportunity. Had a sight picture on an armed man in a hunting jacket when he saw the gun lock open. Still looking at him as the man slammed home another magazine. Hensley shot him through the throat before he could rack the slide.


Doc and McGinniss flanked the entrance to the main room, waiting for Trettle with word from the video center. Sisler trotted up, AR-15 at port arms, just as the first shots sounded.

Doc turned to McGinniss. "Raise Trettle and find out what the fuck is taking so long." To Sisler: "Get to that position where you can see everything. Cover us the best you can."

Chris Trettle stormed up the hallway, mad as Doc had ever seen a human being. "Miserable chickenshit sons of bitches. They panicked and barricaded themselves in the video room. Won't even let me in and they can *see* I'm a cop. What do you want to do?"

Nancy Snyder approached the door before Doc could answer. Doc waved her over. "Deputy Snyder! We have shots fired and the video room went barricade on us. Get the number there and see if anyone can tell us what they see. We're going in."

Snyder already had phone in hand. "Got it. Go."

The gaming floor was pandemonium. A few people kept their wits and found places to shelter in place. The vast majority panicked and ran for the nearest open space. For some that was an emergency exit, which set off alarms. Others ran for the restaurants that connected the gaming and slot areas of the casino. The rest came straight up the route the champion would have taken, where his car sat waiting, valet still holding the door.

Doc pointed to a bank of exits at the back of the room where most of the action seemed to be. "Those doors are the rallying point. We'll split up and work our way back there as quick as we can. Keep funneling civilians this way to get them out of the line of fire. Sisler will cover us." Didn't wait for acknowledgment.


Took Tucker a few seconds to decide the confusion caused by the gunfire and alarms was good for him. Easier to slip out unnoticed, and, if he was lucky, fewer shares to pay. "Where's the closest exit?" The security man nodded to his left. "Pick up the case and let's go."

Tucker rotated to cover fore and aft as they moved, keeping his distance to calm any temptations his companion might have about using the case as a weapon. The security man had cooperated so far, but Tucker knew he was a pro, and assumed he'd be looking for an opening.

The row of offices ended at a corridor twenty feet shy of the outside wall. Tucker made the security man wait while he peeked around the corner. Empty, with a standard panic-bar door at the end. Looked back the way they'd come. Clear. Shoved the security man into the corridor and was rounding the bend when a door crashed open behind him.

Seeing one of the robbers shot encouraged his peers to join the crowd looking for an exit. Hensley grabbed the arm of a security guard. "Give me your card key." The man froze, staring at the gun. Hensley put his badge in the guard's face. "I'm a deputy United States marshal. Either give me the key or open the door for me." The man recalibrated the situation and handed over his card.

The man turned toward the departing robbers. Hensley took him by the forearm. Pointed to a uniformed guard on the floor. "Forget those guys. Your man needs help. Call for an ambulance and see what you can do for him in the meantime."

Swiped the card and kicked the panic bar hard enough for the door to hit the wall and bounce back. No shots. Stuck his head through the opening in time to see a heel disappear around a corner to his right.

Doc was halfway to the back of the room when things started to break up there. Shifted his vision to the gateway that led to the non-gambling parts of the casino—restaurants, rest rooms, cashiers—when Chris Trettle's voice cut through the commotion.

"Freeze! Empty your hands! Do it now!"

Took Doc a moment in the room's odd acoustics to locate Trettle's voice. The three shots turned him in time to see a Bubba throw up his arms and fall, a gun arcing away from his extended hand. Guess Chris shot the right guy.

Doc saw motion and moved to cut off two subjects running for the restaurants. The other side of the wasp-shaped building held the slot machines and had not been closed off during the poker tournament. Doc wanted no part of gunplay there. What he knew about slot players who would come out in this weather was that gunfire, screaming, and commotion were beneath their notice. Prime candidates for collateral damage or to win the hostage lottery.

Nancy Snyder's voice came through a bullhorn. "Near the restaurants! Stop and raise your hands or we will shoot."

One of them yelled something. The next thing Doc heard was a supersonic round zip past him to shatter a mirror the man would have passed in another second. Doc knew the miss was intentional. The man didn't. He raised his gun and turned toward Snyder's voice. Four things happened almost in unison:

1. Doc raised his weapon.
2. Snyder said, "Put the gun down."
3. The man threw two shots in Snyder's direction.
4. Sisler shot him twice, dead center.

The other runner threw up his hands and surrendered before Doc could ask.

Cuffing him, Doc took inventory of the situation. Trettle knelt next to the man he'd shot. Caught Doc's eye and shook his head. Barney McGinniss had two cuffed together and was walking them up what would have been Victory Lane. Doc steered his over to the man Sisler shot. Didn't bother checking the pulse. Cheap dolls had more life in their eyes, the face locked into an expression of disbelief.

McGinniss had two; Trettle one. Doc had one in custody plus one on the floor. Got on the radio. "I count five. We're expecting at least seven. Who am I missing?"

Sisler: "I think there's one down by those doors behind the stage."

Doc gave his prisoner a shove. "See that cop with two of your buddies? Turn yourself in before the guy with the rifle blows your head off." The man staggered away, hands cuffed behind him. Doc made McGinniss aware and turned his attention to the missing robber.

Got Trettle's attention. Pointed to himself, Trettle, then the doors behind the stage. Trettle nodded and moved. Doc still reaching for his mike when Sisler spoke: "Go ahead. You're covered."

# 39.

Karl Tucker heard the door slam open behind him. Saw the *Emergency Exit* sign at the end of the hall and pushed the security man toward it. Ten feet from the exit Tucker put a hand on the guy's shoulder. "Don't make a sound. I'll kill you for the hell of it if you don't do exactly what I tell you." The old guy nodded.

Tucker moved back to within twenty feet of the main corridor. No parabolic mirror meant he couldn't see who might be around the corner; they couldn't see him, either. Held the gun in both hands and aimed for what he figured would be center of mass on anyone turning the corner.

No one came.

He had to risk a peek. A quick jerk of the head around the corner, ready to fire. Whoever he might see would be in a hallway full of locked doors; Tucker could always pull back and take a position. He crept toward the intersection, gun cocked and ready.

James Hensley pressed himself to the wall twenty feet from the branch of the hallway, gun poised and cocked. Someone had gone around that corner, and it was even money there would be an emergency exit back there. Felt a little like Gene Hackman in *The French Connection*. *The sonofabitch is here. I saw him. I'm gonna get him.*

Truth be told, Hensley didn't care who put the collar on

Tucker. He'd be content to accept delivery, drive his man to jail, and give the locals the credit. "I'm just the chauffeur," he'd say. He'd done it before. Part of the reason everyone liked working with him.

His best instincts told him the man around the corner was Karl Tucker, and that the marshal held the most cards. Another alarm would sound if Tucker went out the back. If he came this way, Hensley was ready, pressed so tight to the wall a quick look might not discover him. That would buy a second, and a second was all he asked. He had support behind him and assumed the police had a secure perimeter. He'd wait all night if he had to.

Then an alarm went off.


It crossed Daniel Rollison's mind to give the man with the gun his money's worth when they'd fought. Twenty years ago Rollison would have kicked his ass and hung him from a coat hook for the police to collect. A fifty-fifty proposition these days; the consequences of a loss made it a risk not worth taking. The key to a hostage situation was time. Let things play out until law enforcement's superior resources took effect. Dougherty and Sisler had significant skills, and there were others Rollison felt more than comfortable with not to lose their heads.

That didn't mean he couldn't try to create an opportunity on his own. He'd moved a little slower than requested, not so much the hostage-taker lost patience. Random comments about the hopelessness of the situation without making a federal case of it. Engaged the man enough to distract a small percentage of his concentration. Any edge Rollison could find.

Now he stood holding a million dollars cash in a satchel ten feet from an alarmed door. The man with the gun thirty feet away, creeping farther, his attention elsewhere. Rollison took one last look and bolted for the door.

\* \* \*

Tucker heard the alarm and realized he'd trusted the old guy too much. Turned and fired toward the open door, saw the man stumble. Tucker ran, his only hope to get through the door before whoever was behind him turned the corner. He'd deal with whatever he found outside when he got there.

The exit opened onto a six-foot-by-eight-foot metal landing. Metal stairs against the side of the building on the left led to the pavement. Tucker noticed blood on the door as he pushed it open to run through, wind-blown snow stinging his face. Alone on the landing, he looked down the stairs and saw the man he'd shot sprawled near the bottom. Went down as fast as conditions allowed. Stepped over the man lying at the base and trotted over to the satchel about ten feet away. About to pick it up when he heard a shout from his left. Sent two shots that way, not aiming, just to buy time.

Bent to pick up the case when the snow exploded a foot from his hand. Looked up to see a man on the landing aiming a gun at him and yelling something else he couldn't make out. Tucker had a pretty good idea what the new player wanted and had no intention of giving it to him. Kicked the case down an incline and chased after it.

Another flare of snow, not as close. Tucker kicked again, the case coming to rest at the base of a four-foot fence separating the casino from a residential area. Threw the satchel over the fence before vaulting it himself.


Doc and Trettle burst through the doors in time to see a backside as it turned the corner into another corridor on their right. Reached the intersection in time to see an empty hallway, the emergency exit easing shut. Heard what might have been a shot over the noise of the alarm, then another. Ran to the door and listened for a few seconds before kicking the panic bar.

James Hensley was running toward the fence at the edge of the property. A cop—had to be Holtzclaw—approached from the left, hollering something Doc couldn't make out. There was blood on the door, the snowy landing, and the stairs. A man lay crumpled at the bottom.

He told Trettle to cover him and went as fast as prudence allowed. Arrived at the bottom just as the other cop—it was Holtzclaw—trotted up. Considering the amount of blood on the door and stairs, little had pooled around Rollison. Doc took off a glove to check for a pulse. Paused when he saw Rollison's head turned almost all the way around. Touched his throat to be sure and gestured Holtzclaw closer as Trettle thundered down the stairs.

The rookie stared at the body. "Is that the security guy from the casino?"

Doc felt Trettle leaning in to hear. "Used to be. What happened?"

"I was over there when I heard the alarm and seen him in the doorway. He stumbled and I wondered if he was okay because he didn't go down, not at first. Then he—"

"Get on with it before someone gets away."

Holtzclaw still focused on Rollison's body. "He wobbled a few seconds, then he went down the stairs face first. Right then a guy with a gun, big guy, came down and tried to pick up the briefcase the first guy dropped. Did I say he was carrying a briefcase? Looked like the one they had the tournament money in." Doc tried to will the kid to leave out the parts he'd like to skip. "I yelled at him to stop and he shot at me. Twice, I think. I was going to return fire when I remembered those houses across the way and worried about stray rounds."

"Well done. Then what?"

"I backed off. When he leaned over to pick up the case, someone I hadn't seen before shot at him from the top of the stairs. The first guy kicked the case across the snow down the hill and jumped the fence. The second guy chased him but didn't go over." Pointed to where Hensley stood with both hands on the top rail.

Doc grabbed Holtzclaw's arm, pointed to Rollison's body and up the stairs. "This is your crime scene until I tell you different, or the deputy takes over. Call it in and make sure no one messes with it. Understood?" The rookie nodded, getting better hold of himself.

Doc turned to Trettle. "You're with me."

Halfway to the fence, motion caught Doc's eye. Aimed his weapon, lowered it when he recognized Sisler, once again doing the airborne shuffle he could maintain for hours, rifle at port arms. Trotted up to Doc and Trettle, showing as much exertion as if he'd opened a refrigerator door. Bastard. "The deputy thought you might could use a little help back here. She says things are under control inside."

Doc tried not to show his relief. Chris Trettle was good police and would have a partner's back regardless of personal feelings. Sisler had saved Doc's ass more times than Doc cared to remember. He was safe now.

# 40.

The three cops met Hensley at the fence. Doc asked if it was Tucker they were chasing. "All I've seen are his feet and ass, but yeah, it's him." Pointed across the fence. "I thought about going in after, but I don't know the terrain. All he'd have to do is luck into a good spot and wait to pick me off."

Doc nodded. "The book says to cordon off the area and do a house-to-house. Even if we had enough cops to do it right, which we don't, that's almost sure to create a hostage situation." Turned to Sisler. "Can you track him in this light in this weather?"

Sisler stared into the neighborhood. "If we get a move on. Hard to say if we wait for backup."

Doc keyed his mike. "Deputy Snyder, this is Dougherty."

"Snyder here."

"I need a couple of units to seal off Wildlife Lodge Road from the casino to Snively Hill. No one gets in or out from either direction. We're tracking a suspect on foot and I don't want him stealing a car and driving out."

"On it."

Doc faced his team. "Sisler's on point. We all cover him. Questions?" A thought occurred. "Marshal Hensley? Are you all right with this? All kidding aside, I don't want to violate a protocol."

"Let's say we're a task force created to apprehend a federal fugitive and get going."

Tucker was a large man; the snow was heavy with damp. Even Doc could see the tracks in decent light. Sisler was in his element. "He's running. Not a sprint, but we're losing ground. So you know."

"Move quick as you can but don't get carried away."

They walked between two houses toward Fairhaven Lane. Hensley asked where the street went.

Doc said, "Nowhere. It's a loop that runs back to the road that passes the casino. We're about a quarter of the way along."

Sisler veered left, away from Wildlife Lodge. "He either doesn't know the way out or he's looking to go to ground."

"We can't let him do that. Keep pushing. We'll drive him like a deer if we have to."

Dan Knipple and Michelle Busowski took advantage of a mild increase in temperature as the front passed to enjoy an evening walk in the snow. Dan could have lived without it, snow at least a foot deep even on the street. Still, there wasn't much he wouldn't do for Micki, the wedding set for the spring, the house theirs since mid-December.

A few cars had left fading tracks, which made walking easier on the street than the sidewalk. They completed the loop and started home. Walking three-quarters of the way around and back would be a nice bit of air, after which Micki would make hot chocolate and want to snuggle. Dan knew what came after that, which was why he'd put up so little resistance to the excursion.

They saw the man with the metal attaché case coming toward them down the center of the street. Dan wondered if the poor guy got stuck and was walking home. Ten feet away he waved and said, "Hell of a storm, isn't it?"

The man replied by pulling a gun from his pocket. Pointed it at Dan. "Where do you live?"

This was not the response Dan expected. "Uh, around the

corner." Pointed past the man.

The man gestured with the gun. "Let's go. You first. And don't be all night about getting there."

Sisler stopped in the middle of Fairhaven. Pointed to the street. "New set of prints. Two people walking together."

"What about Tucker?" Doc sure it was him now.

"He's following them."

"Fuck." Doc looked both ways. Pointed right. "They came from over there?" Sisler nodded. "So they need to double back. No cross streets for a shortcut."

Trettle said, "They could come up Wildlife Lodge. Make a complete circle."

"They'd be taking their lives in their hands with these roads and visibility." Doc weighed options. "I guess we better follow them."

Hensley said, "Or we could just wait." Pointed up the street. "Here they come."

Karl Tucker knew the odds were good he'd run into cops coming back this way. Didn't see any other options. He had no vehicle and no knowledge of this part of town. Considered pulling these two off the street and waiting for the cops to go past when the one in civilian clothes pointed.

Options reduced to one, Tucker wrapped an arm around the man's throat. Put the gun to his head. "Nice and slow and we'll get past them."

The man handled it well. The woman's eyes got big as dinner plates. "What are you going to do?"

"Get lost, honey. Don't make me shoot you just so I don't have to keep track of you."

\* \* \*

Doc spoke to his team. "Stop here. Let's see how close he wants to—"

"That's far enough." Tucker's voice was muffled, his head tucked behind the much shorter hostage's shoulder.

Thirty yards. Maybe a hundred feet. The front had passed, the wind calmed; the evening was still as a photograph. The snow slowed to random flakes. What was already on the ground reflected streetlights and emerging moonlight to provide surprising visibility. Even so, long shots for cops with handguns. Too hard to consider with Tucker holding a gun of his own to a man's head.

Sisler had a rifle.

Doc lowered his voice. "Sis, can you get a head shot from here? One of those 'cut his strings' jobs?"

Sisler hesitated. "Probably. Maybe."

"That's not good enough."

"That's the best I can do unless you can get him to stand up."

Tucker spoke. "I'll keep this simple so you don't get confused. You let us pass or I blow his head off. You follow us, I blow his head off. You don't let us drive out of here, I blow his head off. We get stopped anywhere along the way, I blow his head off. Anything that doesn't end with me getting away clean, I blow his head off."

Doc spoke to Sisler again. "I need a shooting exhibition. What's the most impressive shot you can make from right here? Smallest target and greatest distance."

Sisler surveyed the area. "Over there. What's that? Dorothy Street?"

Tucker: "Time's wasting."

"The house all the way at the end still has its Christmas decorations lit up."

"I see it."

"How far you figure that is?"

"Two hundred yards, at least."

Trettle said, "Closer to two fifty."

"See the hand Santa's holding the reins with?"

"Sort of."

"The wind doesn't kick up, I can take his thumb."

Doc looked again. Santa's hand didn't get any clearer. "You're sure."

"Sure enough for a demonstration."

"You miss and we're in the shitter."

"Have some confidence. Besides, even if I miss, we're no worse off than we are now."

Doc nodded. "Karl Tucker. This is not going to be a long, drawn-out negotiation. Release the hostage or Officer Sisler will blow *your* head off so quick you won't have time to pull the trigger." To Sisler: "Sight him up."

Tucker spat out a laugh. "You're that sure you'd risk the hostage?"

"The only person at risk here tonight is you, Tucker."

"Oh yeah?" The humor in Tucker's voice was obvious. "How's that?"

Doc hoped Tucker had decent eyesight. Pointed to the house on Dorothy Street. "Look down that street across the way there. Last house still has Santa on the roof. He's holding the reins in his right hand. Watch his hand."

"Thumb," Sisler said.

"Even better, watch Santa's thumb." To Sisler: "Make the shot and bring the rifle right back on him."

Sisler shifted his aim downrange. Stood stiller than Doc had ever seen a living creature. His finger caressed the trigger as if stroking a baby's face. For the second time in less than two hours Doc heard a supersonic round whiz past. Still forming the thought he never needed to hear it again when Santa's hand exploded. Turned his attention to Sisler, already re-sighted on Tucker and standing as still as before.

Doc hadn't been to church since Drew got married twelve years ago. Now he prayed Hensley had been right when he said Tucker would rather jail than die. "The next shot goes through your eye."

A week passed in the next ten seconds. Tucker raised his hand away from the hostage's head and let the gun dangle from his middle finger. Released the man's throat and raised that hand as well. "What the fuck. It's only a million bucks. Not worth dying over."

The other cops left Sisler a clear line of sight as they approached Tucker. Hensley had his cuffs open and ready when Doc laid a hand on his wrist. "He's mine for now, Marshal."

Hensley didn't seem mad, but Doc could see it coming. "We had a deal."

"That was before he killed a man in my town. Let me at least get him arraigned before I hand him over. I want to be sure there's a Penns River cop with a warrant waiting for him if he ever steps out of a federal prison."

Hensley nodded. Trettle was cuffing Tucker as Sisler trotted up. "Sully's been trying to call you for half an hour. Snyder says you're to get your ass to the house forthwith."

Two *forthwiths* in as many days. *Now what?* Doc took Tucker by the shackles. "Sounds like he's pissed. Maybe I should bring a peace offering."

# 41.

Brendan Sullivan felt a combination of pride and sadness as he watched Dougherty frog-march his prisoner through the station. Not accustomed to seeing Dougherty in uniform—never seen him in riot gear until the previous day—Sullivan was impressed by how well the detective played down his profession when in plain clothes. Easygoing, polite, putting people at ease until he got them in the box, where he could be whatever was necessary.

Today Dougherty looked like he'd been born in the bag. Blood on one sleeve—Burrows's?—wet spots on his knees. Outer jacket unzipped, tactical vest peeking out. Different set to his face and posture. This was not the guy to fuck with.

Sullivan waved him in as he passed the chief's office. Dougherty held up a finger. "Let me stash this one in the interview room and I'll be right there." Never stopped walking.

Back in less than a minute. Sullivan said, "Close the door, please." Pointed to a seat.

Dougherty adjusted his holster to accommodate the arm of the chair. "Sorry I wasn't answering my cell, Chief. All the excitement, I left it in the car when I ran into the casino. My bad."

"Don't worry about it." Sullivan had had half an hour to decide how to handle this. Would have called Stan Napierkowski in if the weather weren't so bad. Decided to rip off the Band-Aid all at once. "Doc, I'm sorry to be the one to tell you, but your father's dead."

It took a second to register. Sergeant Dougherty stayed in the chair a few seconds before Benny Dougherty—who his father's friends used to call "Little Doc" due to their resemblance—replaced him. The transition accelerated as it progressed. "What happened?"

"He had a heart attack." Then Sullivan told his first lie. "I don't have any more details than that. Your brother's at the hospital with your mother. Go on over. We'll clean up here."

Dougherty rubbed an index finger along his lip and chin, his mind far away. "You mind if I take a minute to call my brother?"

"Go see him at the hospital."

"I'll call first. See if he needs anything." Dougherty had his hand on the doorknob when he halted. "Any word on Burrows?"

"She'll live. How well she'll walk is still too early to tell."

"Can she still police?"

Sullivan shrugged. "She may have to be a house cat, but I'll find something for her if she'll take it."

Dougherty stepped into the hall, looking at the phone in his hand as if he'd never seen one before. Sullivan asked Maureen Tilghman to come to his office ASAP.


"Drew? What happened?"

"Benny? Are you okay? I heard what's going on at the casino and when we couldn't reach you—"

"I'm fine. What happened to Dad?"

Drew took a deep breath. "Mom says he got dizzy and almost fell. She helped him into his chair and tried to call you."

"Not nine-one-one."

Drew sighed. "You know how she is. She tried you first. Said it went to voice mail."

Doc's eyes rolled shut. He'd seen missed calls from his mother. Didn't check voice mail. She rang every time she worried about him. On a day like this, five calls would not have been unusual.

Drew: "She called me and I called nine-one-one. I tried to get to the house but got hung up in the hollow by the softball fields. I had to call Bobby d'Alessio and he came and got me on his snowmobile. Dad was on the floor and blue. Me and Bobby took turns doing CPR."

"Jesus Christ. The ambulance *still* wasn't there?"

Doc heard his brother holding back tears. "Tony Lutz said they were on a false alarm call and couldn't take a direct route because of how things were jacked up around the casino. He had to go down the bypass and come in the back way on Spooky Hollow Road, and you know what that's like in this kind of weather. He did everything he could, even took Dad out through Freeport and the Heights to get to the hospital on flatter roads."

"Where are you now?"

"At the hospital."

"How'd you get there?"

"Bobby brought me on the snowmobile."

"Where the hell's Mom?"

"Sitting right next to me. Tony let her ride in the ambulance." Against policy; maybe illegal. There were people on the EMT side who owed Doc favors if Tony caught any blowback.

Doc dry-washed his face with his free hand. "You guys okay over there?"

"I got this and Paula's with the kids. Do what you have to do, but I need a small favor first."

"Name it."

"Talk to Mom. Just for a minute. She's right here."

"Put her on."

Muffled voices. Then, "Benny? Where are you?"

"I'm at the station, Mom. We had a busy day."

"Tom's dead, Benny. I need you and Drew over here."

"I'll get there soon as I can. I got kind of a situation going on."

"How soon will that be?"

"Not long. Honest to god, Mom, I'll be there quick as I can. Put Drew back on."

"Benny, you should come over right now."

"Mom, please put Drew back on the phone. I need to talk to him."

"Benny—"

"Mom, I can either talk to you on the phone or I can finish up here and come over. I can't do both. Put Drew on."

His brother came back. Doc said, "I know it's a shitty job, but I need you to keep her calmed down for a while. I'll get there soon as I can."

"Don't worry about it. Just be safe getting over here. It's a bastard out."

Doc no sooner off the call when the cell buzzed again. Tony Lutz. "Do you have a minute?"

The Doughertys and the Lutzes went way back. Tony and the old man had been close. "Sure, Tony."

Tony's voice broke over the occasional sob. "Doc, I'm sorry. We tried everything to get there."

"It's okay. Drew just filled me in. You did all that could be done."

"I was afraid we wouldn't get there soon enough, but Drew and Bobby did a great job on the CPR. We did the best we could to get him to the hospital on time but with the weather and roadblocks—"

"Wait, what? He was alive when you got there?"

"Barely, but the tough old bird was hanging in. Drew and Bobby should be in my job, keeping him alive long enough for us to get there."

Tony kept talking; Doc stopped listening. Made an apology— *I have to get going, I'll call you, thanks for everything*—broke off the conversation. Absence of mind passed for thought. Then he started for the interview room.


Sullivan watched Dougherty through the open door. Heard snippets of his end of the conversations. Hoped he wouldn't get the whole story until after leaving the station. Such was life. Sullivan waved him in again. Asked him to shut the door.

Dougherty's irritation over the diversion showed in his posture. Sullivan waited for eye contact. "I'll give you five minutes. Uncuff him first, then cuff him again when you leave. Either Tilghman or I will be in after six minutes. We see what we see." Waited for Dougherty to realize what he'd been told. "Be with your family. We got this."

Dougherty nodded a quarter of an inch, then left the room.

Rick Neuschwander had to step aside to let Dougherty out. "I see there's a guy in the interview room. You want me to get the equipment ready?"

Sullivan shook his head. "The video equipment is malfunctioning."

Neuschwander showed surprise. "It was fine yesterday when I—"

"It's malfunctioning, Detective. I'm sure it will be fine in the morning. Find something else to do."

# 42.

James Hensley felt odd, standing outside a courtroom with no weapon. On administrative duty pending an investigation of his shooting at the casino, the chief deputy granted permission to go to Penns River as a spectator while Karl Tucker was taken into federal custody. Neshannock County had agreed to arraign Tucker first so the marshals could get him out. The locals would be into the afternoon clearing the weekend's backlog.

Bullshitting with another marshal when Hensley recognized a man lingering alone near the doorway to the courtroom. Excused himself and went over. "Spencer Richards?"

Richards seemed pleased to be recognized. Did not extend a hand. "Yes, I am. And you are…"

"Deputy United States Marshal James Hensley." Richards's enjoyment of the chance encounter dropped several notches. "You caused a lot of trouble here this weekend."

"I came for a friend's funeral."

"Did you know Richard Johnson? Ever lay eyes on him alive?"

"We have—had—acquaintances in common. I was showing my support and respect."

"You always encourage as many of your white supremacist buddies as possible to go to funerals for friends of friends?"

"This was a special occasion."

Surprised Hensley a little, not objecting to *white supremacist*. "How so?"

"A line had been crossed. White people's rights have eroded since the sixties. We've been forced into fighting holding actions ever since. We prefer to pick our spots, but allowing a police assassin to kill a brother could not go unanswered."

All Hensley could do to keep from chuckling over Richards's lack of any sense of irony, appropriating *brother* in this context. Nodded into the courtroom instead. "You here for Tucker?"

"Potentia Albus is paying his legal fees and will guarantee his bail."

"What for? He's here for robbery and murder. Nothing to do with your activities over the weekend."

"Karl Tucker is a valued member of our organization who is unjustly accused. I would do the same for any of us." Then, as if reciting a legal disclaimer. "I had no advance knowledge of the casino robbery."

"You sure were involved in creating diversions for it." Richards shot Hensley a look. "Did you think we wouldn't have people on the inside this weekend?" All hate groups were born of paranoia. Few things worked better against them than spreading internal distrust.

"Karl and his friends found opportunity in what we would have done with or without him."

Hensley peeked through the doorway. Still a few minutes from showtime. "Was he robbing the casino for personal profit, or for the organization?"

Richards allowed himself a superior smile. "Why do you insult my intelligence? You'd take anything I'd say to the U.S. attorney to use as foreknowledge in one of those conspiracy charges the federal government loves to manufacture against patriots."

"Are you doing the same for everyone else on the docket today? Lawyers and bail?"

"Potentia Albus does not have unlimited resources. I'll start an online fundraiser when I get home. Everyone will be taken care of."

"I'll bet they will."

"I don't like the implication in your tone."

"That doesn't make you special. How do you think things went this weekend? I saw your spiel on the internet. I'm thinking you expected more than a couple hundred fellow travelers in this five-state area."

Richards appeared to have anticipated the question. The disdain showed in his voice. "Even though the weather held down our numbers, we still drew from as far away as Illinois."

"How about those that did show up? Raise enough hell?"

Richards's patience began to fray. "We didn't come here to raise hell. We came to show there are limits to what white people will tolerate. Push too hard and we'll take back what has been taken from us with whatever force is necessary."

"Good luck with that. If what I saw this weekend is any indication of your organization, you'll need it."

Smug dripped from Richards like melting icicles. "Underestimate our capabilities at your own risk." Hensley let a corner of his mouth show a smile. "That amuses you?"

"You still don't recognize me, do you?" It was clear Richards did not. "We had dinner together Saturday night at the Longhorn next to the Springhill Suites. You had a filet, I had a New York strip, and Tucker ate a porterhouse. Here we are, not forty-eight hours later, and you don't remember me. Those keen powers of observation are going to get you locked up some day, Mr. Master Race."

Activity in the courtroom. Hensley said, "Thanks for the conversation and insights. I have to go, but so you don't think I'm a complete prick, I want to let you know the Marshals Service is doing Potentia Albus a favor."

"A favor?"

"It's already been arranged for the judge to remand your boy Tucker into federal custody. That'll save you thousands in bail and legal fees. He's still here so the locals can file charges that'll be waiting for him if he ever gets out." Hensley gave a half bow.

"Have a nice day. You know, fourteen words and eighty-eight and all that good shit."

# 43.

Brendan Sullivan noticed Barney McGinniss coming out of roll call. Called him into the office. "I hear you got cut the other day."

"I'll live."

"I also hear you got your money's worth."

McGinniss pretended to speak under his breath. "Fucking Dougherty."

"Dougherty's on bereavement leave. My information came from outside. What happened?"

"He didn't leave a report?"

"He's been busy." Barney disappointed Sullivan. Department this size, everyone knew about Tom Dougherty's death by roll call yesterday. "I'm giving you a chance to get ahead of it before paperwork starts to show up."

McGinniss exhaled with force. "We were at the playground Saturday. Half a race riot going on and some Estates dweller pulled a blade and sliced me. I affected an arrest."

Sullivan waited for more. There wasn't any. "The report I have says Dougherty had to pull you off the guy. Said you were administering a grievous beating." The report came from Christian Love, who'd called Dougherty Monday morning only to learn of Tom's death. Love gave his condolences and called Sullivan before setting down the phone.

"He assaulted a police officer with a deadly weapon."

"Understood. He paid for an ass-kicking and you fulfilled

the order. We wouldn't be having this conversation if you had the good judgment not to do it in front of witnesses."

McGinniss had no answer for that. Sullivan went on. "That's not why I called you in. We'll let the process take its course. I also hear you and Dougherty had words."

Watched McGinniss's ass crawl onto his shoulders. "He showed me up in front of other cops and civilians."

"How?"

"He pulled—put hands on me and read me the riot act."

"Pulled you off?"

"I would've stopped."

"Did he tell you to stop before he put hands on you?"

"Not so I heard." Sullivan left the comment to sit so Barney could gauge its reception. "I got thirty years in, Sully, and not in some pisspot town. Who the fuck does he think he is?"

"He's a sergeant, Barney. You don't have to like him, but you do have to respect the rank." Cut off an interruption. "How much do you know about Dougherty."

"I know everybody here kisses his ass." McGinniss's tone implied *including you*.

"He's got nine years in the Army. Two tours of Iraq and a Bronze Star. The government and NGOs were lined up to recruit him when he got out."

"What's he doing here, then?"

"He was born here. Grew up here. Goes to all the football and basketball and wrestling. Works on the committee that's trying to put together a hockey team. Belongs to the school booster organization that helps raise money for the band, for chrissakes. The old chief is a family friend going back since before he was born. Shot it out with four Russians at his parents' house a few years ago. That's why everyone feels the way they do about him. I could live without some of it myself, but I can't say he hasn't earned it."

"He might want to turn down the volume on those stripes. It's overbearing."

Sullivan wished Barney would take his medicine and shut up. "He'd give them back in a heartbeat. It shouldn't have been him who was out there, but every account I have says he kept things from getting too far out of hand."

Saw the look on McGinniss's face. "I know this job isn't what you expected. Same here. There still has to be order. You disagree with a superior, you take it up later. In private, like we are now. You can call me Sully in here and when you're over to the house, but with anyone else around it has to be 'Chief.' I know you get that."

"Yeah. I get it."

"Okay, then. Back to work. I'm not doing anything about this incident unless the civilian files a written complaint. Till then, don't worry about it."

Sullivan leaned back in his chair. Blew air from his cheeks. Mike Zywiciel had been waiting for him Monday morning, retirement papers in hand. Sullivan persuaded him to stay another six months to complete forty years and teach his replacement the ropes. They both knew it was lip gloss on a sow, a translucent way to allow Zywiciel to save face while letting him give the replacement the appearance of a blessing.

And who would the new patrol sergeant be? Barney was too new to Penns River to have much respect from the rank and file. The potential for an excessive force complaint didn't help. Besides, Sullivan couldn't in good conscience promote a man to a position of authority in a town he'd just referred to as a pisspot.

Straight seniority wouldn't work, either. George Augustine, Skip Speer, and Dave Wohleber all had good records and plenty of time in service. All were close to their own retirements and were too tight with cops who would no longer be their peers.

Chris Trettle was a solid cop in mid-career who had shown a willingness to disrespect Nancy Snyder in her role as deputy chief. Sullivan wasn't about to reward that kind of behavior and risk the signal it might send to some other members of the department.

He had the perfect patrol sergeant right under his nose: Nancy Snyder. She had been an outstanding street cop by all accounts. Acquitted herself well as deputy under difficult circumstances. Too well. The deputy chief's job was, in practice, to do whatever the chief didn't want to do himself. Snyder carried it off without a complaint and with apparent enthusiasm, but it was a waste of her talent.

The issue was that moving her to a position where she'd be more valuable wouldn't only seem like a demotion; it would be one. A pay cut and stripping of authority, even if much of that authority was titular. Maybe he could have her fill both roles on an interim basis to buy some time.

He liked that idea the more he thought about it. Attacked the pile of paperwork. First up were Kathy Burrows's rehabilitation leave requests. All formalities—her injuries were as in-the-line-of-duty as it gets—they reminded Sullivan he'd have to decide what to do about her.

He'd stopped by the hospital on his way in. Found her in good spirits looking tired and pale as hell. Said she was looking forward to getting back to work and would do whatever rehab would be necessary.

Sullivan had no doubt she had the want-to. He also knew she'd lost a chunk of hamstring and suffered nerve damage. The odds she'd walk again were good. Without a limp, not as good. Well enough to police? Shitty. He'd sign for her to receive a full pension if she asked. Knew she wouldn't.

He'd make a place for her if he had to. It didn't help that Penns River was too small to have the administrative jobs big city departments had. An unsworn assistant handled the property room. No public information officer. No school resource officer, though Sullivan could make a valid case for one.

This was supposed to be a retirement…Caught himself before finishing the thought.

# 44.

Press conferences were worse than testifying. Courts had rules and judges enforced them. The prosecutors had your back. Usually. The media were...not vultures. More like dogs in a shelter. Some were friendlier, some were better looking, some barked, but they all wanted the same thing. Shelter dogs wanted out. The media wanted information. If they could pull something from you that was better left unsaid, that's how careers were made. And ended.

Sullivan stepped onto the low riser erected in the multipurpose room. Tapped the microphone. "Thank you all for coming. I'm sorry we had to keep pushing this back, but I wanted to give as thorough a report as I could, and I know you'll have questions. We tried to split the difference between how complete our information was and how quickly it needed to get out."

Paused to line up his notes. At least two dozen reporters and support people in the room. All four local TV stations. A couple of network heads he recognized from the evening news. The young woman Dougherty sometimes fed information to. A few he didn't recognize and assumed were out-of-town print people. A shoulder-held camera off to the side displayed the logo of a fringe operation that claimed Newtown and the attack on the Capitol were hoaxes. Couldn't wait to hear what he'd ask.

"As you know, we had a busy weekend. I'll start by commending the entire department for working above and beyond the call of duty. Several individual awards are pending, but I'd like to point out the selfless devotion of Officer Katherine Burrows, who was seriously injured while protecting a fellow officer during a domestic call on Sunday. Unknown to Officer Burrows and her partner," the more Sullivan learned of the actions on Esther Avenue, the less he intended to give Obidowski any mention at all, "the man of the house had already killed his wife and was waiting for them with a shotgun. Officer Burrows underwent surgery at Allegheny Valley Hospital and is resting comfortably.

"I mention that first not only to draw attention to Officer Burrows's heroism, but to remind everyone that, no matter what else went on over the weekend, we still fielded the routine calls, any of which can turn out not to be routine. With that in mind, I'd like to thank the police departments of Tarentum and Plum Borough for their assistance. Their willingness to share resources allowed us to better deploy our officers as events required."

Paused for a sip of water. Cleared his throat. No one seemed anxious to ask questions. Yet.

"On Sunday, seven armed men tried to steal one million dollars designated as prize money for a poker tournament at The Allegheny Casino. Penns River police responded to a call from casino security and intervened to stop the robbery in progress. Three suspects were shot and killed, two by Penns River officers and one by a deputy United States marshal. Also killed was Daniel Rollison, chief of security at The Allegheny Casino. A guard was shot; his wounds are serious, but not life threatening."

Sullivan read the names of the dead robbers, then those who were arrested. A hand went up near the back of the room. "Chief, was the robbery connected to the demonstrations that occurred here over the weekend?"

"Please hold your questions till the end. I'll do the best I can to anticipate what you'll want to know in the interest of saving everyone some time."

And he did. As well as he could. He knew it wouldn't be enough. In addition to the robbery and the events surrounding Burrows's shooting, there had been:

- A riot at the JFK Playground that led to multiple arrests and several injuries.
- Six arrests later that night near the same playground for carrying concealed weapons, including Molotov cocktails.
- An attempt to breach the City-County Building.
- Seventy-five calls, including at least fifty false alarms, in addition to the typical volume on a bad weather weekend.

"In total, thirty-seven arrests were made. Among those arrested was Karl Tucker, currently Number Two on the FBI's Most Wanted list. Tucker was taken into custody in a joint effort that included Penns River police and the U.S. Marshals Service. Neshannock County has charged him with inciting a riot, making terroristic threats, robbery, conspiracy, kidnapping, and murder. Additional charges are under consideration as the investigation continues. He was arraigned yesterday in Neshannock County court and was immediately released into the custody of the marshals to face his pending federal charges."

Paused for a long drink of water. "Are there any questions?" Like there might not be.

The line-jumper got in first. "Chief, was the robbery connected to the weekend demonstrations?"

"That is under investigation."

Same reporter: "Isn't Karl Tucker associated with Potentia Albus, whose leader, Spencer Richards, called for the protests?"

"I'm not in a position to speak to anything in connection with Karl Tucker except the robbery and homicide. We are working with the FBI and the Department of Homeland Security to close the loop on any...entanglements, for lack of a better *word.*" Another question half out of the reporter's mouth when Sullivan decided he'd had enough. "Let's get to someone else." Sullivan pointed to a woman from a local TV station.

"Chief, was anyone other than the robbers and Mr. Rollison killed or injured at the casino?"

"One casino security guard suffered a gunshot wound and is in Allegheny Valley Hospital in stable condition. A few casino customers sustained relatively minor injuries in the confusion. Cuts and bruises from falls, mostly. One man broke his nose, and another may need dental work. Two others were held overnight at Allegheny Valley with possible concussions. We're keeping in touch with everyone and all casino injuries will go on Mr. Tucker's tab. Over here, on the left."

Sullivan recognized him from the national evening news. "Will there be charges against Potentia Albus and its leaders for the casino robbery?"

"We're investigating specific individuals for specific crimes. The Department of Justice will look into any conspiracy-related charges."

Same reporter, before Sullivan could move on: "Do you think the robbery is related to the other disturbances over the weekend? Might they have been coordinated?"

Sullivan gave a tight-lipped grin his cops had come to know well. "I'm not going to speculate in front of a roomful of reporters."

A voice from the back: "How will the weekend's events affect the Richard Johnson murder investigation?"

Any vestige of a smile disappeared. "That's a state police matter. They were not involved in our efforts over the weekend."

"Can you tell us the status of that investigation?"

"Ongoing. That's all I can say and, frankly, that's all I know. As I said, this department has nothing to do with that investigation beyond providing support when requested."

The questioner got the next one in before Sullivan could move on. "Why were the state police called in? Isn't Penns River competent to investigate one of its own? Or can it not be trusted?"

This drew the full Sullivan glare, another look his subordinates were not unfamiliar with. "We're not a big enough department to have an Internal Affairs Bureau. I don't know of any of the towns around here that would handle an internal case such as this."

"Springdale is smaller than Penns River and they didn't request state police when they had a shooting last year."

"Springdale is in Allegheny County and the county police and, I believe, the DA's office handled their case. Penns River is about all there is to Neshannock County. Do your research and you'll find asking the state police to handle officer-involved shootings has been standard practice here for quite a while." Turned and pointed. "Over here. Ms. Jackson."

"Can you tell us the identity of the woman who was killed in the incident where Officer Burrows was injured?"

"That's a...sad, I guess, is the word I want. We have not yet been able to locate any blood relatives to make notification and we won't release the name until the family is aware. There are two grown children who became estranged and lost contact. We're still trying to get ahold of them. We'll release the name as soon as they're notified."

"Doesn't the husband know where they are?"

Sullivan didn't bother to hold back his disgust. "He's not saying."

"Can you tell us anymore about what happened there before the police arrived?"

Bless her for caring about something that wasn't national news. Sullivan made a mental note to feed her a scoop when he got a chance. "As far as we know, the husband's plans to go to the casino to see the poker tournament fell through because of the weather. He started drinking early in the day and something, we don't know what, sparked an argument that became physical. She called nine-one-one and he shot her before the officers could arrive. Down here in front."

"What's the status of the three officers involved in the shootings at the casino?"

"Only two were Penns River officers. Both are on administrative leave pending investigation by the state police. You'd have to check with the marshals for their man's status."

This went on for another half an hour before Sullivan decided he'd done his duty. Reporters asked about things he'd answered in detail during his opening statement. About questions that had already been asked and answered. No one asked how he planned to staff all his shifts after the extraordinary hours worked over the weekend, four patrol officers either on admin leave or in the hospital. Dougherty had already requested to burn a week, probably two, maybe more, of his accumulated lost time as extended bereavement leave to get his mother squared away.

Personnel never ran this thin in Boston. An idle thought: maybe they had a captain's billet open. Never mind. Brendan Sullivan wouldn't have a metal plate in his hip if he ran from tough situations.

# 45.

The state troopers, Thornton and Rothermel, knocked on Sullivan's door Wednesday morning, ten o'clock. He waved them in. "You missed all the excitement."

Thornton took the lead. "We got enough. You have a minute?"

Sullivan gestured to his visitors' chairs. Thornton sat, adjusted his tie. "We have a preliminary report. It's still pending final lab results, but I don't think anything material is going to change."

"That was quick."

"Like I said, it's preliminary. We wanted to give you a heads up of what to expect."

"Still, it hasn't even been a week."

"No witnesses. Very little physical evidence. You want us to take it with us, wait for the lab reports, then bring it back and tell you the same thing I'm going to tell you today right before the media gets it, we can do that. We thought you might appreciate the courtesy of knowing what to expect."

Sullivan didn't mind a heads up. What he appreciated was good police work. "And?"

Thornton looked toward Rothermel as if offering the opportunity to go first. Rothermel focused on a plaque hanging on the wall behind Sullivan.

Thornton said, "We have no evidence Johnson had a weapon. We have a statement that Boston left the bar vowing violence."

"That's not in any of the statements from the scene."

274

"Someone came forward."

Sullivan looked at Rothermel, who refused to make eye contact. Gestured for Thornton to continue.

"Combined with Officer Boston's history of excessive force—"

"There are no reports of excessive force in his record. I checked it myself the other day."

"Again, someone came forward."

Sullivan tried to remember who was with him the day Boston got rough with a corner boy. Thornton appeared to anticipate a comment and waited. Sullivan chose not to.

Thornton said, "Chief, we didn't come in here to argue. You seem to have made up your mind which way we decided. We can leave now and send you the final report and recommendations when they're ready."

The condescending tone brought Sullivan's Irish all the way up. Accompanied, as always, by his Boston accent. "Listen, Troopah, you don't come into my office and tell me how to compaht myself." Punched a button on his phone, frustration growing until Maureen Tilghman picked up. "Mo? It's Sully. Is Shimp there? Round her up and tell her to get her ass into my office forthwith. She can wipe later."

Thornton breathed to speak. Sullivan raised a hand. Spoke to Rothermel. "What's your story, Teller? You weren't so close-mouthed the other day."

"I go with my partner."

"A rousing endorsement."

Thornton's irritation showed. "What is this, Chief? We came in here to do you a courtesy and you don't let us get as far as the preliminary findings."

"Relax, Trooper. I'm doing you a favor. You give voice to anything you're implying in this preliminary report, you're going to have to walk a tightrope if it blows up in your face." A knock on the door. "Come in."

Teresa Shimp entered. Saw who was there and flushed a little. "You wanted to see me, Chief?"

"How much time have you spent with these two?"

Sullivan was a little surprised to see Shimp's face redden for real. "Thursday afternoon and evening. Pretty much all day Friday."

"Over the weekend?"

"I worked intake for the protests all weekend."

"Did they call you? Ask for anything?"

"No."

"You spend any time with them yesterday or the day before?"

Thornton spoke before Shimp could. "We didn't need her. Not that she wasn't helpful. We knew how to find her."

Sullivan spoke to Shimp. "Detective Shimp, you've worked several homicides. Been lead on one last summer. Based on what you've seen of this investigation, how close would you say they are to a resolution?"

Thornton came out of his seat. "This is bullshit and you know it, Sullivan." Realized what he'd done. "All due respect, Chief. This isn't a murder investigation, as such. We're here to determine if the shooting was justified. We have no obligation to coordinate with your liaison. As I keep trying to say, this is a preliminary report and won't be finalized until all the lab work is in."

Another knock. Sullivan wasn't in the mood for interruption. "Who is it?"

"Rick Neuschwander, Chief."

"Later, Rick. We're in the middle of something here."

"With the state police investigators?"

"Yeah."

"You're going to want to see this."

Sullivan pinched the bridge of his nose. "All right, but make it quick."

Neuschwander entered carrying an evidence container the size of a shoe box. Placed it on Sullivan's desk. "I've been working on this since the shooting, whenever I had time."

Sullivan respected Neuschwander's work too much to rush

him. "What is it, Rick?"

Neuschwander put on a pair of gloves. "Johnson fell to his knees, then straight onto his face, right?"

Sullivan deferred to the troopers. Rothermel showed interest for the first time that day. "There are impressions where his knees hit the ground, and the injuries to his face are consistent with someone who fell from that height without doing anything to lessen the impact."

Neuschwander's turn. "There's all kinds of debris back there. A lot of it's glass. I noticed quite a bit stuck to Johnson's clothes and face. I picked up everything left on the ground and asked the ME to take special care that whatever was on his clothes or embedded in his skin came back to me just as it was, including whatever they vacuumed out of the body bag at the morgue."

Thornton projected indifference, though not as cocky as before. "Is there a point here? You already impressed us with your evidence collecting skills."

Neuschwander lifted the top from the box. Took out what appeared to be about three-quarters of a longneck beer bottle. Cradled it in his gloved hands like it had come direct from Tut's tomb. "This is what Johnson had in his hand when he was shot. I pieced it together from fragments on his clothing and at the scene."

It took a lot to impress Brendan Sullivan. This qualified. He stood for a better look. There were small seams and tiny pieces missing, but there was no question this was all from the same bottle, down to the dirty label fragments. Sullivan spoke as if in church. "Please tell me you got prints."

Neuschwander nodded. "No full sets, and there are prints I can't identify, which makes sense given the number of people who must've handled it. I was able to match two of the prints to Richard Johnson."

"Did Johnson leave the bar with a bottle?"

Rothermel spoke first. "No one said he did."

"So he almost had to've picked this up outside the building."

"Makes the most sense."

"Knowing Boston was coming right behind him."

"I don't see how he couldn't."

Sullivan kept his eyes on the bottle, putting his thoughts together as he went. "Johnson runs around back. He knows Boston is coming. Doesn't have a weapon on him so he picks up whatever comes to hand and waits. Takes a run at Boston when he sees an opportunity."

Thornton said, "Oh, for Christ's sake. Really? Little shit like him is going to take on an armed police officer half again his size?"

"How drunk was Johnson?"

Rothermel picked up the file. Shimp said, "Point one three."

Rothermel nodded. "That agrees with the witness statements. Says here he was 'drunk off his ass.' Other similar comments."

Shimp said, "More than drunk enough to impair judgment."

Sullivan: "Which he had already displayed in spades by how he responded to events in the bar, including striking a police officer in front of witnesses."

Thornton wasn't ready to give up. "There is no physical evidence that indicates Johnson came at Boston with that bottle. Not to mention a beer bottle's not much of a weapon, especially against an armed police officer."

Sullivan raised a finger. "No offense, Trooper, but how many violent assaults and homicides have you worked."

Thornton's ire was instant. "I'll put my experience up against anyone you have here."

"And you'll lose if you've never seen the damage a beer bottle can do. I broke up my share of bar fights in Southie when I was a patrolman. Some guys, a broken bottle is the weapon of choice. Makes it hard to prove premeditation or even predisposition.

"It doesn't matter anyway. We're having a different discussion now. So long as Boston thought Johnson was coming at him with a weapon—any weapon—he had cause to believe he was in physical danger. Possibly mortal danger."

Rothermel flipped pages. "We have multiple accounts of Johnson making racist comments in the bar when the original fight blew up."

Shimp: "And he had a few choice words for Boston. I took two of those statements myself."

Full circle to Sullivan: "And Johnson had already assaulted Boston inside the bar. In front of witnesses."

Thornton tossed his folder on Sullivan's desk. "You've already written the report and made conclusions. You might as well type it up."

Sullivan pushed the folder back. "I just want you to do your job. If you complete a thorough investigation that shows Officer Boston used unnecessary force and went out there with violence in mind, I want him out of my department. You haven't shown me anything like that."

Hensley's comment on Sunday morning came to mind. "I don't know if there's another dynamic in play here, but if there is, I don't want any of it to be reflected in this report or I'm going to have something to say about it."

No one spoke. Neuschwander beamed. Shimp had an expression Sullivan couldn't read. Nothing new there.

Rothermel said, "Thanks, Chief. We have a much clearer picture now than we did even an hour ago. We'll run with it from here. You ready, Evan?"

Thornton was. Sullivan spoke before anyone left. "Trooper Thornton. May I have a minute after I finish with Detective Neuschwander? It won't take long." Thornton nodded and stepped outside.

Sullivan waited until he and Neuschwander were alone. "I never saw better police work in thirty years in Boston."

Neuschwander blushed. "Thanks, Chief. I know Trevor pretty well. I didn't think he had something like that in him."

"He's lucky. We're lucky. The department owes you. Besides the commendation I'm writing, you and I are going to lunch."

Neuschwander picked up his box. "How long do you think it'll be before they wrap this up?"

"A few weeks. They'll give us a clearance to okay him to work before that, but they'll need time to cross the Ts and dot the Is." Sullivan looked at his watch. "Come by around twelve thirty. You pick the place. I'm not talking about McDonald's, but it has to be in town. And Detective..." Waited for Neuschwander to turn. "Do not let anything happen to that box."

Neuschwander tucked his prize under an arm. Sullivan said, "Send in Trooper Thornton on your way out."

Thornton stepped in. Sullivan asked him to shut the door. Thornton began talking before he was all the way facing Sullivan. "No disrespect intended, Chief, but it's not your place to tell me how to run my investigation."

"Have a seat." Sullivan waited for Thornton to settle. "I haven't tried to run your investigation, and I'm not going to. I called you back to ask a question: where have you been staying while you're in town?"

"Trooper Rothermel and I have rooms at the Comfort Inn."

"What were you doing at the Springhill Suites in Tarentum Saturday afternoon around five, a little after?"

Sullivan caught the *oh shit* expression before Thornton could control it. "Conducting my investigation. As I said, I don't have to account to you for any of that."

"You were seen riding an elevator with Spencer Richards and Karl Tucker."

"I got on an elevator with two men. A third man got on the next floor. I had no idea who they were."

"What did they talk about?"

"I wasn't paying attention."

Sullivan allowed the comment to ripen. "You're a cop. You say you were there as part of your investigation. You knew what was going on here and you expect me to believe you weren't paying attention to what was said around you?"

"My mind was occupied with my own case."

"Which took you to a hotel room—I assume it was a room, coming off a floor like you did—without your partner."

"He was following up on something else."

"Did the lead pan out?"

"You know I can't say anything about that."

"All I'm asking is if it was worth the trip."

Thornton made a point of showing his forbearance. "All right. This one time. It was a dead end."

"It'll be in your report, though."

"There's no need. Nothing came of it."

"It's in your notes, right?"

"You have no right to my notes."

"Boston's lawyer will. Who's your boss?"

"Goddamnit! Chief or not, you can't talk to me that way."

Sullivan kept his Irish under control. "I'm just asking a question. It's not like I can't find out with a phone call. Now who do you report to, Trooper?" *Troopah.*

# 46.

"Robber" Barron gestured coming through the door for Igor behind the bar to get two Iron Cities. Kept walking to where Chonker Hannah sat at a table near the back of Igor's Bar and Grille in Ambridge, soon-to-be ex-hangout for the Steel City Disciples.

They clasped hands and did one-armed bro hugs. Chonker said, "How'd it go?"

"Wait for the beers so we won't be interrupted. I'll miss this dump, but I got quicker service from my old lady." Saw Chonker's expression. "That's why she's my ex, right?"

They talked about bikes and potential runs until Igor brought their beers. Robber said to Chonker, "Get this round, will you? I'm a little short after this morning."

Chonker handed Igor a five. Igor looked at it, shrugged, and walked away. Chonker nodded after him. "He wants a tip, he should show a little tit. How'd it go this morning?"

Robber took a long pull. "The real-a-tor was about what I expected. Dried up old prune of a bitch. Sixty, at least, and showing every minute. Looks like her old man hasn't put it to her in about thirty years, and I say good for him. You could tell she didn't think I had the earnest money. About shit when I started pulling out cash."

"You had enough? I knew it was gonna be close."

Another swallow. "I'm down to about three dollars in the

bank and I sold that old Indian engine that was sitting in the garage."

"Fuck, man. You gave up on rebuilding that monster?"

"For now. If we pull this off, I'll be able to buy another one and get good reconditioned parts instead of having to make do."

Finished his beer. Yelled for Igor and held up the empty bottle and two fingers on the other hand. Igor nodded. Robber pointed to Chonker's beer, still half full. "Take your time. The old bastard'll be half an hour bringing the refills. About that real-a-tor. Like I said, she about pinched a loaf when I started dropping hundreds on her desk. Didn't mind the fifties. Had a look like her dildo batteries died when I counted out that last handful of fives." Laughed at the memory. "I saw her puss and reminded her she said cash was okay. She didn't say dick about denominations or conditions or shit."

"You paid for it yourself? All of it?"

Robber shook his head. "It was mostly club money. I found a lawyer that helped me set up some kind of corporation LLC limited partnership sole proprietorship holding company thing and made me the CEO. We need to get you and Brute up there the next couple days to sign as president or chairman or janitor or something to make everything legal. What we did today was enough for me to sign papers to start the process but we have to close the loop before anything gets finalized."

"What'd that cost? The lawyer?"

"Couple hundred. The rest is COD when the deal closes." Igor brought their beers. Robber nodded to Chonker. Chonker handed Igor another five. Igor left no happier than before.

Chonker said, "How'd you get a lawyer to work on the arm like that?"

Robber drank half his bottle in one pass. "I think he sees visions of us busting up the town and him being our Perry Mason." Snorted. "He has a better chance of being that chick in *Law & Order* you're hot for."

"You mean Angie Harmon?"

"Whatever. All the trim on that show runs together after a while. Alls I'm saying is he's about half a fag. You'll see when you go up there. He might not take it up the ass, but I'm sure he hums a sweet tune."

Chonker finished his first beer, reached for the second. "You think we'll get the mortgage?"

Robber nodded while swallowing. "The current owner is so desperate to unload the place he says he'll carry the note himself. Even going to let us set it up so the early payments are cheap so long as we pay the taxes and upkeep. That'll give us time to get things running at least enough to be a front. It'll be tight at first, but we'll be fine once we get established and can use the bike shop to launder the money."

"How long do you think it'll take?"

Robber not so glib with this answer. "Depends on how much time we spend there. You and Brute have construction backgrounds, so I'm hoping you two can do most of the heavy work to save money for materials. Knucks went to electrician's school—"

"Knucks flunked out of electrician's school."

"It's not like we're asking him to rewire the scoreboard at Heinz Field. We'll recruit prospects that have skills we need. They'll practically be slave labor. Nothing goes wrong, I see no reason we can't be up and running by the fall. Maybe even sooner."

Robber took another swig. Hoped Chonker didn't push for details. Already the second half of February and they hadn't closed yet.

Chonker held his bottle by the neck. Swirled it around. "When can we get in for a closer look?"

Robber relaxed. Chonker talking logistics meant he was in. All Robber had to do was lay out however much of the plan he'd already come up with. The Chonk was a good soldier. Point him at what had to be done and no one would work harder. Didn't matter if you were putting up drywall or knocking heads.

Any questions Robber didn't know the answer to, he'd task Chonker with finding out.

Half an hour and two more beers each later, they sat back with satisfied, half-drunk, shit-eating grins. Chonker burped. "I think it'll work. We just have to get the product side up and running for cash flow. Take some time, though."

"I don't mind spending time on this. I just don't want to do any."

# 47.

Doc was deep not in thought when Stush Napierkowski squeezed his shoulder and slipped into the seat next to him. "Remember the last time we were here?" Meaning the function room of the Penns River American Legion.

"Your retirement."

They sat a minute in silence. Doc nursed a beer he didn't want. Stush's attitudes about day drinking had relaxed since he retired. "He was a good man, Benny."

Doc pretended to drink. "I never heard of him doing anyone dirt."

"That's because he never did. Always had time to help a friend. I remember, back when he still played golf, before his hands got bad, I'd make some casual remark on the course about a household thing that needed doing. He'd say that was no big deal and practically lead me home so he could help with it. A man who never left a task hanging."

"He mellowed over time, though. I remember when Drew and I were kids helping install those kitchen cabinets he built. Our standards of level didn't meet his, so he looked us right in the eye and said, 'Any time you say a job is good enough, it isn't.' Fast forward twenty-five years and I'm fixing up my new place, sweating bullets to show him I met his standard, and he comes over. Steps back, takes a good look, and says 'You know, someone driving past at sixty mile an hour will never notice that.' I just stared at him."

Stush laughed. Took a healthy swallow. Swished the remaining beer in the can. "This keeps up, I may need a ride home. Me no longer having professional immunity an' 'at."

"I'll take you. We just have to make a quick stop at the funeral home on the way. Bill Pfeffer says the extra death certificates are ready."

"It's not like I'll be in a hurry." Stush crushed the can. Waved over Drew's older daughter, Elizabeth. "Lizzy, do your Uncle Stush a favor and get me a cold beer. Tell Doris it's for me and she'll look over so I can say it's okay."

Elizabeth looked at Stush like he'd asked her to kill a snake and strip it. Still, she went to the bar.

Doc said, "Jesus, Stush. You know how shy she is."

"This'll be good for her." Stush gave the high sign to Doris the barmaid.

"You're also the only person in the world who can call her Lizzie and get away with it."

"Like how I call you Benny."

"At least my family calls me Benny. Drew and Paula can't call her anything but Elizabeth. They tried."

Elizabeth handed Stush his beer. He kissed her on the forehead and she went off. "It's not like your dad knew everything. He was over the house one day, this was years ago, I was having trouble with a ceiling fan. I asked and he told me he didn't know anything about them. I said, 'I knew you were overrated.' I guess it broke his balls. Next time I saw him he knew more about ceiling fans than an electrician. I think he was half pissed off when I told him I just replaced the bastard and called it done."

"You weren't at his Uncle Cooper's funeral, were you?"

"I went to the viewing the night before."

"We're sitting around my grandma's living room, all Dad's brothers and sisters. I remember this because I was just old enough to be allowed to stay. Anyway, everyone's sitting there, kind of like we are here, but no one has anything to say. Finally my Uncle Lee speaks up. 'It's kind of sad,' he says. 'We're all here to say goodbye to Uncle Cooper and no one has any stories to tell.'

"Quiet for a few seconds, then Dad says in that voice of his, 'Well, Uncle Cooper was a son of a bitch.' That got the ball rolling. *Everyone* had stories about Uncle Cooper being a prick."

"That's the kind of person he was. Do anything for you, but no bullshit. I'll miss the hell out of him." A short swallow. "How are you holding up?"

"I'll be okay. Still a little raw. It's the damnedest thing. Worried as I've been about him, first thing that came to mind when I saw him laying there in the hospital was, 'Mom can't stay in the house anymore.'"

"How is she? Been a while since I seen her before today, and today don't count."

Doc sighed. "I don't know how blind she really is. She swears she can't read things on the television, but I'll be driving her somewhere and she'll read the signs on the sides of trucks. Her mind is going, though."

"Alzheimer's?"

"Parkinson's induced dementia."

"She has Parkinson's? I haven't seen her shake."

"She's on meds. It shows itself differently for different people."

"They ever follow up on getting her into one of those assisted living places?" Doc shook his head. "I know Julie Ondako at River Manor pretty good. She'll get Ellen in if they have a spot." Stush paused. "No offense, Benny, but it's pretty pricey."

"None taken. For two people who had working class jobs all their lives, they're in pretty good shape. Add in Social Security and she should be fine."

"What are you gonna do about her in the meantime?"

"Sully's letting me cash in an assload of lost time, so I'll live in Drew's old room for a while. I spoke to Julie myself the other day. She says they'll take Mom, but it'll be a few weeks until they finish renovating a room that isn't already spoken for."

"I shouldn't have to tell you this, but you need anything, call me. Me and Helen will take Ellen for a few days if you need a break. We'd be happy to have her."

"Thanks. I'm hoping Julie has something before it comes to that."

Stush gripped Doc's shoulder again. Stood. "I guess you tuned up that white supremacist the other night."

"A little."

"So you know, that's a dead issue." Doc arched an eyebrow. "I ran into your marshal friend leaving court on Monday. Said he convinced what's his name—Tucker?—that it must have slipped his mind how strenuously he resisted arrest. Told him if he pressed the matter the marshal could make sure to have him processed in with a bunch of Crips and Bloods before the Aryan Brotherhood could protect him. Mentioned that a respected marshal such as himself could always arrange for something like that if he felt the need. He's good people, that marshal."

They shook hands. Doc forced himself not to choke up. Not over his father. Tom was where he'd be forever; Ellen was Doc's focus now. The feelings that almost erupted came from knowing the time was coming when Doc would be in this room for Stush's send-off. Except Stush wouldn't be there to help him through that one.

The reasons Ben Dougherty had returned to Penns River were themselves dying, or leaving of their own volition. More and more he was caretaker for people who couldn't—or didn't want to—take care of things themselves. He knew at some level this would happen when he decided to come back, but the reality, and accelerating pace, gave him pause.

He stood to look for his brother to see about settling up with the Legion. His left knee made a noise like crinkling cellophane.

# ACKNOWLEDGMENTS

The actual writing of a book takes place when the author is alone, but no book comes to life without plenty of people who each have a role in making it so. For this book, these include:

Eric Campbell, Lance Wright, and everyone in the Down & Out Books family. It is a family, and I am delighted and grateful they invited me into it.

Editor Chris Rhatigan. He finds my errors, challenges my assumptions, and always finds ways to make each book better then what I submitted, always with good cheer and in a cooperative spirit. I'll be happy for Chris to be my editor for as long as he wants to do it. For details on Chris's work, check out his website, https://chrisrhatiganediting.com/

The friends I have made in the law enforcement community. Never having been a cop myself, I'm an interloper and a bit of a dilettante for having the presumption to write police procedurals. Their insights, encouragement, and friendship keep me from hitting the wall.

The Southern Poverty Law Center. Their exhaustive research has saved me countless hours of Internet wandering.

Next to last, but certainly not least, The Beloved Spouse™. She helps with the plotting, listens to the first and final drafts, assists with problems as they arise, and, most important, makes it a pleasure to get up every day I'm with her.

Last, and definitely least, white supremacists. Whether you

call yourselves the American Freedom Party, Aryan Brotherhood, Storm Front, Patriot Front, The Base, or Proud Boys, anytime I thought I'd written something here that might have gone too far, a little research showed I'd not even scratched the surface. Folks wouldn't be reading this page if not for you evolutionary dead ends.

*White Out* is **DANA KING**'s seventh Penns River novel. He also writes the Nick Forte private investigator novels, two of which earned Shamus Award nominations from the Private Eye Writers of America. His work has appeared in numerous anthologies, most recently *The Eviction of Hope*. You can get to know him better on his website (https://danakingauthor.com/), blog (https://danaking.blogspot.com/), Facebook page (dana.king.735), or Twitter (@DanaKingAuthor).

BOOKS

On the following pages are a few
more great titles from the
Down & Out Books publishing family.

For a complete list of books and to
sign up for our newsletter,
go to DownAndOutBooks.com.

*The Damned Lovely*
Adam Frost

Down & Out Books
May 2022
978-1-64396-253-5

"She wasn't pretty but she was ours…" Sandwiched between seedy businesses in the scorching east LA suburb of Glendale, the Damned Lovely dive bar is as scarred as its regulars: ex-cops, misfits and loners. And for Sam Goss, it's a refuge from the promising life he's walked away from, a place to write and a hole to hide in.

But when a beautiful and mysterious new patron to the bar turns up murdered as the third victim of a serial killer terrorizing the local streets, Sam can't stop himself from getting involved. Despite their fleeting interaction, or perhaps because of it, something about her ghost won't let go…

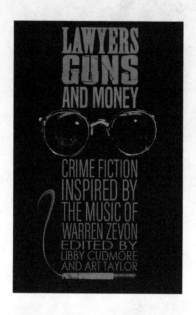

***Lawyers, Guns, and Money***
Crime Fiction Inspired by the Music of Warren Zevon
Edited by Libby Cudmore and Art Taylor

Down & Out Books
June 2022
978-1-64396-266-5

The songs of Warren Zevon are rich with crime and intrigue and suspense—guns and gunners, assassins and drug dealers, a supernatural serial killer, and a heap of hapless losers along the way too. And Zevon himself was a fan of crime fiction.

15 fantastic writers offer fresh spins on his discography with tales that span the mystery genre: caper, espionage, noir, paranormal, private eye, and more. Contributors include Gray Basnight, William Boyle, Dana Cameron, Libby Cudmore, Hilary Davidson, Steve Liskow, Nick Mamatas, Paul D. Marks, matthew quinn martin, Josh Pachter, Charles Salzberg, Laura Ellen Scott, Alex Segura, Kevin Burton Smith, and Brian Thornton.

*Scar Tissue*
Jeffery Hess

Down & Out Books
June 2022
978-1-64396-267-2

A forty-year-old self-cutting workaholic abandons everything she knows for a stripper with a death wish. Both lives change, only one ends.

*Scar Tissue* is a psychological noir novel that stunningly brings to life a world others dare not dream of. This is a vivid and memorable portrayal of desire as seen through the eyes of two women with dark hearts and very different goals who cross paths at critical moments in their lives. The power of their hopes and despair, their weaknesses and strengths is a testament to the yearning that resides inside all of us.

*Swing Gang*
A Vince McNulty Thriller
Colin Campbell

Down & Out Books
June 2022
978-1-64396-268-9

Titanic Productions has moved to Hollywood but the producer's problems don't stop with the cost of location services.

When McNulty finds a runaway girl hiding at the Hollywood Boulevard location during a night shoot e takes the girl under his wing but she runs away again.

Between the drug cartel that wants her back and a hitman who wants her dead, McNulty must find her again before California wildfires race towards her hiding place.

9 781643 962696